Fylgia

Fylgia

BIRGITTA HJALMARSON

Bink Books
Bedazzled Ink Publishing Company • Fairfield, California

978-1-945805-70-7 paperback

Cover Photo
by
Ing-Britt Hjalmarson

Cover Design
by

DESIGNS

Bink Books
a division of
Bedazzled Ink Publishing Company
Fairfield, California
http://www.bedazzledink.com

To Birgit and Arvid, my parents.

While the author spent her childhood summers in a village much like Hult, the characters and events are entirely fictional. Her research on time and place served only to set the stage.

Acknowledgments

My mother mentioned the child almost as if in passing. I had moved to California, but at the time I was visiting her in a small town in Sweden. When I questioned her on the details, she was unsure.

And so I went back to the village where Anna had lived. Suspicious of strangers and protective of their own, the villagers did not allow themselves to be rushed, nor did they speak easily in front of a tape recorder. Year after year I returned. Perhaps it was my refusal to give up that eventually swayed them. Stubbornness, I believe, was something they respected and understood.

Gun and Folke Karlson put me up, as did Kerstin and Bengt Börjesson. Of the other villagers, there were too many to thank by name. Some of the stories they told were based on hearsay, others on recollections that even the villagers themselves would question when pressed. But glimpses of Anna always shone through, and as a writer of fiction, I did not hesitate to make use of it all.

I'm also grateful to Laurie Barkin, Mary Hower, Giana Miniace, and Pam Reitman, all members of my San Francisco writers' group. Sven Thorén and Marion Abbott helped in the early years as the book took shape. Leslie Martin read draft after draft, as did Sigrid Blumberg, Marie Grönvall, Jo Hoffman, and Birgith Siberg, a child of the village herself. Susan Malone, with her unerring sense of story, saw what was missing and made me see it too. Bert Holtje offered friendship and advice, Ing-Britt Hjalmarson took the cover photograph, and Daphne Reece always stood by. Most of all my heart goes out to my husband Phillip, who waited at the San Francisco airport each time I came home.

I'm honored and proud to see *Fylgia* published by Bedazzled Ink, whose take on "women's fiction" is the same as mine. There's no such thing.

Prologue

ONCE, WHEN I was eight, my father took me to a church to see the wooden Christ.

"This is your grandfather's Christ," he said. "Don't ever forget."

I drew back. The Christ hung tortured on a cross. Thorns pierced his scalp. Iron spikes bored through his palms and feet. Blood, black with age, spilled from the gash in his flank.

None of this surprised me. I had seen the pictures in the Bible and heard the vicar talk about it many times. What I was not prepared for was the defiance. This Christ had not submitted. This Christ had fought. His flesh had torn, and his wounds had festered. Death had been slow. In the end, when he could no longer push himself up to block the pain, he had stopped gasping for air, and his head had slumped to his chest. Even then, when he must have known that death was close, his faith had not been in heaven but in earth.

I crawled under the wooden Christ the better to see his face. He gazed down in astonishment as if he could not believe I was there.

Chapter One

I STILL GO to the grave. My younger self runs ahead. I follow, cutting through the forest and staying away from the country road. An old woman in a beret and a tweed jacket.

Anemones cover the graveyard in the spring. Songbirds nest in the church ruin and the bird-cherry tree smells of bitter almonds. By midsummer the dog rose blooms. Dry branches crack in the meadow below, as the brown cows seek shade under the old apple trees. Buttercups and thistles still stand after the cows have grazed around them. Newborn calves, hidden by their mothers, lie motionless in the underbrush.

In the autumn, when the birches blaze orange and red, school children come through the gate with their notepads and crayons. Their voices ring in the air, high and eager. As I watch, they copy the writings on the granite slabs that mark the graves. They scream and run when they think they see ghosts. I recognize the fear in their eyes. And I remember.

In late October snow begins to fall. For a few months the graveyard is draped in white. A fir shakes, as a solitary moose pushes out of the forest, snow stippling his tufted winter coat. He stops and turns his head in the direction he came from, his nostrils quivering, as if something back there still holds his attention. His dark antlers catch the light, and he trots down into the meadow, whirling up a cloud of powdery snow.

The grave is marked by an iron cross, the letters raised and covered with gold. "Ingrid, 1918." She was not long on this earth and yet she suffered more than any human should. I failed to protect her once. I cannot leave her now.

Fredrik, the child's father, is buried next to her. They carried out his wishes, even though the soil was much too shallow and the rock underneath made the coffin tilt. This morning some animal, most likely a badger, had dug ruts around his stone. I have heard about badgers burrowing under graves and bringing up bones. As far as I am concerned, they may as well finish their task. I did not want him buried here.

THIS SUMMER AFTERNOON I sit outside Gustafa's cabin. I still call it that, even though Gustafa died in 1936, and I moved in two years later. Now, in 1974, I am a woman in my early eighties, by all appearances content. I live in Hult, a village hidden in the forests of southwest Sweden. I grow my own potatoes, carrots, radishes, and strawberries. Johan sends up his farmhand to mow. He says he will install an indoor toilet. I have not told him, but I shall miss the old outhouse and the thump of acorns landing on the tin roof.

Across from a field of tawny wheat, I can see Ramm, the farm that Johan bought from my brother. My mother's cherry tree is gone. There are still a few fruit trees, even some flowerbeds, but Johan's wife has only so much time, and other chores are more pressing. When Ulrika, my mother, was still alive, the garden was lush. White and purple lilacs glowed among the pear and apple trees. Raked gravel paths, lined with larkspur and peonies, stretched as far as you could see. Farther out, beyond the weeping willows, grew gooseberry bushes and black and red currants. Around it all ran a hedge of hawthorn, kept at bay by Elias, my father's farmhand. Whenever my father was home, a white flagpole flew a blue and yellow flag. On days when he was gone, the wind cracked the ropes against the pole in protest.

My father's real name was Grim Larsson, but everyone knew him as Rammen. He was a tall, imposing man, with a high forehead and thick, blond hair. His features were regular, with the exception of his finely drawn nose, which had shifted slightly in one of the fights of his youth—a minor imperfection, yet distinct enough to put you on your guard. Men and women used to come to Ramm to talk about matters great and small. He met with them in his office, the first door to the left, after you crossed the veranda and entered our house. Most, after being in his company, felt their egos boosted and their footsteps lighter. Others, those he did not approve of, said he could fill a whole room with his presence, pushing them out of the way by merely breathing.

He often traveled to Vänersborg, where he represented our region at the Provincial Council. The debates were known to be peaceable, although the villagers had often heard of Rammen's refusals to back down when it came to protecting the interests of his region. For this they praised him, particularly after they learned that members of the Provincial Council received no salary. Some complained that their taxes still paid for his train tickets and his hotel, but almost all agreed that he should travel first class and put up in style.

As a child, I used to tiptoe down the stairs at dawn and join my parents in their bed. The sheets would be twisted and sometimes damp. Ulrika's flowers were on the bedside table, lilies of the valley in the early spring, cornflowers and bluebells in the summer. Rammen would hoist me high into the air, but his gaze would follow Ulrika as she dressed and sat by her desk, checking the records for her henhouse. When Ulrika left for the kitchen, I would lie on the still unmade bed and watch Rammen shave.

After stropping his razor, he would walk over to the dresser, take down his gold watch from its nail, and wind it. As he paced and practiced his speeches, every sentence seemed to resonate with his concern for the village and the country. Yet, with the intuition of a child, I sensed that something was wrong. The years to come would prove me right. Rammen, who was supposed to provide for us all, had failed to provide for himself.

Chapter Two

I WAS TWENTY-TWO years old when I first saw Fredrik. It was late 1913, the land frozen under the snow. A tramp came before him, as if to prepare the ground.

That morning, when I came down to the kitchen, the tramp sat on a chair just inside the door, his red hair knotted and parched. None of the tramps advanced any farther, which was as much in consideration of them as it was of us. We knew our place in those days, and that applied to high as well as low.

I joined Rammen at the round kitchen table. He was watching Ulrika, who stirred a pot on the cast-iron stove. I watched her too. Even on mornings like that, when all appeared to be well, we kept an eye on Ulrika.

Ulrika brought the tramp a bowl of steaming porridge, sprinkled with cinnamon and thick enough to stand a spoon. Rammen's wool coat, a gift to the tramp from Ulrika, lay folded on the floor. The tramp would leave his old one behind for Elias to burn.

Ulrika opened the grate and added more wood to the stove. When she made no sign of serving Rammen and me, I brought us some porridge myself. I did not want the tramp to notice that Ulrika paid less attention to her husband and her daughter than she did to a vagabond.

The tramp's bowl was already empty. "Best porridge in the parish," he said, his beard grizzled and his face blotchy from the cold.

Gustafa, our servant, walked in with a bucket of potatoes. She glared at the tramp, her thin hair pulled back so hard that the skin stretched at her temples. Poverty to her was a disease. You never knew when you might catch it.

"Seen any saw sharpeners?" she asked, her voice as haughty as that of a judge interrogating a common thief. We all knew why she asked. Again and again the newspaper wrote about Russian spies, who had been spotted all over Sweden, offering to sharpen saws and other tools, although secretly they spent their time peering through binoculars and drawing maps.

"Not hereabouts," the tramp said. "Saw one on the coast. Wasn't sharpening any saws when they caught him. Last I heard—"

"Hush, hush," Gustafa said, holding the bucket in front of her as a shield. "No need to go on and on. Bad luck it brings. Before we know it, the real Russians will come through, shooting people and animals both. They make no distinction, no distinction at all."

Gustafa was not the only one who expected to hear cannons any day. In sermon after sermon the vicar warned us of the coming war. Russian soldiers would slaughter our cattle and steal our horses. Should we demand payment, they would beat us with their rifle butts. When at long last they moved on, the land would be scorched and no cocks would crow. All that was left would be the stench of corpses and the flapping of wings as the ravens came to feed.

Ulrika ladled more porridge into the tramp's bowl, her olive skin flushed in the light from the stove.

Rammen conversed with the tramp, the way he would with any other guest. "Where are you heading?"

The question seemed innocent enough but the tramp must have known its implications. Tramps might be well looked after but they were always expected to move on.

"Heading north," the tramp said. "Unless the road takes me south."

Rammen frowned and pulled out his gold pocket watch. Most tramps would do their utmost not to offend. They were remnants of their former selves, or so they would say, claiming that their lives had turned bad through no fault of their own. This man was different. Apparently he saw no reason to explain himself. Even as he appealed to our pity, he scarcely concealed his contempt.

"Have you ever been lost?" I asked, trying to strike as light a tone as I could.

The bucket banged as Gustafa stood it in the sink. "This man needs to leave. For all we know he may be Russian too."

"Lost?" the tramp repeated, eyes wary under bushy brows.

"Have you ever looked around and wondered where you were?"

"Ah," he said. "Can't say I have. One step leads to the next. It's an odd kind of freedom but it's the only kind I've got."

The tramp rose, fresh straw escaping from his boots. Gustafa wiped the seat of his chair and tried to shoo him out the door. Baring a row of strong, yellow teeth, he crouched and curled his upper lip. When he lunged, Gustafa screeched like a rabbit swooped up by a hawk.

The tramp turned to Ulrika and bowed. "Won't keep you good people from church."

"So much to talk about," Ulrika said, in her soft, melodious voice, "but now is not the time."

Rammen's old coat was too long, and the tramp had to tie a rope around his waist to hoist it up. Pressing a tattered hat on top of his straggling lichen hair, he studied me rather too closely, at least for his own good. Tramps had been run out of villages for less.

"Dance and laugh," he said. "We all reach our destination whether we aim for it or not."

"Godspeed," Rammen said and put away his watch.

We could see him through the window, the bulk of him descending the kitchen steps. Up toward Gustafa's cabin he carved a sign in one of the fence posts telling other tramps that the people of Ramm would treat them well, and all dogs were chained.

We saw them often in those days, a ragtag succession of lonely men. This was a new kind of poverty, not brought on by crop failures but by markets and trade. More and more people were on the move, mainly from the countryside to the cities, where the factories swallowed them up. Most tramps walked with a determined step, the goal well in sight. They stayed on the highway, only stealing into the forest when someone approached. This man would surely walk with no particular goal in mind, carrying his pots and his knife. Whether begging for shelter or for bread, he never apologized or cringed. Nor would he cross the road when he saw us come, much less hide among the trees. There was always the threat of the quarry, forced labor that would break a man's spirits as well as his back, and yet the pull of the road was stronger. People would taunt him and throw stones, but he was too proud to swat at flies, and so he would laugh in their faces and walk away. Even then, as I watched him disappear across the field, his feet moved as in a dance.

His words took root. I thought I could find my own way, but all the while error crept in, and before it was over, a child had to die . . .

LONG AFTER THE door closed behind the tramp, Gustafa kept rocking and crying.

Ulrika put her arm around her shoulders. "Today, Gustafa, you sit with me."

A short while later my sister Disa joined us, all bundled up against the cold. My three brothers, who had been out doing chores, had already left for the morning service. It was only then that we missed Ulrika.

I found her at the upstairs window, where she often sat looking toward Brunnsdal, the large farm where she grew up. After I managed to coax her downstairs, I waited in the hallway while she changed. When she finally came out, she wore a purple jacket, as tight a bodice as the riding habits of her youth, when her figure, always sumptuous, was still firm. A green pheasant feather swayed from her hat, large gold rings dangled from the tips of her ears, and her long black skirt was hemmed with a new strip of fur. All the other women, except Mrs. Holmberg, the mill owner's wife, would wear shawls instead of hats, and not even Mrs. Holmberg would wear anything but black.

"They're much too thin for the snow," Disa said to Rammen as soon as she caught sight of Ulrika's calfskin boots.

Rammen shook his head. "Best leave well enough alone."

"At least they're black," Disa said, always wanting the last word.

Gustafa waited outside, clutching her book of hymns, her many underskirts layered wide over her hips.

Again Disa looked to Rammen to intervene.

Rammen grinned. "A promise is a promise. She'll sit with us."

Ulrika reached for Rammen's arm, and we started down the hill. Ulrika's foot slid forward on a patch of ice but Rammen grasped her with his other hand, and she held on.

As sharp as it was, the sun lacked warmth. Below us the frozen river curved and shone. Red farms hibernated under the snow, the animals penned up in dimly lit barns. Craggy mountains reared in the distance, and a blue sky vaulted boldly over everything, as it did in the domes of glass that Holmberg sold in his store. Shake them, and snow would fall over animals and people, and we all admired the spectacle, or at least pretended to, for that miniature world might well be our own, sealed off and at the mercy of a giant hand.

Horses stood tied along the road that led to the yellow-brick church. Most were of mixed and uncertain origin, their coats shaggy, their heads too large. A few were Ardenners, a Belgian breed of draft horses, which, as Rammen liked to point out, had once been used to move Napoleon's troops. They stood immobile as we passed, their fetlocks weighed down by ice, their lashes rimmed with frost, our reflections but shadows in their faraway eyes.

The church was octagonal with a tall central tower and turrets and spires to the sides. Lars, my grandfather, had been against it from the start, his resistance strong enough to delay its construction for years. The only church where he would ever worship was the old one across the road, the one with the wooden Christ.

As we approached, my brother Björn was playing the organ, the same hymn over and over. Later I learned that only Karolina, the schoolmistress, had kept singing. After three or four repetitions even she had given up.

"No need to apologize," Rammen said as we readied ourselves to enter the church. "Remember who we are."

Rammen, Ulrika still on his arm, led us up the aisle. Björn stopped playing. On the men's side someone spat and worked the saliva into the floor planks with his clog.

Gustafa strained as if bracing herself against a forceful wind. Her usual seat was with the other servants up in the gallery, and we all expected Klas, the church caretaker, to stop her. He stood down by the door, holding a long stick, which he used to wake up those who fell asleep during the service. Disa, next to Gustafa, walked with a stiff, measured gait. She appeared to be looking straight ahead, but with her bad eye you could never really tell.

Rammen took his time, his wolf-skin coat brushing the floor. There was always a kind of recklessness about Rammen, not that he would knowingly endanger others, or at least I did not think so, but he always seemed in favor of endangering himself, and as a consequence his entire household was sometimes at risk.

As we reached the pews of the farmers, Henrik Wikander, the parish vicar, watched us through the hole in the vestry wall. He was a follower of Schartau, an orthodox Lutheran, who said we could never do enough to be worthy before God. The delay would set him back. He had three more churches to preach in that day. To reach them he had to travel on bad country roads, his only company being his horse and his thoughts, none of which would offer relief, for he had received his message directly from God, and it was not in his power to change it.

Rammen opened the gate to his pew in front of the other farmers. He nodded to Holmberg, who returned his nod, the two of them friendly enough, although it was no secret that they clashed at the parish council. Shifting a wad of tobacco to his other cheek, Rammen sat down next to my brothers, Wilhelm and Johannes. Knees wide apart, he began to remove his gloves, one finger at a time. From the gallery came the scrunch of paper as maids and farmhands craned their necks and passed bags of sugar candy.

That was when I saw him. Fredrik Otter sat next to Holmberg, his legs crossed as he balanced a black felt hat on his knee. He was Wikander's nephew and had studied farming at Ultuna, an agricultural college to the north. Now, with money inherited from his father, he was looking to buy his own farm. Until he found the right one, Wikander had offered him the lease of Prästgården, the farm that belonged to the vicarage of Hult.

We had all read his article in the newspaper, which was printed in Varberg, a seaside town some thirty miles due west. He wrote about his first impressions of Hult, pointing out roofs that needed repair, fields that were taken over by thistles, and nitrogen evaporating from manure piles that were too loosely packed. Precisely because he did not mention names, hardly a farmer existed who did not think himself a target.

Klas tried to pass to my right but I put out my foot to block him. When he tried to pass to the left, I blocked him again. He must have pulled back for I could no longer smell his sour breath. Seconds later he advanced again, his boots rapping against the floor. This time I waited until the very last moment, using both my elbow and my foot. There was a snarl and a crash and gasp from the congregation. I did not need to turn my head to know that Klas had taken a fall.

Disa held the gate, but just as Gustafa was about to follow Ulrika into the pew, Klas was back on his feet.

"She can't sit here," he said. "Not her place."

Disa fixed him with his good eye, her bad one veering off into the distance. Klas raised his hand as if to ward off evil while Gustafa edged into the pew and took her seat next to Ulrika.

Björn played "Wondrous are your ways, O God," even though it was not listed for this particular service. As the rest of the congregation leafed through their hymnals to find the right page, Karolina sang alone again. Just before I sat down, I stole another glance at Fredrik Otter, who smiled and rubbed his chin. Had he expected a typical morning service, the weight and solemnity of it all, only to learn that this remote village might surprise him?

Disa made room for me, moving closer to Gustafa. Björn kept playing, and finished with a flourish of unexpected notes, confusing even Karolina. At long last Wikander stepped out of the vestry, wearing his black, shirred robe, his bald head glistening in the light of the candles. As pastel-colored cherubs peered down from the ceiling, we all recited the confession, a jumble of voices barely audible in a church that my grandfather Lars had pronounced much too grand for a small country parish. *"For we are by nature sinful and unclean, and we have sinned against Thee by thought, word, and deed."*

They say that before we die we see our whole life flash before us. Perhaps this also happens at birth, only we are too young to remember. All I can say is that I recognized Fredrik Otter that day. I recognized the strong set of his jaw and the way his straight dark hair almost covered his sharp gray eyes. I knew the feeling that took hold of me. The closest I could come to describing it would be to compare it to spring. When it does arrive, it is so sudden and so bright that it almost blinds us.

THAT AFTERNOON I left for the forest, my rifle slung over my shoulder. Normally I would have taken Wilhelm's dog Stella, a white, long-legged harrier with tan marks above her eyes. At the first whiff of a hare she would yelp, and her whole body would tremble as I unleashed her.

Her baying, rhythmical and strong, would ring out among the trees. She would drive the hare in circles, while I selected a place to stand, hidden by a spruce or a boulder. An hour later, perhaps two, the hare would come loping down the path, safe in its ability to trick the dog but unaware of me. After I shot it, I let Stella lick its blood.

But this afternoon, because it was Sunday, I did not take the dog. Even though the snow might have muffled it some, the villagers would have heard her baying. It was bad enough that they might hear the shot. A woman hunting was unusual, but a woman hunting on a Sunday would make them turn their eyes toward heaven to apologize on my behalf.

Dressed in Björn's old jacket and boots, I walked farther and farther into the forest. In some ways I preferred to hunt without a dog. I liked the quietness of it all and having to rely on my own senses. Something happens to me when I enter the forest. I always thought it was the way I was supposed to feel at church but never quite managed.

Snow began to fall, and my chances of finding tracks grew slimmer. Then, in a clearing, I spotted the roe deer. Three does and a buck. The snow was so deep that they could no longer scrape their way to the ground but had to survive on bark. The buck kept his ears pointed in my direction, his nose and eyes black. Since I was downwind, he could not scent me. The does stood like phantoms in the falling snow. Deer are unusual that way. I have seen them hide in a thicket, completely unflappable, when not even the best of dogs could flush them, but I have also seen them panic long before the danger was real.

I raised my rifle and placed my finger on the trigger. The camphor in the gun oil stung my nose. Ever so slightly, the buck shifted his head and looked straight at me.

I do not hunt any more. My eyesight does not allow it. In my younger days I used to be an even better shot than my brother Björn. Death had to be swift. In this I always took pride. Everything I did, and everything the animal did, built toward that one moment when the outcome was so certain that even the animal seemed to know it.

That day in the snow, I aimed for the buck's heart, just behind the shoulder. All I could hear was the rush of my blood. It would have been the perfect shot, but something in the eyes of the buck stared me down, as bottomless as the forest bog. He stomped, swung around, and leapt back in among the trees. The does followed, tails high, hindquarters flashing white.

I once told my friend Samuel about it. He is not a hunter himself so I tried to explain. I said that the absence of a kill makes the hunt incomplete. He said he could see why I did not shoot. Even if we have the power to take a life, we may still decide against it.

Only, I did not think it was my decision to make.

Chapter Three

KARIN AND OLOF are here, with their two small children. Karin is Björn's granddaughter. She studied law and is now an attorney at a large firm in Gothenburg. Olof is a civil engineer and works to develop nuclear power plants for ASEA. His smile, when it does break through, is genuine and broad.

The evening before they arrived, I left my bed and walked barefoot on the grass outside the cabin. The garden chairs stood stripped of their cushions, which I keep inside the cabin out of the moistness of the night. When the clouds parted and the moon shone through, I realized I had almost stepped on two large slugs, jet-black and glistening, one on top of the other, with a wake of silver mucus behind them. As a child I often saw them on my walks through the forest. Gustafa told me that the gypsies kept them in large wooden buckets and used them to lubricate their wagon wheels.

My visitors sleep in my bedroom, which means they must climb the narrow stairs. Olof has to duck so as not to bump his head against the ceiling. Like the kitchen, the upstairs was added before I moved in. There was a great deal of hammering all through that summer. Björn, of course, had his family by then, and I wanted a place of my own.

This morning the cabin fills with life, the boy teasing the girl, and Olof looking for his shoes. Karin scolds the boy and locates Olof's shoes. Her eyes are brown like Björn's, but she is angular and thin, with none of his stoutness and lust for life.

I do not know why they have come. Karin spent her childhood summers at Ramm, but these days I hardly ever see her. Her shoulder blades seem sharp enough to cut her blouse, her nerves as tightly wound as the strings on Wilhelm's fiddle. She leaves her packets of cigarettes on my kitchen table, in the garden, even in the outhouse, strong French Gauloise, the only brand she smokes. When she is out of sight, Olof picks up the blue packets and counts how many cigarettes are left.

The boy brings in a dead slug, and Olof says the ants probably killed it. I keep quiet even though I know that Olof is wrong, not easy for an old woman who is trying to get at the truth. The slugs sometimes turn on their own. What starts as a nibble, even a coupling, leads to real bites. The ants come later, when the slug is already dead.

After Olof throws the slug into the tall grass behind the cabin, the boy will not stop crying. Olof takes the children down to Ramm, the girl riding on his shoulders, her hands holding on to his head. Karin and I stay behind. While she helps me dry the dishes, she tells me she is "on the pill." She wants to know how village women managed in the past. I remind her that contraception was illegal.

We sit down by the square kitchen table, so small that her sharp knees touch mine. Only then does it strike me that she has the same straight eyebrows as Ulrika, the same dark voice.

"But the women must have talked about it," she says.

"Of course they did. Some used a piece of wool soaked in sour milk. It rarely worked. If a birth proved particularly difficult, they thought God had punished them for not wanting to conceive. The midwife tried to convince them that this was not God's way, but few believed her."

I tell her I used to help the midwife fit the village women with diaphragms even though we broke the law. I can still see them, quiet women coming to the bank asking for help. Most of the fittings took place in the outhouse just behind the inn. The stench stuck in my clothes for days.

Karin keeps shaking her head, I cannot tell whether from sadness or disbelief. And as I talk, all this now seems remote even to me. It has, as they say, been resolved. Other matters have not.

She lights a cigarette. Tilting back her head, she shapes the corner of her mouth into a funnel and blows the smoke to the side. I know so little about her.

"How did you and Olof meet?" I ask.

She ignores my question, her old habit of acting as if she has not heard.

"Karin."

"Yes?"

"How did you and Olof meet?"

Her voice has a hint of a smile. "We marched against the war in Vietnam. He walked in front of me, in his old leather jacket."

The children dash in, the boy chasing the girl. Karin pulls back, as if called upon to do something but not knowing what. Olof stands in the door, his blond hair still disheveled from his daughter's hands. He looks at me, and for a moment I catch the bewilderment in his eyes, his pupils widening in the relative dark of the cabin. Something is wrong, and I wish they would tell me what it is.

While Olof loads the car, the boy searches for the dead slug.

I tell him it has probably been eaten. "Nothing goes to waste in the wild."

Was I too blunt? We do not always know what goes on in the minds of children. Death, when I was a child, was ever-present. No one made any attempt to hide it. Perhaps that is why I have no fear. There are already days when death seems more real than life. I look out over the fields and the forest, the lake lucent behind the trees. Soon I will no longer see them. The sorrow is there, but it is not about death, it is about the parting.

Their green Volvo disappears down the driveway, the boy up on his knees in the back seat as he waves at me through the window.

For hours I sit on my sofa, staring at the floor. The lid of the phonograph is up. Early this morning, while Karin and the children were still asleep, Olof came down the stairs and asked if all was well. I had lit a candle and opened the window. I told him I was glad they were here. After Rammen's death, my relationship with Björn was never easy. Still, as I keep telling myself, what he did was not that strange. I have seen farmers' sons live well into their fifties before they could marry and take over the farms. Most villagers would have understood.

I cranked up the phonograph, lowered the needle, and Olof and I danced to *Muzetta's Waltz*. I felt so light in his arms, almost young again. There is not much room in the cabin so we danced in place, swaying and turning, the breeze from the window cool against my skin. I do think Olof is a good lover for Karin. He has a strong body, almost lithe. I sometimes catch myself watching his buttocks, small and firm, as he walks away in those snug blue jeans.

This morning, when I danced with Olof, I was back in Fredrik's arms. I remembered his jacket smelling faintly of earth and the heat of his hands as he placed them on the small of my back to draw me closer. I must not weaken, not now, not after years of hate.

Unlike love, hatred must be fueled or it will lose its grip. That is why I call on it every morning, and every evening before I go to sleep, even though Fredrik is long dead, and I myself am a dry old woman just a step away from the grave.

Chapter Four

HULT WAS ONCE a true village with wooden farmhouses clustered on both sides of the road. The surrounding fields were divided into narrow strips, each strip allocated to a specific farmer. In the early 1800s, following edicts from the king, individual holdings were consolidated and farmhouses moved out of the village to be closer to the land. While productivity increased, the people could barely see from one farm to the next. No longer could workers from one farm call out to those of another, even if only to goad each other to work faster. It was not just a matter of an increased physical distance, but also a distance of souls.

Ramm, because of its large size, was allowed to remain in the village. In Rammen's days it was one of the most prosperous farms in the parish, with sixty-eight acres of cultivated fields and two hundred acres of forest and pasture.

The main house, the back of which I can now see from Gustafa's cabin, was built by my grandfather Lars in 1852. He painted it white, but now it is pale yellow, like butter in the spring. Two stories, my grandfather wanted, and a large veranda, now hidden from my view. All I can see is the kitchen entrance. When the church bells rang on Saturday evenings, my sister Disa would step outside, scattering the cats that lodged on the kitchen steps. She would take off her apron, turn her head toward the direction of the bells, and thank God for another week of work and good health.

A few years ago Johan tore down the old farm buildings and built a large dairy barn and machine hall down the road toward the village. Only the courtyard remains unchanged, the memories imbedded in the cobblestones like fossils. I miss the old buildings pressing against the forest, oxblood red against dark green. The stable and the barn were across from the main house. To the side were the carpentry shed, the grain storage, and the washhouse with the wooden tub and the stone mangle. Whenever I cross that courtyard, I can still hear the voices of the milkmaids, praising or scolding. A cow plops manure into a cement gutter, and jets of milk strike the buckets, at first hard and hollow, more muffled as the buckets fill. Even with the old barn gone, it is no less real than the fog dispersing over the lake or the sunlight falling on my kitchen floor. I do not tell anyone for fear that they will think me mad. If that condition comes, I shall deal with that too. I am well aware that the disease can progress silently for years. Madness is only one of its many facets but as far as I am concerned I am still sane.

I take good care. Every morning I wash my face and my body with glycerin soap and cold water. Until a few years ago I could scrub my own back but these days Fredrik's daughter Ella helps. In the winter I use barely melted snow. Afterward I rub myself with a thick towel until my skin turns crimson. It has been my routine ever since I was young. Fredrik used to laugh and call me ascetic. Once he brought a jar of skin cream from a store in Gothenburg. With long, even strokes, the way you would brush a horse, he spread the cream over my back, all the while talking about the farm he planned to buy and the life that lay before us.

Sometimes, when he fell asleep, I would pace my breathing to his. The doors of the wise woman's stove stood ajar and the light from the fire glimmered on his chest, which was still moist from his exertion. Throughout the summer, bees droned among the wise woman's herbs that continued to grow tall outside the windows, the air heady with bitter wormwood and musky caraway. In the winter Fredrik would balance on the ridgepole as he shoveled large chunks of snow off the roof, while I stood below, imploring him not to slip. Thinking back on it now is like finding an old photograph in a drawer, only to remember why I put it away.

He was not a man to compromise. He kept his focus. He did not rush through life but neither did he let it slow him down. He ought to have been married, or so the villagers said, a man like that, in his best years, and not lacking for means. Women thought him lonely, imagining that they alone could fill the void. I was no exception, although I did not see it at the time.

I heard he died a spectacular death. Ella said he had been out all day. The felling had gone well and the trees lay on the ground, stripped of their branches. He had examined the legs of the horses and checked their harness, greasing the slides so that the collars would not shift and chafe. His steward saw him put his nose to the neck of one of the Ardenners, which I can understand, for there is nothing like the musty smell of a horse in winter. One spruce was still standing. The way I heard it, it was as if the tree aimed straight for him. The men did all they could to free him but it was too late. The forest kept him.

I did not grieve. I was glad he was gone.

Chapter Five

A WHIFF OF scouring soap followed Aunt Alfrida as she swept into the kitchen at Ramm. Disa looked at me and sighed.

"I'm glad it's just the two of you," Alfrida said. "Because of what I've got to say."

It was only two days after I blocked Klas at church so I was not surprised to see her.

She took off her shawl and handed it to me. "There's talk," she said, her double chin bobbing in agreement.

Disa disappeared into the pantry, while Alfrida sat down at the table and motioned for me to join her. She was still out of breath from walking up the hill from Bergvik, the small farm that my grandfather Lars had chosen as her dowry. Keys jangled from her belt. At Bergvik, not even the biscuit jar could be opened without her help. She scrubbed the floors herself. None of her maids had been entirely up to the task.

"Everyone wants to know why you were late for church," Alfrida said as Disa returned with a cake. "Not to mention why you let Gustafa sit in your pew."

I traced the knotty tabletop with my finger, wishing Alfrida gone. Disa folded her arms, pursed her mouth, and stared at the floor.

"They're right, you know," Alfrida said, serving herself an ample slice of cake.

"Right about what?" I asked.

"Klas was only doing his duty. You shouldn't have stopped him."

To gather her information, Alfrida had cut through the forest and rowed across the lake. She prided herself on knowing everything that happened in the village. "The Grand Inquisitor," Rammen called her. If he needed to know from which direction the wind was blowing, especially during election times, his sister was the one to ask.

Behind her back, the villagers talked about Alfrida too. Much was made of her rotund figure, which contrasted so sharply with her parsimonious ways. Theodor Olsson, her husband, was a tall and gentle man, who spoke in terse sentences if he spoke at all. Over the years he had cleared new land, ditched and drained, and made so many improvements that Bergvik had become one of the best-run farms in the parish. Their two sons worked just as hard as their father, whether at home or hired out at other farms. However, with only two children, Alfrida had failed to replenish the earth. Theodor, being such a strapping figure of a man, would not have shied away from his marital duties, but Alfrida, the village women whispered, had surely taken measures to circumvent hers.

"Not even Rammen would want to be late for church," Alfrida said, looking first at Disa, then at me. "Most everyone thinks it had something to do with Ulrika."

It was only natural that the villagers would have mentioned Ulrika. Her oddities were well known, even cherished. Whenever the villagers spoke her name, their voices softened, as if they were talking about a dear departed friend. Some were old enough to remember her mother, the Baroness von Holkenstam, whose ancestors had been wealthy estate owners in Schleswig-Holstein, a region used as a pawn in recurring wars between Germany and Denmark. They still came alive in Ulrika's olive skin and in the color of her eyes, dark brown like the stones on the bottom of the river. Rammen's eyes, in contrast, were midnight blue like mine, although his had a certain hardness that made him all the more handsome and marked him as a man of the world. No, Ulrika was not one of them, on this the villagers agreed. For some reason this also made them defend her. If anyone was to blame, it had to be Rammen. A man so powerful ought to be able to control his own wife.

Not one of Alfrida's informants had put in a good word for Gustafa. Her family background, unlike Ulrika's, was murky at best. Lars had bought her at auction, and she never told him from where she came. A small girl in rags, she stood among feeble old women and men, all of them commodities carefully examined by potential bidders. Lars' bid had been the lowest, representing the money the parish would pay him to let Gustafa live at Ramm. A seven-year-old girl, he had likely reasoned, would not eat much and could more than pay for herself by spinning. Over the years Gustafa had come to identify herself with Ramm. The villagers avoided her company as much as possible, since she was known to cast spells and bring misfortunes on those who crossed her.

"What exactly were you trying to accomplish?" Alfrida asked. "Showing us we all can sit where we want?"

Disa, still staring at the floor, shifted in her chair.

"Anna," Alfrida demanded. "Have you nothing to say?"

I heard the heavy footfall, as Elias, our farmhand, stepped into the covered porch. Groaning, as if he already sensed Alfrida's presence, he pulled off his boots. He washed his hands in the basin, taking his time, sloshing water onto the floor. At last he entered the kitchen in his smelly stocking feet, muttering into his gray beard, less of a greeting than a growl.

Alfrida brushed the crumbs off her skirt, pushed her knuckles against the table, and heaved herself to her feet. She said she had spoken her piece. She had to get back to Bergvik, where people like Elias were not allowed to come and go as they pleased.

Alfrida gone, Elias sat down at the table. Gustafa came in from the parlor and took her seat by the stove. She always found a place to hide when Alfrida paid her visits.

As Disa poured him coffee, Elias flattened his beard and studied us with deep-set eyes. He was back from taking a heifer to the bull at Prästgården. The bull had shown no interest.

"Otter told me to come back this afternoon," he said as he tipped coffee from his cup on to his saucer. "He knows it too. A bull needs his horns. Sawing them off is just as bad as castration. Either way he'll never be the same." With that he placed a lump of sugar on his tongue, put his thin lips to the rim of the saucer, and slurped.

The dehorning of the bull had been done under Fredrik's predecessor, a man ill suited for handling bulls. Elias himself had been ordered to help. The men used iron chains to tie the bull to his stall before they sawed off his horns. His bellowing could be heard all over the village. Afterward the halter hung like an insult on his huge, bloody head.

Elias pushed away the saucer and complained that his coffee was cold. Muttering, Disa put the coffee pot back on the burner.

Gustafa sucked on her upper front gum, where she had lost two more teeth. "Fetch Kristina Andersdotter."

Disa nodded. Having a whore lead a cow to the bull was an old practice, and Gustafa swore by it still.

"Just don't get into any discussions with Erik," Disa called as I was out the door.

Truth was, I could hardly wait.

I HARNESSED CAESAR, a gray warmblood gelding, now in his fourth year. He had been distrustful since birth. Some of us are born that way, no matter what life tries to teach us. Perhaps that was why I took to him the moment he slid out of the mare.

The last time I had been to Kristina's cabin was in the spring of 1912. I had been collecting money for an armor-clad warship that would strengthen Sweden's defense. The Liberals, then in power, foresaw a world of peace, a thawing out of hostilities, an international community where conflict would be solved through mediation, not arms.

The response of the Conservatives, Rammen being one of them, was swift and decisive. The ship must be built, with or without the support of the Liberals. Driving all over the parish, I collected more than a hundred crowns.

Almost everyone contributed, if only a few ören. Erik, Kristina's son, refused. The true danger, he told me, was capitalism, not war. All the ship would be good for was to add a touch of excitement at the bathing resorts when the officers came ashore to dance.

Caesar's breath showed in the cold air as he walked down the hill, snow piled high on both sides of the single-lane road. Once on the main road, he began to trot, extending his neck and lengthening his stride, the sleigh runners humming as we sped along. Around us stone fences ran for miles and miles and ice from the night still coated the birches. Now and then, when we passed a farm, a kitchen curtain moved.

Travelers, particularly people from the cities, would call this part of Sweden beautiful, pointing to the dark forests of spruce and pine and the deep valleys shimmering with rivers and lakes. The people of Hult rarely thought of it in such terms, but rather as their share on earth, from which they had to eke out a living. The soil was sandy moraine on solid rock, mainly gneiss and granite. In the valley, where Rammen had most of his fields, the sediment made the land richer, but even there the land seemed reluctant to cooperate with man. Each spring, as the soil thawed, stones rose to the surface, ringing against the blades of the plows. It was as if the fields actually grew them.

A narrow, winding road took us up into the forest. Caesar slowed to a walk, the iron studs of his shoes gripping the ice. The road was not much traveled although Kristina would be the first to point out that traffic had once been dense.

Caesar shook his head when I pulled the reins. The ramshackle cabin, next to a lake, leaned in on itself, the roof sagging under the snow. Icicles hung like daggers from the eaves, making any exit or entry treacherous. Inside, children's faces pressed against the windows.

Erik came out, bowlegged and gaunt. At nineteen, he was the eldest of Kristina's six children, all by different fathers.

"What do you want?" he asked.

One of his brothers, a boy around eight, came up behind him, shivering and staring.

"Gustafa says Kristina must come. We need her to take a cow to the bull."

"Go tell your mother," Erik said to the boy who ran back into the cabin. None of Kristina's children knew their fathers, which she said was just as well.

"How's the horse coming along?" Erik asked, combing Caesar's forelock with his crooked fingers.

"He still tends to rush, but I've driven him next to an older horse, and that seemed to calm him."

Caesar sniffed Erik's pocket.

"Nothing there, my friend," Erik said. "Barely have enough as it is."

The frozen lake reflected the sun, taunting the cabin with its splendor. In her youth Kristina had used the cabin as a tavern. Not licensed to serve liquor, she ran her own illegal still. Her *brännvin*, made on potatoes, was known for its strength. Rammen once referred to her cabin as *Hôtel du Nord* and the name had stuck. The vicar, the man before Wikander, called it an infamous hideaway where many a man had been robbed of his life as well as his soul. His words proved more of an encouragement than a deterrent. It was not until Holmberg, the mill owner, leased the village inn from Rammen that Kristina's business began to wane. Holmberg made sure he was properly licensed, and even though Kristina's *brännvin* was still the strongest, the competition proved crushing. That was when she took up whoring in earnest, or, as she herself used to say, when she had to gain on the swings what she had lost on the carousel.

"I heard you started a temperance group at the mill," I said.

Erik did not answer. He could have been good-looking, but poverty had left its mark. His growth had been stunted from the start. At school we used to call him a bastard. Johannes and the other boys would pin him to the ground, smear his face with schoolyard dirt, and kick him where his clothes would cover the bruises.

"Rammen thinks it's uncalled for," I said.

"Uncalled for?"

"He says we need freedom, not restrictions. How can we learn to control our urges if we don't have a choice?"

Erik warmed his hand in the soft crease between Caesar's front legs. "Look at the old wretches at the poorhouse. Worked hard all their lives. No one ever called that freedom. The young people don't think it will happen to them. They think they'll put away some money and have a better life. But then the mill begins to wear them down. The noise. The dust. Doffing their caps to the foreman. They have a drink on Saturday evening. Before they know it, they'll have a swig or two on Sunday too. Soon it's all they live for, that one moment when they finally think they count."

Caesar kept nudging Erik as gusts of snow swept across the lake. Two hares chased each other over by the island. Now and then they rose on their hind legs to box.

"I hear the group is a cover-up for socialism," I said.

Erik smiled that wry smile of his, the same tight-lipped smile that used to drive Johannes and the other boys to kick him even harder.

"I saw what you did at church," he said.

Now I was the one who chose not to answer, not sure where he was aiming.

"Caused quite a stir," he said, lowering his voice as if reluctant to show his approval.

"Aunt Alfrida seems to feel sorry for Klas."

Erik laughed. "Wouldn't worry about Klas. All you did was make him earn his keep."

The cabin door opened and Kristina emerged. Without a word she stepped into the sleigh. Even through her thick, woolen shawl, her hair smelled of grime and cooking grease.

She had barely settled in when Erik stepped back, raised his arms, and yelled. Before I had a chance to gather up the reins, Caesar bounded forward. Erik's laughter rang out as he stood by the cabin and watched us disappear.

With Caesar galloping down the narrow forest road, I sawed at the reins, bracing my feet against the front of the sleigh. "Give and take," I heard Elias' voice, "give and take."

While the curves slowed him down, Caesar picked up speed where the road was straight. I shouted to Kristina to hold on as the sleigh swerved and careened just inches away from the ditches. We tore down the last hill, straight across the main road, through an open gate, barely clearing the fence posts.

The field was thick with snow, but Caesar galloped on. I pulled the right rein hard and did not let go. He began to turn, around and around, in ever-smaller circles, until at last he stopped. When I gave him the rein, he stretched his neck and snorted. Kristina had buried her face in her shawl—had I not known better, I could have sworn she was praying. Each time Caesar began walking I made him halt again. All around us the sleigh tracks dug deep into the snow, deeper and deeper as they wound toward the center, where Caesar stood heaving, sweat foaming between his buttocks and his nostrils flaring red. The villagers would see the tracks and wonder. No doubt we could expect another visit by Alfrida.

As we drove up to Ramm, Gustafa was waiting. "I thank you for coming," she said to Kristina. "You're much in demand, I know."

Kristina dismounted, her large breasts wobbling under her threadbare coat. "Won't come again," she said and shook out the folds of her heavy skirt. "Not worth risking my life for."

When Elias brought her out, the heifer pranced and lifted her tail. She was a fine animal, a cross between Ayrshire and Swedish Red and White, with long pointed teats. Clear mucus exuded from her vulva, and a thick rumble rose through her throat, turning into a drawn-out bawl.

"I fed her some beer," Gustafa said. "Close to three liters."

"That so." Kristina placed one hand on top of the heifer's rump and pressed down. When the heifer straightened her back in anticipation of the weight of the bull, Kristina nodded, took the rope from Elias, and began to lead the heifer down the hill. Gustafa followed, birch switch at the ready, should the heifer have a change of mind and try to return to the barn.

"Don't give him any water," Elias said as I tied Caesar to his stall.

I knew better than to water a sweaty horse but did not say so. Elias did not like his horses overheated, and I saw no reason to aggravate him further.

The stable held five Ardenners, all grinding hay between their molars, their joints clicking as they shifted their legs. Across the aisle, in boxes of their own with iron grids in front of the windows, stood Rammen's warmbloods, two chestnut geldings, which only Rammen himself would drive.

I rubbed Caesar with a pad of straw, bringing out the light gray dappling on his withers. In the neighboring stall Elias was spreading fresh straw with a pitchfork, moving the Ardenner this way and that by smacking his lips and touching its haunches. I could hear the bull blowing and bellowing all the way from Prästgården, his interest clearly peaked. Elias must have heard it too but said nothing.

The stars were out when I drove Kristina back to her cabin. Caesar needed rest, and Elias had hitched one of the Ardenners to the sleigh.

"If they were good enough for Napoleon, they're good enough for you," he said and gave me the reins.

Both Kristina and I had wrapped ourselves in blankets, and I balanced a carriage lantern between my feet.

The Ardenner kept a steady walk. Kristina was more talkative now. She and Gustafa had joined Fredrik Otter and his housekeeper for coffee in Prästgården's kitchen. "That Agnes is as fine a woman as I ever saw. Sliced the bread thick as my hand and put out real butter."

She reached into the folds of her skirt. "No heating of the syrup either. I just slathered it on, as thick as it came, and she still told me to have more. I saw her drop two pieces of sugar into Otter's coffee and take her own sweet time stirring it. Bet you anything she sleeps with him too."

She pulled out a small tin flask and took a swig, as the sharp smell of *brännvin* mixed with the bitter cold air. "A real gentleman, Fredrik Otter. Treats everybody the same. Steps back in the store while the rest of us do our business. But he's not making friends, all them articles in the newspaper. Even takes on Wikander. I hear the two of them stay up late at night debating religion. One man enjoys himself as much as the other. More often than not, or so I've heard, Otter wins."

The light of the lantern shivered on the snow. Kristina pushed out her lower jaw, forming a bowl into which she managed to shake a few more drops from her flask.

"Wouldn't mind keeping him warm myself," she said. "But even whores wear out. Was a time when I could accommodate a man in any position, propped up against a barn, a tree, you name it, as long as the footing was good. Never bothered with drawers, still don't."

She tucked the empty flask back into her skirt, and her laughter faded into the dark. I slapped the reins against the horse's back.

"Ah yes, my beauty," Kristina said, wrapping her blanket tighter. "We all have needs. I bet Mother Ulrika never told you. A little of this, and a little of that. Make way for the Lord and lower the bridges. I know a good man when I see him. Fredrik Otter takes his time. Enjoys getting there just as much as arriving. Thinks about his women too. Most men around here are only concerned with their own Hallelujahs."

We turned off the main road and continued up into the forest. I was glad that Kristina thought well of Fredrik Otter, even though, as cold as it was, my face burned. For all her faults, Kristina certainly had to know about men. Once, when the bishop had traveled to Hult to determine how well we obeyed God's laws, she had proudly told him that there was not a man in the parish who had not come to see her, except one who could not rise to the occasion and one who lacked the funds. Like everything else about Kristina, this might have been an exaggeration, but, then again, who but Kristina should know?

At the cabin Kristina stepped down without saying goodbye. It was as if the *brännvin* had worn off and her hostility had returned. I held up the lantern as she walked to the door.

Inside, shadows moved in the light of a tallow candle. The same pale faces pressed against the windows, black holes for eyes and mouths.

Chapter Six

ELLA ARRIVES ON the bus, and I am waiting with coffee. She works at the hospital in Varberg, her nurse's persona crisp and to the point. She does remind me of Fredrik. He too had that quality of standing back and surveying a situation, before he would decide on a course.

As always she goes to visit Fredrik's grave. She says she saw no recent sign of badgers but she covered up the old ruts.

She has turned into a badger herself, rooting around in the past. "You never talked about feelings," she says. "None of you did."

Well, I almost add, your father least of all, even though I know she is not talking about him.

"What I do remember is the silence," she says. "You'd all be sitting around the table and sigh. If you did talk, it was about the weather and the crops. You, Anna, were no better than the rest. You never told me how you felt."

What can I say? Even now it seems absurd that I should sit here and talk about my feelings. What good could it possibly do?

"I know you think me repressed," I say. "But there's also a kind of fortitude in that. You look around. You assess your life with all its limitations. You find a way to get through."

Ella keeps telling me she was too young to remember. I say her brain may not remember but her body does. That kind of evil does not go away. That is why she keeps asking all these questions.

"The village was different back then," I say. "All of society existed according to rules that had been tried and fixed over the ages. Not all were written down in the law books, or even in the Bible. I was taught early that what was good for the family and the village was also good for me. Feelings would only confuse."

I tell her I should never have allowed it to go as far as it did. Fredrik used to say it had nothing to do with me but he was mistaken.

"And the other girl?" she asks. "Did you ever find out who she was?"

"Never did. I know I've been accused of imagining things but Rammen saw her too. He said she tried to make them stop."

Ella seems to ponder this. "You gave up so much."

"I had no choice. Guilt spreads like a weed, suffocating everything around it. I had seen it happen to Rammen and Ulrika, although I didn't know the full extent of it yet."

As always, before she leaves, Ella insists on examining me. She keeps asking me about my heart. I know why. There is not just the possible deterioration of the brain, there is also the concern that my aorta may tear and cause sudden death.

As always she puts away her stethoscope and reassures me that I am as healthy as a bear. As always I tell her she may have gotten that wrong.

Chapter Seven

AS A CHILD I would visit Gustafa in the evenings. The shoemaker, who used the cabin during the day, had gone home, but his tools and his materials were still here and everything smelled of leather.

Much of the time Elias would lie on his cot, morose and drunk. Gustafa would be sweeping the warped wooden floor so the fairies could dance on it during the night. She did not fear Elias.

"He won't hurt me," she said. "He's too busy hurting himself."

She dreaded the dusk, as she dreaded all transitions, not just those between light and dark but also those between the living and the dead. As much as she was a Christian, her heathen ways ran deep.

"We must fear not only God but other forces too," she said. "Good and evil. We must make sure we don't offend them."

I would sit on Gustafa's cot, wriggling my toes inside my shoes. Sometimes we heard Wilhelm play his fiddle at Ramm, softly and mournfully, burdened by the responsibility of being the eldest son. Soon Gustafa's voice would take over, husky like a man's, and my heart would settle.

On occasion Gustafa showed me my caul, a shriveled membrane that had covered my head and my face when I was born. Some day, she said, I would have to guard it myself but for the time being she kept it in a tin box under her cot. It resembled a piece of lace, so dry that it would turn to dust if I tried to touch it. When a child was born, Gustafa said, God gave it a *fylgia*, a shape that rose from the waters and soared across the sea. Because I was born with a caul, my *fylgia* was more potent than others. It would follow me around, know my thoughts, and warn me in my dreams. Most of the time it would be invisible, but once in a while it would appear as an animal or even as a person. It would only leave me shortly before my death, when it would hurry ahead to make room for me in the life hereafter, or disappear forever if I were to be damned.

This is my last summer, I feel it in my bones. Memories of situations long ago come before me with such vividness that I can no longer push them away. If I fail to grasp their meaning, they always come back. Over and over I hear Gustafa's voice: "Start from the beginning. Always start from the beginning. Nothing is as it seems."

BEFORE HE CAME to Ramm, Elias was a soldier. Under the old allotment system, he received a salary, a cabin, and a small plot of land. Once a year he packed his rifle and his cooking utensils and departed for military exercises on a distant moor. All that came to an end the year he arrived drunk and insulted one of the officers. After Rammen hired him, he moved in with Gustafa in her cabin. The arrangement met with Rammen's approval—may well have been his own suggestion—and the current vicar found it useless to object.

As a child, I used to follow on Elias' heels wherever he went. He never moved his arms when he walked.

"All those buckets," he explained. "Arms got stuck for good."

Alfrida claimed it was not normal for a small child to spend so much time with a discarded soldier. Seeing one of us meant that the other could not be far away. Still, there were times when he would be gone for days, and no one seemed to know where I could find him.

Even at church I could keep an eye on him. Elias himself was in the gallery up by the organ, but he was in the altarpiece too. The artist who painted it had used the barn at Ramm as his studio. For months I watched him work, as the hens clucked in the courtyard and Elias poured kitchen scraps mixed with oatmeal and water to the pigs.

Unbeknownst to the villagers, the artist used some of them for models. Like it or not, they found themselves in full view above the altar, wearing headdresses and robes. In the background was Elias, a tall man in a hood, his long beard flowing. Jesus was the only stranger, a beautiful young man, one hand to his chest, the other pointing toward the sky, the sun lighting his forehead. At his feet sat Ulrika, looking straight at the artist, her robe intensely blue. "My very own Mary of Magdala," Rammen said when he first saw the artist's work. "Sinner and penitent both." I had no idea what he meant, my main concern was that I myself had not been included.

As soon as I learned to read, I helped Elias prepare for the house examinations. We sat outside the barn while I questioned him on the catechism. He struggled to remember the answers. Even when I gave him the first word or two, just to get him started, he kept shaking his head. Gustafa had shown him pictures of hell, men and women roasted on spits, or walking around with their heads in their hands, and when he described them to me, he trembled.

"God will save you," he said, "but he won't save Elias. All these years I've confessed my sins but never once have I repented. Same old sins, same old Elias."

On the day of the examination, always the first week of June, I watched for Wikander from the parlor window. Even as a child I was aware that Ramm was situated higher than the church, not the other way around, and I feared it might pit him against us.

He came driving up the hill, the rod of his whip swaying in its stand. Even his horse looked small in comparison, for he had gained weight over the years, no doubt due to the rich fare he had to endure after christenings and funerals.

Everyone had gathered in the parlor, where chairs had been brought down from upstairs. The crofters sat in the back, the men with their hats in their laps, for once without snuff pushed thick against their gums. The women had brought as many children as there were clothes for. They all lived on Rammen's land in exchange for their labor. Even the children weeded turnips in the spring.

Throughout the afternoon Wikander reminded us all, including Rammen, that all power was of God. He told husbands to be the heads of their wives, wives to submit to their husbands, children to honor their parents, and servants to obey their masters. Anxiety, he kept repeating, was a good sign. It meant we were aware of our wretchedness and rightly feared for our souls.

Wikander called Elias' name.

Elias lumbered to his feet, almost knocking over his chair.

"Why is life so important?" Wikander asked.

"Because it is a time of grace."

"Why a time of grace?"

"Because it is a time when God may grant us mercy."

"And why, Elias, is it called important?"

By now Elias shook like an old horse being led into a knacker's yard. "Because all of eternity depends on it and it will never come again."

After the examinations we gathered in the garden, where the table was set with Ulrika's best silver and china. There would be gingerbread cake and rhubarb juice instead of coffee for us children. Elias was nowhere to be seen.

Rammen once went to look for him. While waiting, I straightened nails in the shed. I placed nail after nail on the anvil, bent side up, and hit them with a hammer, just as Elias had taught me, turning and hitting, until the nails were as good as new.

When Rammen returned, he said Elias was fine. "He'll be back," he said although he would not tell me where he was.

I pictured Elias like a wild animal in the forest, hiding behind trunks and boulders, while God's voice thundered above.

At long last he came shambling across the courtyard. I took him by the hand and dragged him toward the storehouse. "Let's check the traps."

The traps in the grain bins often held four or five big rats. I was right behind him when he carried the cages up to the edge of the forest. As if dazed by the sudden light, the rats sniffed the air, their pink noses twitching. When Elias placed the cages on the flat granite rock, the rats clung to the sides with their forelegs stretched out like the arms of the wooden Christ. I did not blink when Elias put his rifle to their stomachs, nor did I cover my ears when the shots shattered the air. One by one the rats tumbled backward, their furry stomachs spotted with blood. I thought it helped Elias, and I felt better too, for such was the nature of redemption that even rats could die for our sins.

Chapter Eight

TODAY, WHEN I walk past the inn, I stop to peer through the window, the only one that is not boarded up. Past the piles of newspapers on the windowsill, I can see the room that used to be the bank.

Chairs are stacked on top of each other and covered with dust. The wallpaper hangs in shreds where the large wall clock used to measure the time. The desk, where I cleared vouchers and filled out column after column in large black ledgers, is turned upside down, some of the drawers missing. The numbers always held my interest, the way they formed patterns on the page, row after row, revealing what was entrusted and what was owed.

The door to the right used to lead to the inn itself, where customers discussed grain prices and Holmberg filled glasses with foaming beer. Upstairs Rammen entertained guests in a private room, and I could hear his laughter when I worked late. I can still see him coming down the narrow staircase, lit from behind, walking sideways with a glass of cognac in hand. In the courtyard, so desolate now, a coal fire burned in a barrel. Coachmen would be on duty, taking frequent drafts from their hip flasks. The horses, associating the smell of *brännvin* with abuse, flattened their ears, flung their necks upward, and bit the air in thwarted aggression.

As I stand there looking through the window, a tractor comes chugging down the road. The driver touches his cap in greeting, no doubt trying to make sense of an old woman staring into a deserted building. He wears earphones, probably listening to the radio, most likely a soccer match or some man from Stockholm reading the news. I have my own radio in the cabin. I never miss the opera hour, and I sometimes turn it on so loud that I wonder if Johan and his wife Greta can hear. Ella brings me records for Björn's phonograph. She says she buys them used from a record store in Varberg. I still listen to Caruso, although the sound is scratchy and the needle tends to stick.

On my way home, I see no one at the gas station. The village store is just as empty. Change has been as relentless as a sow that turns and crushes her young. Many farms have been abandoned. Some are rented out as summer houses to people I do not know. Others are gone altogether, with only a few lilacs and berry shrubs bespeaking a settlement that was. At the church, which used to be filled to capacity, the young vicar preaches to an almost empty house. His sermon plays over the loudspeakers in the nearby old people's home, where men hide liquor in their rooms and women answer telephones that never ring.

I remember them as if it were yesterday, those auctions where entire farms were sold off. Whole families left with nothing but the clothes they wore, the farmers' wives intent on keeping up appearances, putting out coffee and cake and thanking everyone for coming. I can still hear the auctioneer's rolling voice as he pointed with his hammer and fired off jokes, while children played hide and seek in the crowd. The auctions usually began in some shed with the axes, the saws, and the spades. Then it was time for wagons, sleighs, harrows, and plows. Finally came the turn to the animals, their value debated and weighed, the bidding always in favor of the buyers. The cows, penned up too long, would pull their handlers in wider and wider circles. The horses, shown at a walk and a trot, whinnied and shook their heads, stately Ardenners and the more agile *Nordsvensk*, ideal for hauling logs out of the forest. At day's end, when the auctioneer sold off the hens, most people had already left. How do we account for tragedies like that? I sometimes stayed behind, not as a representative of the bank but as someone who might be able to help, if only to return the cups and saucers to the neighbors who had loaned them out for the day.

Some of the wild animals are disappearing too. I hear the hazel snake is on the verge of extinction. I see one sunning itself outside Gustafa's cabin almost every day. I pick it up and hold it, a fluid creature of polished brown. It is harmless to man, although often mistaken for a viper. The two of us look at each other, woman and snake, old adversaries, the woman not as clever as the snake. What happened to Eden after the man and the woman left? Perhaps it still exists, guarded by the angels with the flaming swords.

On my way back to Gustafa's cabin, I see Samuel, the old Jew. He stands in a field sifting the soil between his fingers, his face roughly hewn and bronzed by the sun. "That by which you shall know me," he once said when I commented on the extravagance of the red handkerchief he always wears around his powerful neck. I think he knows that I approve. We can use some extravagance around here.

I do not call out to him. He needs to be left alone with his memories too.

Chapter Nine

In February 1914, some thirty thousand farmers from all over Sweden were to march in Stockholm in support of a stronger defense. For weeks Rammen had been working behind a closed door. Hult alone would send twenty men, a large number for such a small village. Being the eldest son, Wilhelm would represent Ramm. While most of the other farmers were to lodge at hotels and military barracks, Wilhelm would stay with our sister Tekla. Rammen himself would not participate. Like a general he would watch from afar.

War was nothing new, Rammen used to say. For centuries it raged right outside our windows. As the Danes pushed north, intent on conquest, omens were plentiful. Church bells chimed on their own and large flocks of doves arrived and disappeared as quickly as they came. Men armed with swords left to plow their fields at dawn. By nightfall their widows reclaimed their mangled bodies. The region became a no-man's-land, wedged between Denmark and Sweden. Fortresses and palisades burned in the night, huge bonfires that could be seen for miles. The men who lit them vanished into the forest. Rammen called it the village way. The art of ambush always suited us best. Now, he said, we were about to be tested again.

Two days before the march, defense festivities were held at the vicarage. Rammen stood tall in the middle of the room, his blue eyes slightly hooded with age. All around people were talking. Björn kept close to Emma, who had come to Ramm to help her aunt Emilia, the village midwife. Wilhelm twirled his mustache as he listened to Susanna, one of the Holmberg girls. Rightfully, he should have been the man to lead the farmers to Stockholm, but Rammen had surprised us all when he selected Fredrik Otter instead.

"He's not one of us," Rammen had told Wilhelm over supper. "This will give the rest of you a chance to keep an eye on him."

Wilhelm did not seem to mind. As much as he resembled Rammen in appearance, he was by temperament a different man.

Water trickled down the windows, condensed from hot coffee and human breath. Disa, wrapped in the Swedish flag, walked from man to man, offering snuff out of a silver box. Ulrika had stayed at Ramm, and Johannes, my youngest brother, had decided to keep her company. I often heard their voices from the parlor, long after Sara, our maid, came upstairs in the evenings on her way to her bed in the attic. I wondered what they talked about. Ulrika once told me that Rammen was in the grip of something larger, and that

Johannes was too. I did not understand what she meant, and when I asked, she just shook her head and sighed.

Disa stopped before Wikander, who hawked and took a good-sized pinch. For the past twenty years he had served us well. On Sundays, women would follow him from one parish church to the next, walking miles just to hear his strong singing voice and to shudder at the severity of his sermons. His private conduct was not always exemplary since he was given to card games and drink. To the church, such shortcomings were of little significance. Once a man was ordained, his divine authority remained undisputed. Nor did they bother his parishioners, certainly not the men. Sure, he drank too much, they said, but so what? There was plenty of liquor for all.

I kept looking for Fredrik but he was nowhere to be seen. For all her efforts, Alfrida had not managed to find out a great deal about him. He was not born in our part of the country, nor anywhere else as far as she could tell, since he never said a word about himself but always talked about farming.

"And how have you been doing, Anna?"

It was Emilia, her voice kind and bright. She had been the first village woman ever to ride a bicycle, a practice that many villagers, particularly the women, disapproved of. Still, she was a good midwife, and her unconventional manner of transportation had been put down to youth rather than immodesty. Besides, most of the roads were too rough to accommodate a bicycle, and more often than not she had to walk like everyone else.

I told her we were all doing well. Of course, even if there had been trouble, as with Ulrika, I would not have let on, not even to Emilia.

"I want you to meet Emma," Emilia said and took me by my arm.

Björn frowned at the interruption. I could hardly keep from staring. Emma was the most beautiful woman I had ever seen, her bosom high, her skin pure, and her lively brown eyes set off by her rich auburn hair, which was pinned loosely on top of her head.

"Emma will be of great help," Emilia said. "Unless, of course, Björn here decides to snatch her away."

Björn chuckled, but Emma's smile was oddly reserved, as if Emilia's words had caused her more embarrassment than pride.

Rammen called for everyone's attention, grasping his lapels with his smooth, white hands—never the hands of a farmer, the villagers used to say, but the hands of someone who worked with his brain.

Heads turned when Fredrik arrived. While the other men wore suits, he wore plain woolen trousers, his waistcoat unbuttoned over a white, collarless shirt. In his early thirties, he was not an impressive man as far as his build was concerned—not much taller than I—but every inch of him seemed charged. Standing by the door, he surveyed the room with his sharp, gray eyes. There was hardly a woman, young or old, who did not lose her train of thought.

Disa stepped up to Fredrik and held out her box of snuff. He smiled at her and declined. Not even Disa proved immune to that penetrating gaze, for she stood as if rooted before she got a hold on herself and moved on.

Fredrik took his place among the other men, his fine, dark hair long enough to cover the back of his neck. He had been a bachelor too long, or so Alfrida had told us, his bad habits accumulating over the years. Agnes had to get down on her hands and knees to retrieve the dirty clothes under his bed. He also used to visit a prostitute in Gothenburg, which in itself was not that remarkable, but what did seem remarkable, not just to Alfrida but to us all, was that he had set her up with a small porcelain shop and even hired a lawyer to get the police to remove her name from their lists.

Rammen nodded to Wikander's housekeeper, a middle-aged woman with swollen ankles, and she poured red wine for the men, spilling some of it on the Persian rug.

"The guns of Russia are aimed at Sweden," Rammen began. "The king is nervous. He doesn't get along with his prime minister, nor with his cabinet. We must let him know that he can count on us."

Fredrik spoke in a strong, clipped voice. "To be fair, the danger may not come from Russia. Germany and England are also preparing for war."

The other men shuffled uneasily, but Fredrik stood with his feet slightly apart, his head canted back.

"Russia wants access to the North Sea," Rammen said. "I don't think we have anything to fear from Germany. It may in fact prove a valuable ally."

Several men shouted, "Hear, hear!"

Rammen's tone turned conciliatory, a tactic that often served him well, for he was never as dangerous as when he appeared to concede. "Whoever the enemy is, we must be ready. The Liberals have lived in peace too long. They've forgotten the first rule of war. He who makes himself a sheep, the wolf will devour."

Fredrik's muscles tensed around his jaw. "I'm all for strengthening our defense. What I object to is the rhetoric that has come to surround this march. The newspapers are full of it, and, sad to say, I hear it again this evening. Truth is, to some this march has very little to do with the threat of war. Rather it has everything to do with weakening the current government. As much as I would like to see the Liberals go, I don't believe in mongering to people's fears to achieve it. The Swedish people need information, not propaganda. Unless those of you bound for Stockholm agree with me on this, I won't join you."

"I declare!" Alfrida spoke from the back.

The men shuffled some more, while the women whispered among themselves, a ripple of voices surging through the room, excited and nervous both. Wikander, for reasons of his own, decided to lead us all in prayer, which made the men more awkward yet, for they had to find places to put down their wine glasses before they could clasp their hands.

After the prayer Rammen expressed his regrets that Fredrik had chosen not to participate and appointed Wilhelm the new leader. With this he raised his glass and wished the men success. "My son will get you safely there and home again."

Fredrik bowed slightly and joined in the toast.

When he turned to leave, he looked straight at me, those granite eyes shifting gold. He did not smile the way he had smiled at Disa. I looked straight back, and as he walked toward the door, I wanted to follow, the way a man and a woman would leave a room together, side-by-side, and everyone else thinking it was just as it should.

Björn placed his hand on my shoulder. "Time to go. Mustn't keep Ulrika waiting."

THE FOLLOWING MORNING I drove Wilhelm to the railway station in Håstad, about an hour away at a fast trot. I watched as he stood on the platform, counting the men and giving out cardboard badges.

"Would you help me with this?" he asked, handing me a blue and yellow badge. It read: "With God and the Swedish farmers, for the King and the country."

I took off my mittens and pinned the badge on his lapel, my fingers stiff from the cold. He looked particularly smart that morning in his oval Astrakhan hat and his new black overcoat with a glimpse of his crisp white shirt underneath.

As Wilhelm gave some last-minute instructions, the men stomped and beat their arms against their sides in an effort to keep warm.

"Upon arrival, proceed immediately to your lodgings. Beware of exaggerated friendliness, be it from women or men. Avoid walking alone. Cross the street only when necessary. Whenever you step off a tram, watch both ways for motorcars and carriages."

The train blew its whistle as it approached. Brakes squealing, it came to a stop. Windows were pulled down, and men leaned out, smoking and laughing. Many of them had never been outside their villages or parishes, but now they were all swept along by this grand notion that farmers would march in Stockholm to aid their king.

Two days later I was preparing a hare by the kitchen counter. Stella bayed up in the forest, almost singing, light enough to let us know that she was on the trail of a deer.

Ulrika and Gustafa were making a *Salade Russe*, something Ulrika's mother had taught her, Gustafa still insisting that potatoes should be eaten warm, not cold. Over by the pantry Disa was kneading dough for rye bread, now and then stopping to spread more flour on her board or using her knuckles to push up her eyeglasses.

"You could help in the barn," Disa said to Johannes, who sat by the table and was the only one idle.

Farmhands and farmers' sons were known to milk but Johannes considered milking beneath him. Even Disa would have to admit that she had yet to hear about a man who prided himself on being a good milker. Elias would brush the cows and feed them, and if one or two needed special attention, perhaps because they were kickers or slow to let down, he would offer advice, but it was always Sara and Lina Lind, a crofter's wife, who sat down on their three-legged stools to do the squeezing and the pulling.

Johannes walked over to the stove and poured himself more coffee. A few weeks earlier he had moved to a cabin behind the main house, where the farmhands used to sleep. He shared it with Konrad, a new farmhand, who was timid but courteous and always a hard worker. In the early mornings Johannes would stand outside the cabin door, knocking out his pipe, his suspenders dragging. He came to the main house only for his meals, sometimes staying in the evenings to talk to Ulrika. When I tried to join them, he always found an excuse to leave.

I chopped off the head of the hare. Disa scowled when I severed the thighbones and broke the back. She always insisted that a hare should be cooked whole, but I had found that the heat spread more evenly if I cut it into pieces.

By now Wilhelm should be at Tekla's. I had not seen her since the wedding, which had been held at Ramm. The wedding dinner was served in the large upstairs *sal*, a room reserved for formal occasions. Holger Danell, a friend of the groom, sat to my left. He talked about studying at the University of Lund, how every night the watchman blew his horn from the southern tower of the great cathedral, how he and his friends gathered at Tua, a small and not-so-clean restaurant, where only professors and students were allowed, and where they debated philosophy and law. Tekla had written that Holger still asked about me. Knowing Tekla, I could only assume that she felt free to answer, and that by now she had told him more than he could possibly want to hear.

Just as I began to remove the membranes from the meat, Rammen entered with the newspaper. He took his seat at the table and gave the newspaper to

Johannes, who barely looked at it before passing it back. The relationship between Rammen and Johannes had always been strained. Johannes had been born before term, small and cold. Ulrika had wrapped him in swaths of unrefined cotton wool, which helped keep him alive but never warm. While the rest of us children rewarded Rammen with early and frequent smiles, Johannes never complied. Even now, he rarely smiled. All his life he had been a loner, and we had all come to accept it.

Ulrika and Disa joined Johannes and Rammen at the table. Gustafa poured herself some coffee too and moved to her chair beside the stove, as always wiping the seat before she sat. Of late she took breaks when the rest of us were working. Ulrika humored her, and even Disa pretended not to notice.

As I continued to tend to the hare, Ulrika held up the newspaper so I could see. On the first page was a picture of King Gustaf V, tall and skinny, in his mid fifties. His wife, Queen Victoria, often traveled to her native Germany, and not even Gustafa, to whom the royals could do no wrong, could rightly explain why this should be so.

Rammen told us he had been on the telephone with Stockholm. The weather could have been better, he said. The Stockholm sky was gray, the flags not as bright as they would have been in the sun, but people seemed to be everywhere, watching from balconies and rooftops. The farmers had gathered by provinces in churches around the city. After the services, they marched through the streets, six by six, in close columns, a black mass of bowlers and overcoats. Crowds cheering them on, they made their way toward the royal palace, past the proud facades of old mercantile houses, and across the bridge over Strömmen, which connected Lake Mälar with the Baltic Sea. The flags whipped in the wind. Only a few stones were thrown. A young socialist shouted, "Long live the republic!" and had to be protected from angry bystanders.

Gustafa studied the picture of the king. Whenever she had a chance, she would pore over the photographs in Disa's magazines, the king at the hunt, the king at the tennis court, the king at royal functions at home and abroad. Once my Aunt Hedvig, Rammen's eldest sister, wrote a letter from her villa in Gothenburg, where the king had come for dinner. Apparently the king had spilled soup on himself, dangerously close to his crotch. A servant girl was called in with a towel. While she bent over his lap, the king leaned back and puffed on his cigarette. "Press harder!" he said, and ordered her to rub a little more to the left. Gustafa said it was all lies. It was not right to tell such stories about a monarch. Besides, she happened to know that the king did not like soup, so it was highly unlikely that Hedvig would have served it in the first place.

"The king should know that heads will roll," Johannes said. "Just like they did in France."

"On the contrary," Rammen said. "A republic would never work in Sweden. It's incompatible with the Swedish temperament. Republics lack imagination. Look at the Swiss and the Americans. No sense for pomp and circumstance, only the everyday and dull. And don't let the French fool you. As soon as someone sufficiently brilliant rises above the masses and has the brains and courage to take advantage of the moment, the republic will be ashes. Man has a right to dream, especially when times are hard. He needs to believe in gods and heroes, and he longs to be among them, not just in the hereafter but also here on earth. The king understands all this. He's not as weak as you think."

Yelping came from the covered porch and the kitchen door flew open. Björn entered with Stella and Stoj, a young harrier he had bought from the butcher. Thickset and barrel-chested, Björn threw his leather-strapped hunting jacket on one of the empty chairs and tied the dogs to the leg of the stove.

Disa stepped around the dogs and lifted a pan of potatoes on to a burner. The dogs pulled at their leashes, their claws scratching the freshly scrubbed floor. Sara would have to scrub it all over again. As always she would not complain.

His cheeks still red from the cold, Björn sat at the table as Disa brought his supper.

"Did they say anything about the queen?" Gustafa asked Rammen.

Björn speared a slice of pork. "I'm sure Wilhelm gave her your greetings. No doubt she's been wondering how you're getting along."

"Be quiet, Björn," Ulrika said with a smile. "I'll have no such talk in my kitchen."

Björn sopped up the pork grease with a piece of bread and winked at Gustafa, who tried to shoot him an angry look. Björn laughed, and Gustafa blushed like a young girl who had just been given a compliment. She had loved him since he was a boy and would continue to love him for as long as she lived, and the feeling was always mutual.

Disa put kitchen scraps and the head of the hare in a bucket and placed it by the door.

"No food for the bitch," Björn said and nodded toward Stella. "Bayed without reason. Stoj took off after her. Went on for at least an hour, dumb dogs running 'round and 'round, until I realized that whatever they were chasing didn't exist."

I seared the hare in butter while Rammen continued his account. He said the farmers had filled the inner and outer palace courtyards as well as the surrounding grounds. In the inner courtyard a stage had been built from which the king would speak. White handkerchiefs waved from the palace windows, and behind a curtain there had indeed been a glimpse of the queen. Shortly, King Gustaf, in full military dress, had entered the courtyard. This was the moment everyone had been waiting for. The 1809 constitution, still in effect, stated that "the King alone shall rule the realm," but in reality the power had long since shifted to the cabinet and the *Riksdag*. The king, however, was known for his efforts to assert his supremacy. In this, if in nothing else, his queen stood behind him.

Björn pushed back from the table, propped up his feet on an empty chair, and contemplated the gentle rise and fall of his stomach. Although he always gave the impression of a man well fed, he carried no superfluous fat, no more than he would allow an unneeded thought to crowd his mind.

In a speech, which Rammen called a rhetorical *tour de force*, the king referred to the bond that had always existed between the Swedish farmers and their rulers. The king's cause, he said, was the cause of the farmers. His convictions were their convictions and could never be compromised. "The defense question must be solved, fully and without delay." Shouts of hurrah echoed within the courtyard walls. The farmers sang "A Mighty Fortress is Our God," bared their heads and bowed in prayer while the queen reportedly wept.

Björn hauled himself up from his chair, untied the dogs, and grabbed the bucket by the door. "Hand me the lantern!" he said to Disa who still looked askance at the dogs. As soon as he left, I asked Gustafa to keep an eye on the hare.

The snow creaked under my clogs when I walked over to the doghouses. Stella whined as Björn dumped half the bucket into Stoj's bowl.

I took Stella over to the other doghouse and snapped the chain to her collar. After licking my hand, she trotted back and forth a few times. The chain slid along a wire some six feet above ground, and she seemed to know by force of habit exactly how far she could go.

Björn tossed the head of the hare to Stella, the part that all dogs seemed to prefer.

"Wilhelm ought to shoot her," he said. "Only hunts well when by herself."

Behind the kitchen window, Gustafa was swirling her coffee by the stove. Johannes was gone, but Rammen was still talking.

"Please tell me what's wrong," I said.

Björn pushed his hands into his pockets and looked up at the starless sky.

"We used to be able to talk about everything," I said.

"I saw what happened at the vicarage. He's known to hold women's eyes longer than necessary but this time you were the one holding his."

"Didn't think I was breaking the law."

Björn's voice bristled in the dark. "He's not for you. Simple as that. He's taken."

Stella was gnawing on the head when Björn kicked it into the ditch and out of her reach. With that he gave me the lantern and headed back to the house.

His words stayed with me as I climbed down into the ditch to retrieve the head. Both dogs were watching, tails stiff.

Apparently Björn knew about Agnes sharing Fredrik's bed. Still, a bachelor sleeping with his housekeeper was not unusual. As Björn himself used to say, it was the only entertainment the poor women could expect. As striking as she was, Agnes had to know that she could never marry Fredrik. Marriage was meant to be a union of equals, at least as far as material assets were concerned. Agnes' father was only a tailor, and she would bring nothing by way of dowry other than her looks and her skills. Granted, she had attended a cooking school in Gothenburg and Kristina was not the only one who said that Fredrik was fortunate to have her, but this made her a good housekeeper, not a good wife.

Icy water began to seep through my socks, as the head slid out of my hands and lodged itself between two stones. I gripped the ears, but the skin pulled away, exposing the muscles and the flesh, making the head more slippery yet. After I fit two fingers into the eye sockets and clamped down with my thumb, I finally managed to grasp it and throw it back to Stella. Her jaws closed down on the skull, as easily as Ulrika crushed eggshells for her hens, the same eerie, brittle crack. Perhaps it was the dark, or the acrid smell of mud and slime, but the chill that ran through me had nothing to do with the cold.

Two days after the farmers' march about fifty thousand workers staged their own march in Stockholm. The Varberg newspaper chronicled the events blow by blow. The leader of the Social Democrats urged the Liberal prime minister not to yield to the pressure exerted by the king and the farmers. From the prime minister's point of view, however, it was no longer only a question of defense. The greater question was who would rule the country—the king or his cabinet. At the prime minister's request, the king conceded that his position in the defense question was not locked in by his courtyard speech, but he refused to surrender his right to speak uncensored to his people on matters that concerned them all. Stockholm was in an uproar, bordering on revolution, or so we heard.

Still, as Rammen put it, "reason prevailed." After the prime minister resigned, the Conservatives were back in power. Rammen celebrated at the inn, handing out cigars to farmers and mill workers both.

Chapter Ten

THIS MORNING GRETA, Johan's wife, walks up from Ramm and knocks on my door. She wears a light summer dress, a green sweater, and rubber boots to protect against the dewy grass. She and Johan saw my light on in the night, and she wants to make sure that all is well.

We have coffee and twice-baked bread. I tell her about the dead wood grouse hen I found up in the forest. The hen lay on her back, with a dead viper wrapped around her wings. Three wood rats had bitten into her breast. Even in death they had refused to let go.

"What do you think happened?" Greta asks.

"Someone must have put out fox poison. The grouse ate it first, and then it spread to the others. It's the only explanation I can think of."

Johan signed on as a farmhand in 1952. He was fresh out of agricultural school and much too tall for the doorways. With Ragnar, Björn's son, showing no interest, it soon became clear that Johan was the one who would take over Ramm.

After Johan and Greta bought the farm in 1968, they leased additional land for pasture. These days they milk thirty-two cows and breed steers on the side. They continue to grow grass and grain. Other farmers are less traditional. They no longer keep cows, claiming it is not worth the labor.

The storm in 1969 reduced the forest by half. Björn walked around in a stupor, lost in what used to be his forest. We all have one great catastrophe to live through. There may be others, but this one is always the greatest. After that storm Björn was never himself. I think it was the sight of all those broken trees that ultimately killed him.

Wasting no time, Johan replanted with spruce. Just the other day I found him marking trees to be thinned this winter. He said I should not walk too far into the forest alone. I laughed, would have ruffled his hair if I could have reached it. I told him I had been through far greater dangers than that.

"Come have supper with us tonight," Greta says.

Now and then I do accept her invitations. She is a good cook and we eat in what used to be the parlor. To honor the old house, they have taken out the old tile stove and replaced it with the kind of open fireplace that was there in the beginning.

When I grew up, the parlor windows were hung with white muslin. Ferns and geranium occupied the windowsills. The tiles of the stove repeated the soft green of the walls. A large gilded mirror hung above the sofa, along with tapestries and sconces and a painting of a woman and a child. The black harmony organ stood by the door that led to Rammen and Ulrika's bedroom. The wooden floor, painted white, was all but covered by Ulrika's rag runners.

One of those runners was woven in a range of muted mushroom dyes with strips of red from a velvet dress I wore at Susanna Holmberg's fourteenth birthday party. I was the only girl from the village. The other girls came from Gothenburg and would stay the night.

When Susanna asked us to write in her new poetry album, I drew a picture of a man trying to catch a small girl who seemed to dodge him at every turn. Underneath, in that leaning script Karolina still taught us, even though German doctors had identified it as a possible cause of myopia and crooked spines, I wrote, "Heigh-ho cried the wench and pinched the vicar!" If someone had asked me where those words had come from I would not have been able to say. They jumped up like a jack-in-the box and demanded to be written down.

The day after the birthday party Mrs. Holmberg came to Ramm and asked to talk to Ulrika. Ulrika received her in the parlor and the door was ajar so I could hide in the hallway and watch. Mrs. Holmberg whispered and shook her head but Ulrika laughed so hard she could not stop. Mrs. Holmberg tried to calm her but to no avail. Someone fetched Rammen, who asked Mrs. Holmberg to leave, which she seemed all too happy to do, still shaking her head. That evening Rammen sent for Lina, the crofter's wife, who came and sat with Ulrika by the upstairs window. I expected him to scold me but he never did.

"Anna." Greta speaks softly, as if to remind me of her presence.

"I'm sorry," I say. "I thank you for your invitation, but I'd like to come some other time."

I do not tell her that I had heard the child. I often hear it in the night, a keening in the wind that blows across the grave.

Chapter Eleven

ULRIKA USED TO gather flowers in the meadows. As a child I watched her take the plants out of the tin tube and place them in a wooden press. She told me their Latin names and made me repeat them. They seemed more important after they were dried. She said they now represented their species, not just themselves. Other children's mothers did not have time to collect flowers, nor did they seem to have the inclination. Ulrika's scent was different too, a scent of dusk and roses. And her step was soft, much softer than the clatter of the maids. On days when I felt I needed her more than usual, I would follow her from room to room, the low sound of her voice sending waves of pleasure through my body. But when I caught her eye, she would often look past me, as if I were the one who was not there.

I still have her weaving book. She began it when she was a girl. Her handwriting is forceful, yet ornate, with few mistakes and scratch-outs. It contains detailed instructions with precise amounts of rye flour and linseed oil used to size the yarn, and it stresses the importance of keeping the warp taut and the borders straight, something she always tried to teach me.

The cover of the book is a muted brick red, embossed with elaborate designs like those of rich Victorian velvets. Glued to the inside is a black and white print entitled "Coimbra." Peasants work by the river, and Coimbra itself rises like a magic mountain in the haze behind them. Inside the back cover is another print, called "Dublin." Here too you see a city in the distance. To the right picnickers rest on a grassy slope. Below them, to the left, a man herds cattle. It seems fitting that neither Coimbra nor Dublin is depicted up close. Ulrika once told me that she would have wanted to see more of the world, but her longest journey was with Rammen to Gothenburg on the day of their betrothal.

When Ulrika married Rammen, she was already pregnant with Wilhelm. As with every future farmer's wife, she had to prove that she was fertile and able to produce heirs. The custom was as old as the village. Wikander called it "an abominable stain which the parish must do its utmost to wash away." Like all vicars before him, he found his words went unheeded.

The wedding, held at Brunnsdal, was a grand affair with many guests. On the morning of the second day, the wedding party rode from Brunnsdal to Ramm in a long row of carriages pulled by horses with ribbons braided into their manes and tails. Rammen and Ulrika rode first. Rammen drove himself, with Ulrika next to him. In the seat behind them two fiddlers tuned their instruments, trying to find common ground. The rest of the carriages were so crowded with friends and relatives that the iron wheels dug deep into the gravel road.

At Ramm, the women lingered in the courtyard to admire the view. The men inspected the barn, walking with their hands folded behind their backs to mark that this was a day of leisure. The large barn, with more windows than most, was freshly scrubbed. Three pairs of long-horned oxen stood on peat and freshly hacked twigs. The dunghill in the back was raked, and cows grazed on the strip of grass between the dunghill and the forest. Healthy and serene, they had weathered the winter well. Rammen always did take care of his cows. Other farmers might run low on fodder and underfeed their cattle until some of the animals no longer could stand. In those barns, the first chore of the morning was to "lift" the cows. The last resort was feeding them thatch from the roof.

Ulrika set about to change the rooms at Ramm, making them airy and bright. The chairs in the upstairs *sal*, with their turned legs, lyre backs, and soft yellow upholstery, were inspired by the French style of furniture that King Gustav III had introduced in Sweden in the late 1700s. Ulrika brought pictures to the village carpenter, who measured and copied and at some point even journeyed to Stockholm to see the originals. Ulrika's taste may well have been too extravagant for a farmhouse but it was never pretentious. There was a playfulness and a sureness of style that would deflect even the harshest of critics. Even so, we lived in a make-believe world, like a stage set at the opera, that last splash of splendor before the curtain comes down.

The years to follow would wear her down. By the time Johannes was born, all her energy was spent. The doctor used to tell us that she suffered from a weakness of the will. We had no name for it ourselves. I now think of it as a kind of innocent shamelessness, a sensuality of the soul. The doctor said she would sometimes lose the feeling that she existed at all. The present would have the effect of an intrusion, and while the rest of us would wake up from a dream and know that we were awake, she could not be sure. He said the only possible cure would be talking. A doctor in Vienna had achieved some remarkable results with patients suffering from similar afflictions. Rammen always said no. He said Ulrika needed to forget, not remember. Digging up old hurts would truly push her over the edge. Besides, he could not bear the thought of her being away, for this would be part of the treatment—to take her to hospital and not let the rest of us see her.

SYLVIA, MRS. HOLMBERG'S sister, was a frequent guest at the inn. As a girl I sat in her room and watched her put on rouge. When she met my glance in the mirror, she turned her attention to me.

"We should all have such skin," she said and pinched my cheeks. "And those eyes!" she added. "Lucky the young fellow who gets to plumb those depths."

She bound up my long, blond hair, and said I was pretty. Not like Tekla—everyone knew that Tekla was beautiful—but more in a general sense, perhaps more lasting. When Elias saw me, he laughed and said he had never seen anything like it.

Sylvia staged *tableaux vivants* at the inn. Björn played the piano. His feet did not reach the pedals, and Sylvia told him not to strike the keys so hard. The rest of us children sat on the floor, staring at the sheets that served as a curtain. Once, when they drew apart, we saw a gypsy camp with swarthy men around a fire. Another time we saw fairies and elves and a milkmaid herding cows. In my favorite scene Disa wafted back and forth among the roses, touching the petals with her magic wand and making them unfold.

Sylvia attended my first communion. I remember this well because I heard her gasp.

That morning, as we left for church, Elias had trapped a lynx. The pelt hung on the barn and was soaked by heavy rain. The lynx, Elias said, had not put up a fight. A wildcat would have spat and clawed, but the lynx sat motionless as he lowered the rope into the cage.

At church, the candles trembled in the dusk, like the lanterns of the mill workers when they returned home on foggy evenings. Standing in front of the congregation, I wore a new black dress and ribbed stockings that itched. I was thirteen years old.

Rammen sat in the first row, his usual seat over by the pillar. Just before we left that morning he had presented me with a silver brooch. "Better not wear it to church. Wikander wouldn't approve."

Ulrika sat on the women's side, in front of Mrs. Holmberg and Sylvia. Of late she had begun to check my underwear at night, although she never told me for what. School was no help either. The book on the human body had chapters on bones and joints and muscles. It had pages and pages about the ear, the eye, and the nose. Women, it said, had a stronger sense of feeling than men. Their capacity to tolerate pain was also greater. But never once did it mention the small mound between my legs, the one that had begun to grow soft, curly hair.

Wikander sounded far away even though he was standing right before me. "What sin does God forbid in the sixth commandment?"

"Whoring," I answered, my voice barely audible in the vastness of the church.

"Speak up."

This time I spoke so loudly that even the cherubs in the ceiling must have heard me.

"What else is a sin against the sixth commandment, other than the coarse deed itself?" Wikander asked.

"Everything that leads up to it."

"And what leads up to it?"

"Gestures that cause foul thoughts in oneself and others."

That was when I heard Sylvia gasp.

Perhaps it was less a gasp than a protestation. Later, when everyone gathered at Ramm, she said that some day it would all be revealed, just like everything else that was written in the Bible. Then, making sure that only I could hear, she leaned over and whispered, "Take heart, little one. Don't believe a word they say."

After the guests left, I walked out to the barn and stroked the pelt of the lynx, now drying in the sun. Elias found me there and said I had better get back to the house.

"Is it really true that it didn't put up a fight?" I asked.

"Never flinched. Just poked its head through the noose so I could hang it."

I was still too young to understand. Through the years I would often ask him to tell me the story again, and each time he stuck to his first account, that the lynx had chosen death.

The following summer Sylvia married. She and her husband, Manfred Josefsson, rented a summerhouse at Ramm. It was just a small cottage but they called it a summerhouse. Alfrida had heard that Sylvia and Josefsson slept without clothes.

"I wonder who told her," I said to Disa when I was washing up in our room one evening. Disa was already in her bed, her thick glasses on her nightstand next to her book of hymns. She did not answer.

"Perhaps Sylvia did. Either that, or someone spied on them through the summerhouse window."

Disa turned to the wall and pretended to snore.

I bent over the enameled basin, splashed water on my face, and reached for a towel. "What if some of the villagers try to sleep naked too? Just imagine Alfrida and Theodor without clothes."

"A fool who's silent may be considered wise," Disa muttered. "A fool who keeps talking is still a fool." Soon her sleep was real, her cheek scrunched up against her pillow.

That night I slept without clothes myself. I did not think that Disa would notice. I lay very still, my gaze fixed at the ceiling. After a while I must have fallen asleep, for in the early hours I woke up shivering, my nipples hard against the touch of the sheet. I found my nightgown under my pillow and put it on. It was still an experience, I told myself, lying naked until dawn.

One day, when Björn and I were drifting in a rowboat on the lake, we saw Sylvia and Josefsson swimming close to the shore. I was at the stern, rescuing bees that had landed on the water, carefully scooping them up and depositing them on the railing. Björn lay on his back, his left foot cocked on his right knee, a fishing line tied around his big toe. While he talked about the universe, I watched the swimmers. There was laughter and splashing, as you might expect, but much to my disappointment Sylvia and Josefsson both wore clothes.

Manfred Josefsson came to Ramm for milk and eggs. He talked to Elias, trying to strike up a conversation. Elias never said a word, other than naming the price for what Josefsson wanted to buy. One afternoon I saw Sylvia and Josefsson in the woods. Instead of making my presence known, I hid behind an elderberry bush. Sylvia sat on a blanket, holding a book. I was almost close enough to read the title. The sun shone among the birches, and Sylvia's blue dress was mottled with light. Josefsson had stretched out on his back and seemed to be asleep. When Sylvia reached out as if to wave an insect away from his forehead, he caught her hand and drew her close. She plucked up her skirts and straddled him like you would a horse. The pungent smell of elderberries all around, my body rocked with Sylvia's, as my hand found its way inside my underwear and pressed down on that small secretive spot. Sylvia must have known I was there all along, for she caught my eyes and smiled.

After that I never talked to Sylvia again. Whenever I heard that she and her husband were in the village, I took care not to cross their paths.

Chapter Twelve

I HAVE BEEN reading *Zarathustra*. As always, I do so with pencil in hand. The margins are crowded with my questions and comments, erased and rephrased over the years.

When I hear the knock on the cabin door, I hope it is Samuel. It is the young vicar. He has taken to visiting us all, high and low. Some of the old people are suspicious.

We talk about last week's service. He asks why I think so few of the young people come to church. I tell him I can only speak for myself. The only reason I still attend Sunday mass is that it gives me an opportunity to be alone with my thoughts and yet remain in the company of others. As for his sermons, I say they are too long. He does not seem to take offense.

I ask about his wife. Samuel visits her often. The last time I joined them, Samuel was restoring the old altar cloth. As a stagehand in Salzburg, he learned to mend just about everything. The young vicar was working in his office, door closed, but I was with Samuel and the vicar's wife in the drawing room, where the altar cloth was spread out on a large table, green and red on white linen, hand-embroidered with flowers and vines and grapes. I sat in a yellow armchair with my back against the open window, the scent of lilies drifting in from the garden. The vicar's wife played the piano, Grieg it was, *Remembrances, Opus 71, No 7*, and *Norwegian Dance, Opus 47*. The light fell on her slender neck, her skin white against her black hair and dress. Samuel's hands—large and tanned—moved with the music as he sewed.

The young vicar stays for an hour. The unicorn on the windowsill catches his interest. He says it is a symbol for Christ. I do not tell him where I found it.

When he asks if I have considered moving to the old people's home, I tell him I have not. And since I now have answered all his questions, I think it only fair that he should answer one of mine.

"In your sermon last Sunday you condemned those who manufacture prophylactics. Does that mean you also condemn those who use them?"

"It is indeed against God's will."

I tell him I used to distribute condoms when I worked at the bank. To his credit, he listens. And yet, like Wikander before him, he has his mind made up.

I ask him what would have happened if Pontius Pilatus had refused to crucify Jesus. Would Jesus have lived to a ripe old age? Or was Pontius Pilatus only acting out what had already been decided? Was he merely the means by which God carried out his divine plan? If this were so, was he not as innocent as his victim? To this the young vicar has no answer.

But then, as he is about to leave, he turns in the doorway and points to Nietzsche's book, which lies upside down on the table.

"Anna," he says, his voice much softer. "There can be no forgiveness unless we first forgive ourselves."

Chapter Thirteen

A FEW WEEKS after the farmers' march the telephone rang in the parlor.

"Raaamm," Disa answered in a low, deceptively obliging voice, riding the vowel as long as her breath would let her.

It was Aunt Hedvig, Rammen's eldest sister, who wanted to know if the invitations had arrived. The School of Home Management was holding its annual ball. When Tekla was a student at the school, she had met Erling at one of these balls. Almost all the men invited came looking for prospective brides. Disa had also been a student at the school but she had not managed to secure a husband. I had refused to enroll, since I saw no point in going to Gothenburg to learn skills that I could just as well learn at home. As for finding a husband I had no doubts that I would be able to locate one on my own. Now Hedvig insisted that both Disa and I attend the ball, which was to be held at one of the city hotels. Hedvig, in her own words, would make "the necessary arrangements."

Disa stayed up late making our dresses on the sewing machine. I decided to wear olive green cotton tulle, while Disa chose a dove gray charmeuse, her only concession to color being a snug purple turban, held together with one of Ulrika's brooches.

One evening, when I kept her company, I hawked in imitation of Wikander. "It's not the dance itself, but the unfo-o-o-ortunate embrace that will lead you into temptation."

Disa did not laugh. "God-given desires must have God-given boundaries," she said as she threaded the needle. "Wikander is a man of God. We're fortunate to have him."

"Hedvig was telling me about a young pastor in Gothenburg," I said. "He says that Luther's catechism lacks support in the Bible. That the emphasis on worthlessness and guilt is harmful and old-fashioned."

Disa sighed. "All I can say is I'm glad he's in Gothenburg and not here."

Pins clasped between her lips, she worked the treadle. I could hear the steady rhythm long after I went to bed.

THE WEEK BEFORE the ball, Tekla arrived from Stockholm to teach me how to dance. Everything changed with Tekla. The house filled with laughter, and Gustafa petted the cats before she fed them on the kitchen steps.

In the parlor Wilhelm played the fiddle while Tekla took turns dancing with Disa and me. Hedvig had made it known that Disa's dancing, what little she had seen of it, ought to be improved. For days we practiced the waltz, the polka, the mazurka, and the hambo.

Once Tekla hummed a foreign-sounding melody, fast and light. Wilhelm joined her on the fiddle. She unpinned her thick, golden hair and shook it free. Still humming, she found a red tablecloth in the sideboard drawer and tied it around her waist. While Wilhelm played on, she danced, using a pot lid for a tambourine and striking it with a spoon.

"I'm Nora!" she shouted at the top of her voice. I clapped, and Disa ran to fetch another pot lid in the kitchen and joined in.

"You too," Tekla called out to me.

I shook my head. Disa was dancing for us all, jumping and spinning, while Wilhelm played faster and faster, as if the music had been locked away in his fiddle and was finally set free.

Alfrida joined us after supper. She and Ulrika sat by the kitchen table while the rest of us cleaned up. It was Sara's evening off, and Gustafa was in her cabin looking after Elias.

"Who's Nora?" I said to Tekla as I dried the plates.

"A character in one of Ibsen's plays. I saw it in Stockholm. First with Erling and then again with some of my friends. Nora left her husband. I was at the edge of my seat when she slammed the door."

Alfrida sighed. "I heard about that play a long time ago, and even then I thought it was unrealistic."

"Why did she leave?" I asked.

"Wait," Disa said. "I want to hear this."

We waited while she walked outside and poured the dishwater down the sluice into a barrel at the bottom of the kitchen steps so that Elias could feed it to the pigs in the morning.

"She had no choice," Tekla said when Disa rejoined us. "Her duties were not just to her husband but also to herself."

Alfrida ran her hand across the table, brushing off imaginary crumbs. "She was weak and selfish, that's all. What kind of playwright would write a play like that? I'd just as soon not hear about it."

Even Ulrika spoke up. "Nora didn't just leave her husband. She had to leave her children too. Where would she have found the money to feed them?"

When no one else was listening, Tekla told me more. Nora's husband had been deadly ill. Only rest in a warm climate could save him. Nora forged her father's signature to borrow money that allowed her to take her husband to Italy. By the time they returned, the husband's health was restored and their

first child had been born. A few years later, when Nora had almost managed
to pay off the loan, her creditor told the husband about the forgery and
threatened to make it public. The husband ordered Nora out of the house,
telling her she was not fit to be a wife, much less a mother. When the creditor
withdrew his threat, Nora's husband begged her to stay. He thought they
could go back to their old way of life. Nora said no. She said their marriage
had been based on lies, and she no longer loved him.

"I can see why she had to leave," I said.

"I'm not so sure," Tekla said. "He was a kind of prisoner too. If word got
out that his wife was guilty of forgery, he feared his career at the bank would
be over. Truth is, he was probably right."

Later she gave me a pamphlet she had brought from Stockholm. "It's
really quite simple. Women must make their own lives, not just as wives and
mothers. But first we have to win the vote."

I wanted to ask her what it felt like when Erling came to her in the
night. But before I could muster the courage, she had boarded the train for
Stockholm, leaving the rest of us behind.

ON THE DAY of the ball, Disa and I arrived at Aunt Hedvig's apartment
in the late afternoon. Hedvig, her white hair neatly parted in the middle,
waited impatiently, as if she already wished us gone.

Her husband, twenty years her senior, had been a sea captain and the
owner of several ships. He had died in 1908, after a childless marriage,
which by all accounts had nonetheless been satisfactory. Hedvig sold
the villa and moved to an apartment in the center of Gothenburg. The
apartment was small but tasteful, with rooms in the back for the cook and
the maid. Disa and I changed in the guest bedroom, and I helped Disa
with her turban.

Even as we followed Hedvig into the ballroom, I wished I had not come.
The orchestra was warming up, and cut-glass chandeliers glittered above a
vast expanse of parquet floor. The flourishes on the cornet assaulted the more
retiring strings, and I heard the pianist threaten to walk away because of some
disagreement with the conductor.

Shortly, the male guests, in white gloves and black swallowtail coats, made
their way around the room, asking to be introduced and signing their names
on our dance cards. From the young women came a continuous rustle of silk
and starched lace, like the sound of the bees flying in and out of the lindens
by our veranda. Whenever a man approached, Disa smiled. She kept smiling,
even when he stopped and bowed in front of me. At one time two men all but
collided before us. After the first man signed for the polka, I told the other

man that my card was full. Disa's eyes lit up behind her glasses, but the man turned his back, and her smile retreated like a scolded dog.

I danced the first waltz with a man whose name I could not recall, although I did remember Hedvig mentioning something about a promising career as a civil servant. He moved stiffly, holding my body away from his, for which I was grateful.

Tekla had not prepared me for this. "Listen to the music and follow the man's lead." She must not have realized that the music and the man might not always agree.

Disa, in the arms of yet another acquaintance of Hedvig's, whirled by in the polka. She kept her gaze down, just as Hedvig had suggested. "No need to look a man in the eye. What the rest of us find endearing, a stranger might find disturbing. You have nice hands and small feet. Lift your skirt when you dance. Nothing is as enticing as a pretty ankle. Whatever you do, don't despair. I married young myself, but others have waited longer."

Hedvig had also dispensed advice to me. "You, my dear, are too thin and your breasts too small, but you still have the charm of novelty, and so we must make the most of it. No doubt the men will have questions. Don't be too forthcoming. Keep them guessing. As for their own backgrounds, they've all been thoroughly checked. Their characters should be beyond reproach. Some will have titles but no money. Others will have money but no titles. Very few will have both. You're not in a position to be choosy. Your father is well known in Vänersborg, but here most everyone will know you only through me. I've done what I can, praising both you and Disa whenever the opportunity presented itself. The rest will be up to you."

Rikard Lilja, the man bowing in front of me, was handsome in his blue officer's uniform, yellow braids across his chest. "I believe I have the honor of this waltz," he said and held out his arm.

As he led me out on the dance floor, the orchestra played a short introduction, which sounded like a distant march. I braced myself for more difficulties of the kind I had just experienced with the civil servant, but when the waltz surged forward, the two of us followed, turning and gliding. The one waltz was actually a series of waltzes, each slightly faster than the previous. When the other couples spun, Rikard held completely still, one foot in the air, until I thought we could not possibly stay balanced any longer. He finally sank backward into a slow, wide turn, and the floor all but disappeared underneath us.

The orchestra paused to rest, and Rikard escorted me to an adjacent room, where the buffet was laid out on a table covered with a white linen cloth. The many dishes formed an impressive display of what the current students had learned to prepare: fried sausages, herring *au gratin*, cold poached eel, pickled cucumbers, and smoked goose breast. Bottles of wine and beer glistened on the sideboard. Small glasses were arranged around two crystal decanters, one with pure *brännvin*, the other with *pomerans*, a *brännvin* flavored with the oil of bitter orange.

Rikard led me to a small table where I waited while he fetched our food. At another table Disa and the civil servant were already eating.

Rikard brought our plates and sat down beside me. "Your aunt told me your father owns a large farm. How long has it been in the family?"

"My great-grandfather bought it from the crown in 1832."

"And before that?"

"The first mention of Ramm, as far as we know, dates back to the wars between Denmark and Sweden. One of the owners was rumored to be an illegitimate son of King Erik XIV."

Rikard leaned forward, his eyes full of mischief. "Really? Tell me more."

Rammen used to say that we could not live without the stories. They dealt as much with the present as with the past. You never knew when he would begin one of them. It could be on a perfectly ordinary day, perhaps just after supper. Gustafa would sit on her chair by the stove and rock. He would talk long into the night until the lamp ran out of oil. He told us about places he himself had never seen, such as England and Madagascar, but sooner or later he would always return to Hult.

Now, even though Hedvig had told me not to talk too much, I told Rikard that the king had been present in the early 1560s, when Swedish soldiers went on a rampage to the south. I quoted the king who said they had burned the region "lengthwise and crosswise and everywhere in between," the words as delicious on my tongue as the sausage and the eel. Nine months after the rampage, a woman in Hult gave birth to a son. The event had not gone unnoticed for a few years later the boy received Ramm as a gift from the king.

Rikard laughed and raised his glass. "*Honi soit qui mal y pense.*"

I laughed too. For a moment I thought of how much he reminded me of Rammen, the way he might have been before the trouble with Ulrika.

Around us the men toasted each other with *brännvin*, bringing the glasses to their lips in grand, simultaneous sweeps. Disa was nowhere to be seen.

"Where did you learn to dance?" I asked.

"In Paris. I wanted to be an artist but I didn't have the nerve for it. So I came home and joined the army. Seemed like the sensible thing to do."

"Was it?" I asked. "Sensible?"

"Remains to be seen. I'm sure we'll have a war. Some of my fellow officers actually look forward to it. They say we've had enough of speeches and marches."

"I just read an article by Fredrik Otter, a man who lives in Ramm. He wrote that war is the failure of human wisdom. Instead of waging war, we should have fewer children and grow better crops."

Rikard nodded. "It's true that war brings destruction, but a peace that lasts too long may cause damage too. War shakes us up, makes us take life less for granted. Almost all great nations have thrived in the wake of victorious wars."

In the ballroom the orchestra began to play. Still no sight of Disa.

"I'm afraid my time is up," Rikard said and swallowed the last of his wine. "I have no right to deprive the other gentlemen of your company. But I'd very much like to see you again. Perhaps I might visit you at Ramm? We could continue our discussion."

The lie slipped out of my mouth as if already shaped and waiting. I spoke fast and out of earshot of everyone else. "My aunt must have misled you. She doesn't know that I'm secretly engaged. It's just a matter of time before I shall marry."

Rikard clicked his heels and bowed. "You're a woman of great charm. Whoever he is, your fiancé is a fortunate man."

Disa stood alone by the door, her turban askew.

LATER THAT EVENING, in the vestibule of Aunt Hedvig's apartment, Disa laughed and said she had come under the influence of too much sherry. Eyebrows raised, Hedvig began to pull off her gloves. This, however, only encouraged Disa further. She announced that she had been kissed, but probably more out of pity than desire.

"Still," she added, turning to Hedvig, "I suppose a thank-you is in order. Wouldn't be surprised to learn that you arranged for that as well." With this she excused herself and went to bed.

Hedvig motioned to me to step into the drawing room. We both sank into large armchairs, and Hedvig took off her shoes. On the lid of a grand piano stood photographs framed in silver, mostly of Hedvig and the captain. In one of them, Hedvig christened a ship, smashing a bottle of champagne against its bow. "Took more force than you'd think," she used to say. "Thankfully I possessed it."

Hedvig rang for the maid, who brought port wine on a tray.

"Your sister is too prone to sarcasm," she said as soon as we were alone again. "No man will put up with that. But you, my dear, were a great success. I'm very pleased. I wasn't the only one who noticed. I can think of several young ladies who wished they could have taken your place."

Hedvig unclasped her pearls and placed them in a porcelain bowl on a small table beside her. The light of the candles filled the room with a restful glow, and a French Empire clock ticked loudly on a table.

One of the photographs on the grand piano showed my grandfather Lars, a solemn man with sideburns and a heavy brow. There was also one of his wife, BrittaLena. For some reason they had decided not to pose together but took turns sitting on the same chair, leaning their elbows on a lace-covered table. Both scowled at the camera, both were dressed in thick black wool, adding to the look of harshness, which seemed so much part of who they were. BrittaLena, already the mother of four, still had a good bosom and a small waist. Her fair hair was pulled back and slicked to her head.

A third photograph showed Lars seated in the middle with the children in a close semicircle behind him. BrittaLena had died five years earlier, shortly after giving birth to Alfrida. Again, all were dressed in black and no one smiled. Lars held Alfrida's hand with a tenderness that I found moving. Hedvig, on Lars' right, wore a pinafore and already appeared to have taken on her role as a substitute mother. Standing in the back, Adolf and Grim had placed their hands on their father's shoulders. The symmetry was complete. They looked as if they could not exist without each other, their eyes searching the camera for meaning, the loss of BrittaLena stamped onto their foreheads, like Samuel's identification number on the inside of his arm.

Hedvig instructed the maid about the schedule for the following day and reminded her to prepare the hot water bottle. Then she turned to me again.

"Rikard is an excellent young man," she said. "I've met his mother on several occasions. It would be a step up for you, my dear. I'm sure you know he's the heir to a large estate. Rammen will be pleased."

"There's a man in the village," I said. "His name is Fredrik Otter. He leases Prästgården but I've heard that he's looking for a farm of his own."

"Björn told me," Hedvig said as she poured herself another glass of port. "He made it sound as if Otter plans to marry his housekeeper."

Not knowing quite what to say, I remained silent.

"Don't make the same mistake as your father," Hedvig said. "He married Ulrika without consulting anyone else. Couldn't get her to the altar fast enough. He should have asked questions."

The Baron von Holkenstam, Ulrika's father, had always been regarded as a man of wealth, but shortly after Rammen married Ulrika, the baron declared bankruptcy and left with the baroness in the middle of the night. Ulrika once showed me a letter from her mother, written a year after her parents' departure. It turned out that they had left Sweden for Schleswig-Holstein, where her mother's relatives still held large estates. Accustomed to what she called "the better things of life," Ulrika's mother now found herself shunned by many of her former friends. As she and her husband moved from one town to another, they were no longer invited to dinners and balls. The letter ended with an apology and an attempt to explain why this would be her last letter to her daughter.

"It is for the best," she wrote, and asked that Ulrika always think of her kindly. Two years later she was dead. Not long thereafter Ulrika learned that her father had died too. She received no inheritance whatsoever. Her father, it appeared, had never found a way out of his debts.

As always, when the subject of Rammen and Ulrika was broached, I came to Ulrika's aid.

"Ulrika didn't know," I said. "She had no part in it."

"Who's to say?" Hedvig shrugged and sipped her port. "But of this I'm sure. That marriage was entered under false pretenses and Rammen paid the price."

The clock struck two. Hedvig stifled a yawn and bid me good night. She said not to expect to see her in the morning. The maid would serve Disa and me breakfast, but Hedvig herself would need to rest up.

"These balls are not for the faint of heart," she said. "I fear it will take me a good long time to recover. But it was all worth it, seeing my youngest niece in the arms of Rikard Lilja."

I stayed in the drawing room and tried to gather my thoughts. My only defense for lying to Rikard Lilja was my conviction that the lie would turn into truth. I pictured Fredrik in his office, writing on his typewriter while the rest of the village was asleep. The light from the paraffin lamp would illuminate his sharp gray eyes, and books would be stacked all around him, not just books about farming, but also books of poetry and fiction, in rich leather bindings with gold medallions on the covers.

A few days earlier, as I stood in line at the store, he had come through the door, his black hat under his arm. While he talked to another farmer, he seemed unaware of my presence, and yet I was close enough to notice that his jacket smelled of earth. The following day I saw him plowing on the far side of a field, the dark soil steaming. I had to restrain myself from running out to greet him. I was still cautious enough not to make a spectacle of myself, but even so, my heart was set.

Chapter Fourteen

I AM HARBORING a fugitive. This morning, in the middle of a downpour, Karin arrives, small suitcase in hand. When I open the door, her reddish brown hair has turned black in the rain and water puddles at her feet. She cups a cigarette, trying to light it.

"Well," I say. "You'd better come in."

She goes upstairs, and I decide not to ask any questions.

When I telephone Olof, he says she left in the middle of the night. He is glad to know that she is with me, and his mother will look after the children.

"Tell her we can work it out," he says, and I can hear that he means it.

What am I to do? Björn's granddaughter is here. When I finally do ask her what is wrong, she becomes agitated just like Ulrika.

KARIN COMES DOWN late in the evening, says she cannot sleep. She curls up in my easy chair and pulls the blanket tighter. She asks me about the old church. She says she used to go there as a child. I never knew.

The old church, I tell her, was built to last. The walls were made of stone and nine feet thick, the windows narrow and small. The crucifix, a life-sized Christ, was carved of wood. During the wars, Danish soldiers used the church to stable their horses. The plague struck in the 1300s and flagellants came to lash themselves and expose their wounds to heaven. When Martin Luther brought about the reformation, the king robbed the church of its gold and silver, except for a few chalices that the villagers had buried in the river sand.

As I talk, I find myself using Rammen's words. At some point Karin closes her eyes. I keep talking, if only to keep her calm.

In the mid-1700s a Christmas storm toppled the stone bell tower and split one of the bells. The bell was recast and housed in a new wood tower, inferior to the original in both beauty and strength. To preserve the bells, the parish council determined that they must toll no longer than half an hour, no matter how important the corpse. The farmers were also ordered not to hammer nails into the sides of the pulpit but find another place to hang their hats. To this they paid as little heed as they did to the request not to shear the lambs before they tithed them to their vicar.

Karin does not move. I think I see her smile. Perhaps it is a glimpse of the carefree young woman who used to come to Ramm, driven by various boyfriends. They would race around the courtyard in their open sports cars,

Karin half standing up. Olof drove a rusty but solid Volkswagen. We were all relieved, including Björn. She never stayed long.

As soon as I grow silent, I hear her small, thin voice. "Don't stop, Anna. Don't stop now."

And so I tell her how water from melting ice seeped through the cracks and rotted the church rafters. By the mid-1800s the church was deemed impossible to save. Despite repeated admonitions by visiting bishops, progress on the new church was slow. Negotiations to buy a building site took years, mired in real or invented obstacles. Time after time Lars was on record, stating that the money required to build a new church was more than enough to restore the old.

"Your great grandfather was always his own man," I say. "His hat was firmly planted on his head. The only time he removed it was when the church bells rang. Even when greeting his vicar, he barely touched the brim with the tips of his fingers."

I tell her how the diocese lost patience and hired an architect from Stockholm to draw up the plans. He used as his model the Greek Orthodox temple rather than the conventional rectangular basilica, arguing that an octagonal church would be cheaper to build. Lars died the day they began to break ground.

The walls of the old church were torn down to supply stones for various construction projects throughout the parish. The pews were sold at auction, along with the bells. The wooden Christ was sold to a church in Ljunga, a parish near the coast, which was where I had seen it. The villagers followed him for several miles. The paint was almost gone, the wood furrowed and gnarled. They said he looked like a scarecrow, his arms stretched out on the cross, rigged high on that cart and pulled by an ox.

"They shouldn't have sold him," Karin says. "Why didn't Rammen stop them?"

"He told me his mind was busy elsewhere, but he never said where."

Chapter Fifteen

IT WAS 1914, close to midsummer, and Ulrika's hens were out. They were all over the barn and into the grain bins too. Elias shouted and swung his arms, the hens squawked and flapped their wings, and for a while neither side appeared to be winning. I found one of the hens still burrowing in Ulrika's flowerbed when I dug up violets for the graves.

That day, on my way to the old graveyard, I chose to walk by Prästgården, not across the field, hoping that Fredrik would see me and follow. I was not about to wait any longer. If he did not seek me out, I would seek him out instead. There was nothing wrong in presenting him with an opportunity should he decide to take it.

I had read his latest article on how to slaughter pigs. "*Cruelty and slaughter need not go hand in hand,*" he wrote. "*The only reliable method is the use of a slaughtering mask. The spike enters the front of the brain, and the pig is instantly rendered unconscious. A strike with a club at the forehead has the same effect, but the use of a mask makes the blood drain faster. A strike in the back of the neck or under the ear is always unacceptable. It immobilizes the pig but does not render it unconscious.*"

The vicarage was three stories high and painted white. Fredrik's house, next to it, looked like a poor relation. It was one level only and painted the same red as the stable and the barn. Three stone steps led up to the front door, and six to the kitchen door, as if visitors to this part of the house ought to expend more effort.

Through the kitchen window I could see Agnes serving the farmhands their mid-day meal. I knew that Fredrik had been away to look for a farm of his own, but the haying was about to begin and now he was back at Prästgården. Word was that he ate alone in his office, not because he thought he was better than the other men, but because their appetites were larger, and he did not want them to hold back. After the meal the farmhands would rest in the brew house while Fredrik wrote at his desk. Each day, at five minutes to one, he rejoined the farmhands in the kitchen, where Agnes put out coffee and fresh cardamom buns.

"Time flies," he said and the men went back to work.

The old graveyard was just behind the vicarage. On Rammen's initiative, I had begun to take minutes at the parish council, and of late there had been much concern about the new cemetery running out of space. Some of the council members wanted to put the old graveyard back in use by adding a new layer of soil, even though such a solution would not be lasting. Rammen had laughed. I did not mention his laughter in the minutes, but even Wikander could see that they had to find a better way.

I stopped under the arched stone gate, where the villagers used to set down the coffins as they waited for their vicar. The wind picked up and cloud shadows chased across the graves.

It was then that I heard the shouting. The wind was full of voices, men's and women's too, alive with excitement and fear. Gustafa had warned me. She said there would be times when I would see far into the past just as I might be able to see into the future. Nothing was old, and nothing was new, and all we could do was pay attention.

Rammen had talked about it many times. The people who knelt before the wooden Christ also burned witches in the commons. To keep the stakes from getting wet, they had decapitated the witches and emptied them of their blood. As the rest of the villagers watched, the witches' relatives were forced to tie the headless bodies to the stakes and light them. When the burning was over, they all went home. The relatives showed no emotion. It was as if the day had been like any other, and now it was suppertime.

Above me, jackdaws shot in and out among the tops of the aspens. I lost heart, and hurried back to Ramm, crossing the field to stay out of sight.

Of course there was talk. One of Fredrik's farmhands had spotted me walk past Prästgården. He told anyone who cared to listen—and there were quite a few—that I had been slinking against the walls like a cat in heat. To this day I do not know if Fredrik heard about it too. Still, from then on my visits to the old churchyard grew more frequent. I kept hoping he would see me, even though I always took the shortcut across the field.

THAT SUMMER THERE was trouble at the inn. A socialist agitator had arrived on his bicycle, his hat pushed down in front, his coat tails flapping. Several mill workers had attended a meeting at the outskirts of the village. Most of the older workers watched from afar, for Holmberg disapproved, and they did not want his informants to see them.

A week or so later Erik, Kristina's son, delivered a letter to Holmberg. Ever since he started the temperance group, rumors about socialism had run rife. Now, in his letter, he demanded that all work at the mill must cease at six o'clock, or the workers would strike. As it was, hours at the mill were long and irregular. No one left until the church bells rang. Each time the bell ringer passed the inn on his way to the church, Holmberg stepped out from his store, exchanged pleasantries, and treated him to a glass of beer. Thus the man was almost always fifteen minutes late. It all added up. Even when the man was on time, a workday rarely lasted less than eleven hours.

Holmberg posted notices at the mill and at the inn.

"*To my workers!*" the notices read. "*Those who know me can testify that my greatest concern has always been the welfare of my workers. This being so, there should be no need for strikes. Anyone who disagrees must seek employment elsewhere.*"

Holmberg dismissed Erik and replaced him with a man from a neighboring parish. That was when Holmberg's life turned unpleasant. A kerosene drum was stolen from the courtyard outside the inn. There was mention of smashed windows and kicked-in doors. Karolina, the schoolmistress, had been walking past the inn on her way home from a funeral, when she heard clamor and curses as if in a fight. One moment, a farmer told the constable, Holmberg had been behind the counter, rustling up glasses from the shelf below and giving them a quick twist with his towel, the next he was knocked down, landing on top of a pile of empty bottles. The farmer claimed not to have seen the attackers. The constable's interrogations never led beyond two railroad workers who said they had been recruited to teach Holmberg a lesson although they would not say by whom. The fact that they had been seen at Ramm shortly before the incident met with a shrug.

At that point Holmberg rehired Erik with promises that his demands would be met. Kristina, for her part, told everyone that she was glad that her son had been reinstated. To bar further trouble at the inn, she requested that Holmberg's liquor license be revoked, making room for some of his old competition, but as always her request was denied.

SUMMER WAS WARM that year and the month of July broke all records. At Ramm the haying had begun, and I helped with the lower field. Fredrik had finished around midsummer, one or two weeks before everyone else. Certainly the farmers had read his article, where he argued that grass cut early contained more protein, but most of them looked to quantity rather than content, and stuck to their belief that nature should not be rushed.

It was a Saturday, and I raked after Elias, who cut around the snags and rocks at the edges of the field. Konrad, our new farmhand, raked after Johannes, who swayed to the rhythm of his scythe, now and then stopping to whet the blade. Sara, temporarily relieved of her kitchen duties under Disa, had been assigned to Nils Lind, one of the crofters. It was a difficult position, for Nils kept racing ahead, leaving his path uneven.

Nils had been a crofter under Ramm for almost twenty years. Lina, his wife, had been his helpmate in every sense. The site that Rammen allowed them to use was nothing but heather and forest. Together the couple put several acres under crops, mostly grass and potatoes. Lina even helped Nils build the barn, while Rammen supplied the lumber. The more the croft grew, the more hours Nils had to put in at Ramm. In the summertime he was hardly home except to sleep. Meanwhile Lina was still seen around the croft, clearing stones and digging ditches. She also took care of two cows, one ox, and an unusually large number of hens, since Ulrika tended to give away chickens as well as clothes. During particularly difficult periods, when Ulrika's behavior seemed more erratic than usual—those hectic red spots on her cheeks gave her away—she often asked for Lina, who would sit with her in the *sal* until the worst was over.

As I raked, I was concerned about Sara, who was thorough and conscientious and could barely keep up with Nils. She was one of those durable girls who were born to crofters and hired out for service as soon as they finished school. Now she kept stopping to rub her hands as Nils left large tufts of grass uncut, which forced her to rake around them.

I called out to Nils to slow down, which only made him go faster. Johannes said nothing, which was probably just as well, since Nils would have ignored him.

I wished Wilhelm had been there but he and Björn were off in another field with the horse-drawn mower. Most likely they had difficulties of their own. Every now and then the mower would run up against a hidden stone and the horses would balk and snort. Elias always grumbled that the mower did not reach far enough into the corners. When Björn said there was plenty of grass to take us through the winter, Elias shook his head.

"Never too much hay," he said. "Mark my word. You'll need it the year after."

In late afternoon we stopped to watch the wagons roll by. The mill workers, all members of the temperance group, were on their way to a dance. The wagons were festooned with birch leaves and ox-eye daisies, and on one of them a man played the accordion. Wikander had opposed the dance, but Rammen had told Erik they could use one of his islands, arguing that fresh air would do the workers good.

Nils pushed back his cap and scratched his scalp. "Not all of us have time to go dancing." He spat and glared at Sara, who had pulled down her sleeves in an attempt to cover her blisters.

As the swell of the accordion faded into the distance, we went back to work. The wind came up and clouds covered the sun, but we continued to mow and rake. Nils' swaths grew rougher by the minute, and Sara had begun to talk to herself, tears welling up while she kept muttering under her breath.

When I saw the wire, coiled next to a heap of old stakes and almost hidden by blackberry ramble, I knew what to do. I whacked at the wire with my rake and used all my strength to pull it away from the roots and the grasses. The rest was easy. I took two of the shortest stakes, pushed them into the ground where Nils would mow and rigged the wire between them.

A few minutes later, when I was back at Elias' side, Nils began to shout. He held up his blade with the wire all twisted and spiraling around it. Johannes must have approved, for I thought I could detect one of his rare smiles, the kind that lurked at the corners of his mouth and would be gone before you could be sure you had seen it.

THE FOLLOWING MORNING, when Disa and I stood outside the church before the service, I looked for Fredrik. I always did, even though he hardly ever came to church and that morning was no exception.

The butcher and his wife stopped to wish God's peace. I never could stand the sight of Frans, the way he looked at you as if you were next. I suppose his wife felt the same. We all knew that she slept in the kitchen, while Frans slept in their bed with his dogs, although some said that this was the way Frans preferred it.

We had all heard about Fredrik's confrontation with Frans. Fredrik had told him that *brännvin* had no place at a slaughter, certainly not at Prästgården. Frans announced that he knew when he was not wanted and from then on Fredrik Otter could butcher his own pigs.

While Fredrik sent for a butcher in Varberg, everyone else, including Rammen, continued to use Frans. He would arrive with his knives in his belt, stopping to pat the dogs. He butchered cattle, sheep, and pigs, always judging the quality of the animals by how much *brännvin* the owners served him. He drew the line at horses, not just because of their size but also because he believed that killing a horse was almost akin to murder. Horses too old to be useful were given to itinerant horse dealers, who in turn handed them over to the knackers, a godless breed of men who specialized in slaughtering horses and were shunned by society as a whole. Some of these horses were not slaughtered at all but would reappear at horse fairs, their anuses stuffed with tobacco, which made them as lively as colts. "Nasty business," Frans would say whenever the topic came up.

Alfrida approached, greeting the other women as she passed, the smell of scouring soap as strong as ever. Disa tried to escape into the church but Alfrida, surprisingly agile, cut her off.

"There's a man at the creamery who needs a wife," Alfrida said when she finally had us both before her. "A most modest man, and virtuous too."

With no daughters of her own, Alfrida had always taken a considerable interest in her nieces. For years she had tried to introduce us to suitable young men but much to her distress neither Disa nor I had shown any interest. This time even Alfrida herself appeared to have reservations but the number of candidates was dwindling.

"He may not be right for you, Anna, but he'd certainly be a good prospect for Disa. I told him I'd bring both of you over one of these days. So you can see for yourselves."

Nils shuffled past. His left eye was shut and a blood-caked rag covered his left ear. Lina walked behind him, and the children hung onto her skirt.

"A fight outside the inn," Alfrida said and winked at me. "I heard they joshed him about some wire getting caught in his scythe."

As I entered the church, I heard soft snoring to the left. An old woman from the poorhouse was already fast asleep, her chin close to her chest.

Theodor, Alfrida's husband, served as churchwarden and was hooking metal numbers to a board, identifying the hymns for the service. The numbers dangled slightly before they came to rest.

I could not forget the sight of Lina and the children. When Nils had returned to the croft, throwing open the door, blood must have been running down his face and neck. The children, startled out of their sleep, would have rubbed their eyes, sensing their father's humiliation.

Wikander emerged from the vestry, steadying himself as he did. A murmur of anticipation rose. His sermons were never as commanding as when he was recovering from a night of drink.

Having reached the pulpit, he tapped his snuffbox and glowered down at us all. Minutes passed as he placed the snuff on the back of his hand, an act that seemed to require his full concentration. At long last he drew the snuff up his nostril and began to preach.

The members of the temperance group, he said, had boarded a large barge, normally used to transport hay and cattle. During the crossing the weather had suddenly changed. The barge leaned and the water roiled. One woman prayed aloud.

"God shook his fist at them," Wikander said, shaking his as well. "And yet a man kept playing the accordion, the Devil urging him on. They did not heed God's warning but continued with their voyage and their dance."

For a moment he seemed to have lost his train of thought but the congregation silently willed him on.

"The temperance group is not what it professes to be. It is the work of the Devil, and he tells us we do not need God. He makes evil appear harmless, even good. He says he does not seek to drag down the natural man but to improve him and uplift him. He teaches salvation by deeds. He wants you to forget that man is by nature a fallen creature, that in the flesh there dwelleth no good."

A shriek came from the back as Klas prodded the old woman from the poorhouse. Ulrika dropped her sprig of lavender, the one she used to mark the pages of her book of hymns, and I bent to retrieve it.

Wikander drove on.

"The true purpose of the temperance group is to lead you to eternal death. That is why I would rather see a drunk in a roadside ditch than a temperance man in God's temple. I can help the drunkard, but I cannot help the temperance man, for he has assumed the sign of the beast, and he shall be thrown into the furnace to bu-u-u-rn. There is no power but of God. Whosoever therefore resisteth the power, resisteth the ordinance of God, and they that resist shall receive to themselves damnation."

As we walked out of the church, a flock of Holmberg's young roosters were on their way home after sampling the cemetery oats. Wings fanning, they sprung up on the cemetery wall.

There was a commotion to my left. Johannes stood in front of Erik, whose bowed legs made him seem oddly sturdy.

"You heard the vicar's words," Johannes said. "Take a drink and be a man."

Lovisa, one of the mill workers, hurried her children toward the road. Even though she was a couple of years older, she used to be my closest friend at school. She was the only girl who dared climb the large oak behind the schoolhouse. After she finished school, she married Sven, and they both worked at the mill. I rarely saw her now, and when I did, we no longer stopped to talk. Village ways had formed us. The gap between the mill worker and the farmer's daughter had grown too vast.

A group of farmhands gathered around Johannes and Erik. Konrad tried to hold Johannes back, but Johannes shook him off. Erik, so far, held his own, but it was clear that he would soon be outnumbered.

Rammen, tobacco wad pushing out from under his cheek, raised his arms and made his way past the farmhands. Calm and friendly, at least on the surface, he called the men by their names and inquired about their parents. He never forgot a name, not even those of other people's hired help.

"That's enough for today," he said and stepped between Johannes and Erik. "This is the day when our Lord was resting, so let's all go home and enjoy our coffee. If you still want to fight in the morning, so be it."

Later, in the parlor, Johannes talked about America. He said he wanted to join Uncle Adolf in Chicago. From there he would head west and find his own land.

Rammen, reading the newspaper, did not look up.

"Wheat fields forty miles long," Johannes said. "Furrows straight as railroad tracks, all there for the taking."

I shook my head to make him stop but it was of no use.

"All those men," he said, clenching his pipe between his teeth. "Each as good as the next. As long as they work hard and behave themselves. Shocking and pitching and stacking."

Rammen still did not look up. "Don't start what you can't finish," he said, turning another page.

That afternoon I left for the croft.

Lina, wearing a heavy sack apron, opened the door. "Haven't you done enough? Go back to Ramm. No need to bother us here, unless there's something wrong with Ulrika."

I told her I was sorry but she did not ask me in.

I have never forgotten what I did with that wire in the field and what it all led up to. Good intentions or not, we have to tread cautiously here on earth for nothing we do exists in a vacuum. The young vicar buried Lina in 1971 and Nils a few months later. He called them "simple" country people. I told him there was nothing simple about them whatsoever. Their lives were hard, and in the end they had very little, even though Björn let them stay on at the croft. Two children died young, three moved to Gothenburg, and the youngest son moved to America, never to be heard from again. Lina thought he had been in trouble with the law and that the Americans had sent him back to Sweden. He would be too proud, she said, to get in touch. I do not know if there is any truth to this, but she may well be right, for pride is strong among country people and Nils, his father, was as proud as they came.

Chapter Sixteen

KARIN GOES OUT to "jog." I have read about "jogging" but never thought I would know someone who actually does it.

She is back two hours later and sits down with a glass of milk, a thin white line forming on her upper lip. She wears a yellow sweater over faded jeans.

"What was my dad like?" she asks. "When he was a child."

Ragnar, her father, always sensed that there was a problem between Björn and me, and so he kept his distance. Now he is a traveling salesman for a prestigious brand of men's clothing. The company has rewarded him well. He drives expensive cars and stays at the best hotels. Aside from being a hostess in their home, his wife designs window displays for a large store in Gothenburg.

"I'm sorry, Karin, I never really knew him. He was always with Disa, and I was always at the bank."

"Tell me about Granddad then," she says, her tone quite imperious, which I take as a good sign.

"Björn was a difficult boy," I say. "Hid with his air gun when Gustafa went to the pump. Used her buckets as targets, when she picked her way back to the house with that heavy yoke on her shoulders. Elias said he was too young to know better. Don't know what it was about your grandfather but everyone always forgave him. At school he never let a day go by without causing Karolina, our schoolmistress, some kind of grievance. He'd reach in through the side of the outhouse and tickle her pink bottom with a twig. When Karolina complained to Rammen, he laughed and called it an innocent prank."

Karin smiles and takes another sip of milk. "Not very nice, was it?"

"I don't think any of us were ever very nice to Karolina. Her father was the schoolmaster in Hult but he died when she was fourteen years old. The parish council sent her to Varberg to study for her teacher's qualifications, and they never let her forget what she owed."

Karin pulls the sleeves of her sweater over her hands and hugs herself.

I keep talking. "Björn was also the one who taught me to track and hunt. Showed me the badger's sett where we hid for hours to see the badger come out. He identified the bite marks on the rye, which meant that a hare was close by. He took me to see the wood grouse cocks at dawn. Once you've seen them, you'll never forget, those great birds strutting and leaping, their heavy wings a shimmer of green and blue."

Karin has fallen asleep, her mascara smudged around her eyes. I do not dare move for fear of waking her, so I sit motionless in the gathering dark, regretting that I did not try to get to know her better when she was a child.

The telephone slashes the silence. Both Karin and I jump. I answer, and it is Olof.

Karin's thin hands shake out a Gauloise. "Tell him I'll call him back."

Later we make meatballs. She looks as if she might be back to her "old self," which is what Alfrida used to say about Ulrika. She has yet to telephone Olof and the children. I still do not ask what is wrong.

I say, "I cannot begin to imagine how many meatballs I've rolled in my life." Summertime always brought children to Ramm, not just Karin but also Tekla's boys and Wilhelm's twins. They all needed to be fed.

The outbreak of the Second World War came to Björn's aid. This time Sweden had learned from the crisis of the war before. Rationings and price control were introduced already in the fall of 1939, long before the situation had a chance to get out of hand. Industry boomed, purchasing power was strong, and the value of the land was cautiously rising. In 1943 Björn bought the first tractor in Hult.

I was busy at the bank. Perhaps this is what carries us through life, the notion that we serve something larger. For me it was the bank and what we could do for this region, especially in the '40s and '50s, when farming turned prosperous again, not least thanks to government interference, a complex system of quotas, levies, and subsidies. Of course, none of it would last. More and more, politicians had begun to dictate what farmers should grow and how fast they should grow it. Those unable to keep pace were paid to put their fields in fallow. When I was young, closing down a field would have been worse than murder. Yet, as Johan says, "Once you start dancing, the music never stops."

Karin says she does not remember me making meatballs at all. It is her impression that when I was not at the bank, I was always out in the fields.

"Dad says you could have lived a different life."

"I suppose he's right."

"He says you could have married but you never did."

"Marriage is not for everyone," I say.

Karin must have seen me frown. "He meant it as an accomplishment, not a loss. I think he was always a little afraid of you. Probably still is."

And then I am back to talking about Björn, how he slung the heavy collar over the horse's neck, how his hair thinned early, and how he lowered his voice when angry, the quiet before the storm. I tell her about his laughter, booming and free, and yet he was a serious man, his banter serving only to hide his true self, for he was never ever jovial, and those who thought he was, he would secretly scorn. Actually, there was a great deal of scorn in Björn, even scorn for himself. He was the brother I thought I knew, but I do not tell her that, for I sense she has enough on her mind as it is.

Then, this afternoon, she leaves as quietly as she came. She never does press me about the child. I wonder what Ragnar has told her, probably what most villagers would have said, that Fredrik abandoned me for another, and that the child was unfit to live.

"I needed to get away from Olof and the children," she says as the cab pulls up. "They want too much. All I could think of was Ramm."

Chapter Seventeen

THE SUN WARMED my back as I polished the three-foot tall iron cross that marked Lars' and BrittaLena's graves. Fredrik's cows were grazing in the meadow below. I had heard about his method of dividing his pastures into smaller sections and then moving his cows from one section to the next. The other farmers had frowned, saying that the cost of putting up fences was too high, not to mention the labor. But the result spoke for itself, said Arne Karlsson, who was employed by the Farm Management Agency to tour the farms and measure the fat content of the milk. Otter's cows, he said, spent more time eating and less time walking and now they milked better than any other herd in the parish. Emilia, the midwife, who was married to Karlsson, could also testify to the richness of Prästgården's milk, for she gave it to new mothers who needed to rebuild their strength.

I moved on to my sister Helga. Her headstone was of smooth white marble, which Rammen had ordered from Italy. I pulled up the old violets and planted the new.

Helga had died from whooping cough when she was ten months old. Rammen drove all over the parish in search of mare's milk. It was said to be the only cure, but it did not help Helga, her small body cramping each time she coughed and wheezed. Rammen insisted that she be buried in the old graveyard, next to BrittaLena and Lars. It seemed wrong to place her by herself in the new cemetery so long before anyone else was likely to join her.

Rammen had stayed with Ulrika until well after the funeral. He slept in the parlor and would not even go for his newspaper down at the inn.

"Before I knew it," Ulrika once told me, " I was pregnant with you. Rammen carried you everywhere. Refused to put you down, as if he couldn't let you out of sight."

A child dying was not unusual, and death rarely discriminated between rich and poor. But even though I knew I was not to blame, I still felt guilty for living when Helga did not. I would sit with my back against one of those large aspens and wait for a sign that she knew I was there. Even as an adult I would linger in front of her grave, just in case she had something to say. It was not until my own child died that I stopped feeling guilty about Helga.

The pump creaked and boots crunched the gravel.

"Won't hurt to get them started," Fredrik Otter said and placed a rusted watering can beside me. He spoke quietly, as if sorry to disturb.

I had not seen him come and realized that he must have been in the graveyard all along. He stood before me, hat pushed back, shirtsleeves rolled up, leather boots scuffed. We shook hands. His skin felt rough and warm, and the veins protruded on the inside of his forearms.

"I've been reading under that tree," he said, pointing to a large oak in the far corner of the graveyard.

"What have you been reading?"

"Are you familiar with Friedrich Nietzsche?"

I shook my head and brushed the dirt off my skirt. All I read in those days was the newspaper and the letters from Tekla.

The jackdaws cawed from the tops of the aspens. More flew in, bouncing the others off the branches. In the meadow a cow tried to reach the apples on a tree.

"I read your article about slaughtering masks," I said. "I once watched when something went wrong."

"What happened?"

"I was just a child. I barely remember."

When he offered to carry my bag, I let him. We walked side by side toward Prästgården, the path still wet from the night's rain. He must have known that I could have taken the shortcut across the field.

"Tell me what you saw," he said.

A chaffinch flew ahead of us, its white wings flashing. I spotted Elias watching us from the edge of the forest, where red heather fringed the granite rocks.

I said I wanted to know more about his book.

"Perhaps you'd like to read it," he said. "I'd be curious to hear what you think."

He waited while I stopped to pick some bluebells and red clover. The sorrel was past blooming but the leaves made an excellent addition even so.

"I wish you'd tell me what happened," he said as we kept walking.

And so, never having talked about it before, I finally did. "I woke up when I heard the men in the courtyard. Must have been a month or so before Christmas, because it was still dark. I dressed in a hurry and found them behind the barn. They brought out the pig, Elias pulled at the rope, and Wilhelm pushed from behind. The pig squealed but that didn't alarm me. As my sister Disa says, pigs squeal all the time, with or without reason."

"Go on." His voice, lower now, was so close I thought I could touch it.

"Frans swung his club and struck the pig just above the eyes. It dropped to the ground, and I guess we all thought it was dead. Rammen and Wilhelm hoisted it up on the block, and Frans plunged his knife into its chest, and then Gustafa was there with her bucket, catching the blood and stirring."

A sudden wind, thick with the scent of honeysuckle, swept across the path and down into the meadow. As we kept walking, my long skirt swung and brushed against my legs. I noticed that Elias was gone.

Fredrik waited for me to continue.

"All I can say is that the pig came back to life. Kicked itself off the block and took to running in circles as the black mud turned red. Rammen threw himself on top of it and Wilhelm and Elias threw themselves on top of Rammen. It took all three of them to get that poor animal back up on the block. Frans kept thrusting, and Gustafa kept stirring. The pig didn't stop kicking until the blood slowed to a trickle and even then Rammen kept holding it down."

Fredrik was quiet. Perhaps he knew there was more. "It must have been difficult to watch," he said at long last. "Not just for you but for the adults too. Most likely part of the artery had remained intact. The heart kept pumping."

I did not tell him about the scream. I kept screaming long after the pig was dead. That was when they saw me. The scream took on a life of its own and did not subside until Rammen carried me back to the house and put me down in Ulrika's lap.

"*Lilla flickan,*" Ulrika murmured, her breath warm against my ear.

I knew I had gotten in their way, but all she did was hold me and rock me, as I buried my face in her chest.

Nor did I tell him what I saw in the eye of the pig. The night before had been like any other, but that morning the people who had fed it and watered it had turned against it and rousted it out of its pen. They should have known what they were doing but they had bungled the task. I was too young to put it all into words, but I knew I was no longer safe. If they could do this to an innocent pig, what could they do to me?

As we entered the courtyard at Prästgården, Fredrik's farmhand had harnessed two Ardenners and was turning them around to head out for work. Agnes, in a white apron, was watching from the top of the kitchen steps.

Fredrik stiffened, pulled out his watch, and asked me to wait.

"You're ten minutes early," he said to the farmhand, a raw-boned boy from a neighboring village.

The farmhand's face turned red. "I saw more rain on the horizon. Thought I'd get an early start."

"Take them back to their stalls," Fredrik said and put his hand on the withers of one of the horses. "Rain or no rain, they're entitled to their rest."

Agnes gave me a nod, but she was watching Fredrik. Rumor had it that he cared more about his animals than he cared about his men, and his conduct that day confirmed it. He did not seem to notice that I walked up the kitchen steps and gave the flowers to Agnes. She smiled and thanked me, but her gaze stayed on Fredrik, as if she worried what he might do next.

I started toward the road, past the hornless bull that stood tethered to my right.

"Anna!" Fredrik called. "Wait!"

The bull lifted his head at the sound of his voice. In a few long strides Fredrik was beside me.

"I almost forgot," he said and pulled a book out of his pocket.

The book was light but it burned in my palm. The protective cover was made from the same brown wrapping paper that Holmberg kept in a large roll next to his cash register.

"Keep it," he said. "I can buy another copy on my next trip to Varberg."

That evening, as the rain washed down the bedroom window, I began to read. Disa was asleep, her glasses next to her book of hymns, always laid out in the same fashion. As far as I could tell, *Thus Spoke Zarathustra* was about a prophet who left his mountain to let the people know that God was dead. He spoke to a crowd in a market square but they did not understand him. When a tightrope walker performed high above, a jester taunted him and made him fall. The crowd scattered but Zarathustra stayed with the dying man. "There is no hell," he told him. "Life on earth is all we have." Just before he died, the man moved his hand as if to thank him.

The war began in early August, a few days after Fredrik and I had talked. While Sweden declared itself neutral, the *Riksdag* promptly extended conscription and approved a plan to build cruisers, destroyers, and submarines. At Ramm, Elias loaded two rifles. One he kept by the barn, the other at Gustafa's cabin, which frightened Gustafa even more than the threat of Russians. Wilhelm joined his regiment to guard against possible attacks, and a few days later Björn was called up too. Fredrik volunteered for the *Landstorm*, and I heard he was stationed on the coastline facing Denmark.

Every evening I kept reading *Zarathustra*. It was as if Nietzsche had written a new Bible, deriding the old at every turn. Perhaps he had foreseen the war and the extent of the destruction. There was hardly a day without one country declaring war on another. The Balkans were burning. The Germans marched through Brussels at night, the infantry in files of five, the lancers in columns of four, the shoes of the horses throwing sparks. Before long the Russians advanced into Eastern Prussia, and mines were sinking Swedish ships in the Baltic. By early September, when the Germans had reached Paris, most of us were still innocent enough to think that the bloodshed would soon come to an end.

One Sunday Wikander read the marriage banns for Fredrik and Agnes. His words hit me so hard I bent over and almost retched. I walked into the forest to sort things out. Afterward I went about my chores as if nothing were wrong. In this I was well practiced. Only Elias asked what was the matter. When I did not answer, he said I ought to know better than to bother Fredrik Otter, who was an honest man and a defender of bulls.

"Time to wipe your face," he said, dragging his fingers through the length of his flowing beard. "The women need you in the kitchen."

Chapter Eighteen

TODAY SAMUEL FINALLY knocks on my door. From my window I see him approach, and I have already started the coffee. He walks nimbly for such a large man, never mind his age. The top of his head is bald, but he wears his remaining hair like a crown, almost as black as the day I first saw him.

Samuel came here after the Second World War. He used to do odd jobs for the farmers, building troughs and repairing carriages and anything else that was in need of his attention.

The day he arrived in Hult, I watched him from the bank. He stepped off the bus, his gait unsteady as if he had spent too long a time at sea. When he came inside, he asked for directions to the old croft, which he had rented from Björn. His Swedish was sparse but his voice was deep and firm.

These days he lives at the old people's home, even though he is ten years younger than I. I sometimes go to see him. The old women at the home are knitting. Every time I visit, there are more mittens and caps and shawls. I telephone the Red Cross to come and pick them up but they must think the distance too great for no one ever comes.

Samuel says it is not too bad at the home. I tell him I am staying in Gustafa's cabin. In my old age I have a right to be left alone, far away from people who call me by my first name, a familiarity I disapprove of. Ella says I have gone and become uppity in my old age. I tell her I always was. Not that there was all that much to be proud of, but some things are hard to change.

I depend on this man, and I suspect he knows it. Over the years we have had many talks. He says I give him peace.

We could have been lovers but the fear of my disease always stopped me. Even the young Varberg doctor, when I pressed him, could offer no guarantees. Still, I have come to rely on Samuel, more than I have ever relied on anyone else. He often talks of Salzburg and his work at the opera, where he became a director's assistant and wanted to become a director himself. The German occupation changed all that. Now he comes to my cabin and sits in my garden chair. His fire burns low—the flames turning red and stealing closer to the wood—but I trust he will see me safely to the end.

He will not talk of his experiences in the concentration camp, he only talks about his rescue. They marched the prisoners out, but when the white buses pulled up, he was not allowed to board. Over and over the same procedure, until one day, just before the war ended, he was finally allowed to leave. Even now he does not question why he had to wait so long.

"This land of milk and honey," he says in his low, vibrant voice, his vowels still not as honed as those of a native Swede. "This land of milk and honey and you."

Samuel may not question but I do. In 1940, after the Germans occupied Norway, Sweden allowed German soldiers to travel by train through Sweden, either heading out to Norway or going home on leave. Supposedly we had no choice. If we had refused, Germany would have occupied Sweden too. The train drivers did not blow their whistles as they passed through the towns, they just pushed through, shame-like, with German soldiers leaning out of the windows. Though the newspaper wrote about citizens doing Heil Hitler, the trains were mostly greeted by jeers. Most of the villagers detested the Germans, but the saddle maker was a Nazi, and he could jabber for ten. There were others too, but they grew wiser. Only the saddle maker kept on jabbering. In the end he wished he had not, for his business dried out, and he left for good.

Samuel does not ask me why I limp. Never one to pry, he probably ascribes it to old age. I do not tell him about hearing the child. It was dark, and soon after I left for the old graveyard, my foot caught a root and I fell. I lay with my cheek against the moss, the earth spinning, as if I had been hurled over the edge of a mountain, the din so loud that it drowned out the cries of the child. I rose with caution and checked all my bones. Nothing was broken, but my ankle hurt and forced me to turn back.

All I tell Samuel is that I have been praying. He nods. I bring out the Bible and read from Hebrews 9:22, the passage that says there can be no forgiveness without the shedding of blood. I ask him to explain.

Samuel shakes his head. "That was before the destruction of the temple. Animal sacrifices were never for God. They were always for the benefit of the people."

He studies me over his glasses. "Why do you ask?"

Chapter Nineteen

THE FIRST WEEK of 1915 Rammen attended a dinner at the Varberg City Hotel. He gave us a thorough account of the proceedings. The dinner was given by the Varberg bank to celebrate the opening of a branch office in Hult. The cognac glowed and the warm lights defied the winter dark outside. Rammen, one of forty prominent guests, was at the same table as Manfred Josefsson, director of the bank and husband of Sylvia, the young woman who showed me how to bind up my hair. Holmberg, the mill owner, sat next to Rammen.

Josefsson rose to speak. "The war will bring growth, not just for industry, but also for agriculture. The warring powers will outbid each other to secure our goods and services. Although we all wish for a speedy end to the war, we must also make the most of the situation as it now stands before us. Agriculture will need cash to keep pace with the demand, and the bank intends to provide it."

Here Rammen had raised his glass to Holmberg. They had shared a railroad compartment and at least for the evening acted like old friends.

A few days later Sylvia arrived at the Holmbergs. The newspaper reported that Josefsson himself had disappeared. An eyewitness had seen him board a train, carrying a small suitcase. The suitcase, it was thought, contained a large amount of money, which was missing from the bank. A bank official mentioned fifteen thousand crowns, but the article suggested it might be more.

One morning I was waiting in line at the store. Rings of sausages hung from the ceiling and the aroma of roasted coffee blended with the smell of rubber and spices. Holmberg, in a large green apron, ordered his assistant up and down the stairs. Now and then he stopped to roll up sugar candy in a paper cone for a child who hid behind its mother's skirts.

By then Josefsson had been traced to Gothenburg, where he allegedly had exchanged Swedish crowns for American dollars. His villa in Varberg had been confiscated. His servants cited his recent health problems, which brought some doubt to the accusations of theft. His staff at the bank concurred. He had been agitated and difficult to work with. Suicide was not ruled out.

This morning there were more questions yet. A second woman had arrived and not even Alfrida could tell us who she was.

"Heard you have another guest," a farmer said as soon as he put in his order.

Holmberg offered the farmer snuff out of the large box on the counter. "A friend of Mrs. Josefsson. A charming woman, come to give solace in times of distress."

When my turn came, I bought vanilla and gelatin for Disa. Holmberg asked if I had seen the new mill library, which had been set up by the temperance group. I told him it had long been my intention to visit.

"No time like the present," he said and stuck a pencil behind his ear. "Tell the foreman to take you."

The snow was piled high along the sides of the road, and I had to lift my skirt to get across. Björn, who by then was back from the military, had told me that Holmberg had donated several books himself and encouraged others to do the same. Anyone could borrow, not just the workers, which Björn saw as evidence that Holmberg was a true friend of the people, not just those bound to his mill but also those who were bound to the soil. Emma, the midwife's niece, was working on the catalogue, and Björn had helped her carry boxes.

"If she's a socialist," he said, "I'll gladly join the cause."

The foreman, one of Holmberg's relatives, took me through the huge room where the women were weaving. A large clock hung near the ceiling, where everyone could see it. Next door the colossal mangle rumbled back and forth, and those who wanted a word had to shout. The women curtsied when we passed their stations. One of them was Lovisa, my friend from school. Her face, once freckled, was now pale from lack of sunshine and fresh air. Next to her loom a baby lay in a cardboard box. I could not hear the crying but I saw the small mouth open and close. The foreman must have seen it too, because he handed Lovisa a piece of candy attached to a stick, and Lovisa eased the candy into the baby's red mouth.

In the warehouse men and women were sorting and packing tablecloths and sheets. I found Emma at the far end, where books had been placed on shelves attached to the wall.

Emma removed her wire-rimmed glasses, disentangling the earpieces from her lustrous auburn hair. Her dark frock showed off the purity of her skin, and the dust seemed unable to touch her. "Are you looking for anything in particular?"

"Not really," I said as I scanned the shelves.

"Let me know if you want to take one home," Emma said. "They're in alphabetical order, by the authors. When more donations come in, I'll start placing them by subject. That'll make them easier to find."

"Do people borrow?"

"Not as much as we'd hoped. Some are born readers. They just don't know it. I can see it by the way they handle the books, as if they're things of great value. They tell me they would like to read but they don't have the time. Or they're afraid to damage their eyes. They say they can't waste good lamp oil on a book. Still, they keep coming back. I think that's a good sign, don't you?"

The warehouse window faced a row of outhouses, where a man waited, warming his hands in his armpits. The outhouses at Holmberg's mill were known to be comfortable. At other mills the seats were made to lean, and workers had to hold on to wooden bars to keep from sliding, which made reading or any other kind of lingering impossible.

I ran my fingers along the spines of the books, tilting my head to read the titles. The first two books appeared to be part of a series, *The Life of the Animals* by A. E. Brehm. The first volume, according to the faded lettering, dealt with mammals. The second volume was about birds. A third volume, Emma told me, dealt with reptiles and fish but had gone missing.

"Do you have any novels?" I said.

"Wikander had them removed. He said they might incite unrealistic expectations." Here Emma lowered her voice. "I didn't think it was my place to argue, but I don't believe that knowledge, of any kind, can do harm."

I could imagine Wikander going through the books, like Jesus on the Day of Judgment, placing some to his left and others to his right.

"Do you believe in temperance?" I asked.

"I don't believe in being drunk. My father drinks, so I know first-hand what drinking can do. Mother works hard to keep the farm going."

She was new to our village. Most people in Hult would not talk so openly to someone they barely knew.

I pulled out a book bound in red cloth, *Farthest North, Being a Record of a Voyage of Exploration of the Ship Fram 1893-1896,* by Fridtjof Nansen. It had foldout maps and photographs of rugged men on a sea of ice.

Fredrik entered the warehouse, carrying a large box. It was the first time I had seen him since we had talked in the old graveyard. After his return from the military, he and his men had been out in the forest cutting timber, most of it hauled away to the railway station in Håstad.

Rammen had confronted him outside the inn. "In this village, we leave the forest alone."

Fredrik had begged to differ, saying that even the forest could suffer from neglect.

He put the box on the floor and shook hands with Emma. I pretended to study Nansen's book while I tried to stop my heart from racing. By now we all knew that Agnes was pregnant. With a child on its way, Fredrik had done the only honorable thing, and Agnes was thought to have come out ahead, seeing she was past thirty and almost as old as Fredrik.

He nodded to the book in my hand and said it was interesting. It was only then that I noticed that the bookplate had his name on it. It showed a man sowing in a field, spreading the seeds by hand.

I kept leafing through *Farthest North,* while Fredrik pulled more books out of the box and gave them to Emma. She read the titles aloud, as if wishing them a long life and many readers.

Fredrik turned to me and asked what I thought about Nietzsche.

"I can see that he was on a dangerous path," I said. "No one to blame, not even the Devil."

Emma had apparently read Nietzsche too. "Most people find it reassuring to know that if the wicked aren't punished here on earth, they will at least be punished in the life hereafter."

"The need for hell is no proof that it actually exists," Fredrik said. He had let his fine, dark hair grow even longer, and now it shielded his eyes as he kept pulling out books. "Precisely because Nietzsche knew that we're capable of evil, he argued that we must learn to overcome ourselves and work for the highest good."

"And you think we can?" I asked.

"Take the soldiers at Christmas. They stepped out of the trenches and met in the open, unarmed, exchanging addresses. What do you think made them do it?"

I had read about the German soldiers lighting candles on the parapets, and how the French, the British, and the Belgians had joined in. They broke bread, sang Christmas carols, played soccer, and helped each other bury the dead.

"I can only guess," I said. "Perhaps it was the story of the child in the manger, when there was peace on earth and the lion lay down with the lamb."

"I say it was something else. Something inherently human. That's what we need to believe in, not some distant God."

"*Handbook in Geography,*" Emma kept reciting as Fredrik passed her the books. "*The Mushrooms of Scandinavia. Botanical Excursions around Gothenburg. Harmful Insects in the Field and in the Garden.*"

"The fact remains that the war goes on," I said. "We marvel at the truce but we don't marvel at the war. If man is naturally good, it ought to be other way around."

I would have liked to talk to him more but Fredrik picked up the empty box and bid us goodbye. What I did not know then, and what I know now, is that not even Nietzsche could have held his attention for long. He gleaned what he thought was useful and then moved on.

While Emma filled out cards for the new books, I kept looking at the photographs of Nansen's expedition, dogs and tents half buried in the snow, the ship listing and covered with ice. I found it hard to concentrate for I was still thinking about Fredrik, the way the room seemed hollow now that he had left.

"Have you read it?" I asked, holding the book up to Emma.

"I have. Nansen thought the ice could carry the ship all the way to the Pole."

"Did it?"

"The first year was slow. The ice didn't always move with the wind, and the ship drifted backward nearly as much as forward. The second year was better, but Nansen still didn't think they moved fast enough, so he decided to travel the rest of the way by dog sledge. He took one man with him. The others stayed with the ship."

"And that was how he reached the Pole?"

"They got farther than any man before them. Others could finish what he had begun."

I returned the book to the shelf. Disa would be waiting, wondering what took me so long, eggs cracked already and all she needed now was the vanilla. Besides, I did not care to read about a man who had failed.

As I crossed the road, a sleigh came close to running me over. The horses passed at a sharp trot, chased by village dogs. Holmberg's store assistant was at the reins. Two women sat in the back. One must have been Sylvia and the other, I assumed, was her friend. They sat close together and seemed to laugh a great deal. Suitcases were tied to the back of the sleigh, so the two women must have been on their way to the station. I did not think that Sylvia had seen me, and even if she had, I would have looked like any other village woman in my long black coat, my woolen shawl wrapped around my head and all but covering my face.

The newspaper published a few more articles, all featuring the frustration of the police, who finally concluded that Josefsson must have left for America. In retrospect we could all see that the second visitor must have been Manfred Josefsson himself, who, disguised as a woman, had come to fetch his wife. Rammen said it was too good a ruse not to be admired. The fact that we had all been taken in made it even better.

Chapter Twenty

THIS SUNDAY AFTERNOON I try to telephone Karin. It rings several times before Olof answers. He says he will let her know that I called.

"We have some decisions to make," he says.

I hear the rush in his voice, but before we hang up, I ask him to let me know if I can be of help.

With more effort than usual—it seems that way these days—I climb the narrow stairs to retrieve Lars' letter to BrittaLena. Ulrika kept it in her desk drawer, along with the last letter from her mother and the account books for her henhouse. I think it gave her strength. Perhaps it will do the same for Karin.

At the kitchen table, I begin to read.

> *July 23, 1851*
> *Revered and cherished object of my eternal love. Your company has for a long time now given me such merry times that I wished to keep them to the end of life. Day by day I have observed your gentle qualities. Never before have I found greater joy and peace.*

Most men in the village would not have been able to write. Among the women, it was even more unusual. Compulsory schooling had only recently been introduced, but Lars, being the son of a prosperous farmer, had been tutored as a boy. I suspect he made use of a letter manual, for the wording appears rather too stilted for a robust and not-so-young farmer in need of a wife.

> *What is the meaning of your recent coldness, which has hurled me from heaven above into the deep abyss? Why did you in the early days of our acquaintance bewitch me into believing that our future might be shared?*

Here he must have dipped the tip of his pen into the ink well, for a drop of ink has splashed on to the letter, and he writes around it. His writing is almost dainty, as his rough, bulky hand tries to fit the characters onto the paper.

> *Whatever your reason, your welfare is much dearer to me than my own. Should Providence intend to keep us apart, my eyes will never stop shedding tears for you and I shall constantly call your name.*

Before I seal the envelope, I include a few lines of my own.

Dear Karin,

"You ask about the past, and so I'm sending you this letter. Not sure what to make of it, I can only guess.

"Perhaps Lars had a rival. Or he may have exhibited an unexpected brusqueness, a flash of temper, which made BrittaLena withdraw. At any rate, the letter must have worked, for they married soon thereafter. BrittaLena was 19 years old.

"Did they love each other? Again, who's to say? All I know is that they both came from a long line of farmers and that the land itself was bred into their bones. They didn't know about genes back then, but I do think they felt as if they were obeying an inner law, something indefinable, perhaps what Lars called Providence, and what I call fate.

"Being an only child, BrittaLena had been brought up much like a son. Both her parents were dead. She owned 6 farms, all small, and with the exception of Bergvik, quite remote. Her need for a husband was just as great as Lars' need for a wife. She was not pregnant, at least not as far as I know. Miscarriages were common in those days so we can't rule it out. But most of all I suspect she thought about the meadows and the fields, the hay already in the barns and the grain harvest approaching. Whatever had caused her troubles with Lars, her concern for the land was greater still.

"Karin, I don't know you as well as I would have liked, which is nobody's fault but mine. I don't presume to tell you what to do. Still, it's tempting to abandon that which is difficult. We can't bargain with love, the way we bargain with cattle and crops. The debits don't line up with the credits. We can't always expect something in return.

I mail the letter at the post office, which these days is nothing but a desk and two chairs in the back of the village store down by the gas station.

Where can she be? Would she not want to spend Sunday with her husband and her children?

Chapter Twenty-One

IN MARCH 1915, I woke to horses' hooves clipping the courtyard cobblestones. The light from the carriage lanterns flickered on the bedroom ceiling. Disa mumbled and turned over. Rammen was back from Vänersborg. I could hear his brisk steps across the veranda. The front door opened, and the cold air rose all the way to the second floor. Sara, who had stayed up late polishing Ulrika's silver, must have been sound asleep. Soon the stairs creaked as she tiptoed down from her bed in the attic.

The following morning Elias hoisted the flag. The practice was mostly reserved for royalty, and in the countryside it was nearly unheard of. Yet, whenever Rammen was home, the flag flew high for all to see, unfurling itself under a golden knob.

I was with the other women in the kitchen, tending to a newly slaughtered pig. Fredrik's article about slaughtering masks still had not made much of a mark. Word was that Frans, the butcher, had bought one but never used it. Only Karolina, the schoolmistress, had insisted. One of the farmers had given her a small pig that much to her distress had grown too large for its pen.

Disa was scraping the feet. I had offered to scrape the head and the ears, although I always maintained that in the case of the ears the labor was hardly worth it. Ulrika, assisted by Gustafa, was grinding kidneys, liver, and lungs for sausages.

While I always refused to help with the actual butchering, no one could accuse me of being fainthearted when it came to helping out with the rest. My blood pudding, made with oatmeal and milk, was as good a blood pudding as any village woman cared to put her name on. This particular one, flavored with salt and syrup, was already simmering on the stove. Sara was about to leave with baskets of meat for our crofters. What remained of the pig would be packed in salt and kept in the cellar, along with sacks of potatoes, barrels of herring, and large glazed pots filled with lingonberries and eggs. It was dark down there, made you want to leave right away. When we had heavy rains, the floor sometimes flooded. "It's pitiful but true," Frans used to say. "The pork is swimming in Rammen's cellar."

"We have a visitor," Gustafa said, looking out the kitchen window.

A man descended from a wagon, saying something to the coachman. He stood in the courtyard, looking out over the fields below. Wilhelm came out from the barn, twisting his mustache.

"Not here to play cards, I don't think," Gustafa said as she turned the crank of the grinder.

Ulrika kept guiding the ground meat into the intestines. Sooner or later the card players always showed up, summoned by the flag.

Their voices low, Wilhelm and the visitor took off their shoes in the front hall. Most visitors, while waiting to be announced, would have to wait in the hall but Wilhelm took this man straight to the parlor.

Wilhelm entered the kitchen. "A visitor from Gothenburg. Disa, you'd better start the coffee. Anna, would you entertain our guest while I fetch Rammen?" Although he was the eldest son, he never seemed comfortable giving instructions. Björn was different. According to Gustafa, he began to instruct the midwife as soon as his head popped out.

I untied my apron and pinned down a few strands of hair before I walked into the parlor. The man, his back toward me, was studying a wooden chest, painted in various shades of brown and made to look like marble. Perhaps he was looking for antiques? People in the cities had begun to show great interest in old farmhouse furniture, and agents traveled through the countryside buying up clocks and chairs and anything else they could lay their hands on. Tekla had written about her visit to Skansen, a large open-air museum in Stockholm, where entire farms had been moved from other parts of Sweden to show how country folks lived.

The man turned around and bowed. "Gunnar Strid," he said and held out his hand.

I did not shake it.

"A fine chest," he said. "Must be rather old."

"Have a seat," I said and pointed to the sofa. By good luck BrittaLena's woven tapestries were out of sight, as were the pewter chargers and the candlesticks of bronze and silver.

Rammen entered, lowering his head to avoid hitting the top of the doorway. As always, when I had not seen him for a few days, I was struck by how handsome he was. His blond hair was still thick, his step springy, and his eyes as blue as ever. That same morning Gustafa had ironed his suit, and the chain of his watch formed a golden curve against his vest.

At first Rammen seemed good-natured enough. He mentioned the weather, adding that the coachman was drinking hot coffee in the kitchen and Elias had blanketed the horse.

Disa brought a tray with cups and saucers. Since I gave no sign of leaving, she had no choice but to set a cup for me too.

"Germany seems to be winning the war," Strid said, watching Rammen as if to make sure he had struck the right note.

"Not necessarily," Rammen said. "As far as I can see, it can still go either way."

"I'm inclined to agree," I said. "Both sides have dug themselves in."

Apparently Strid was surprised that I had an opinion of my own, for his gaze darted back and forth between Rammen and me, before it finally settled back on Rammen.

Rammen held up a box of cigars. Strid took one and ran it under his nose in anticipation. After Rammen lit one for himself, he placed the matches just out of reach for Strid.

"And what, may I ask, brings you to Hult?" Rammen asked.

"I would like to know if you might be interested in selling the farm," Strid said, his unlit cigar in hand. "If so, I would very much appreciate the opportunity to make an offer."

"Ramm is not for sale," I said.

Rammen raised his hand. "Not so fast, Anna. Let's hear what our guest has to say."

"If what your daughter says is true, I mustn't waste your time. But might I at least ask permission to state how much we're prepared to pay?"

Rammen took a draft on his cigar and blew the smoke at Strid. "I'm listening."

"We're willing to pay forty thousand crowns. No down payment, all cash, the entire sum in less than a week."

Rammen squinted slightly through the smoke. According to official tax records, Ramm was worth about twenty thousand crowns.

"Given the amount you offer," Rammen said, "it's clear to me that it's the forest you're after. Most likely you intend to cut it down."

His cigar still unlit, Strid remained silent.

"I'm sure you noticed that Hult has no railway station," Rammen said. "Right there you should have known. When my father built the inn, he only did so to conform to the law. Considering that this same law has been in effect since the thirteenth century, I'd say the village has been quite successful at evading it. By the same law, the farmers are required to take turns providing the travelers with transportation, a service I can see you're using. This, the farmers will tell you, is a great inconvenience. Both the horses and the coachmen are needed at the farms. Besides, around here most of us are intent on keeping outsiders out and locals in. That's the main reason why the railroad never made it to Hult, though I'm told that the official excuse had to do with the hilly nature of the land and the usual fears of derailments. There were even those who argued that the rails would be stolen, that the steel would be too valuable to be left on the ground. But the real reason was inhospitality, plain and simple, and some of that sentiment still abounds."

Gustafa curtsied as she entered to add another log to the tiled stove. Rammen urged Strid to have another vanilla crescent, all the while praising Disa's skills as a baker.

"Let me tell you about Brunnsdal," Rammen continued. "You may have seen it on your way from the station. Then again, you may not, which is just as well. I recall it as a thriving farm. It belonged to my wife's family for several generations. Because of unfortunate circumstances, it had to be sold. The new owner disposed of the dairy cows, good solid animals, carefully bred over many years. Only the horses were kept for use in the forest. Then the felling started. Sure, time permitting, there was some plowing and some sowing, but on the whole the fields and the pastures were ignored. This went on for about three years. At that time the farm was sold again. Some of the young forest was still standing, so it was not hard to find a buyer. After that Brunnsdal has changed hands as often as bad horses at the horse fairs. Each new owner took what he could. The buildings, once carefully maintained, began to fall apart. The couch grass crowded out the grain. The weeds in the pastures suffocated everything else. And where there used to be forest, there's now nothing but clear-cuts with stumps and stacks of deadwood that no one has bothered to remove. So you can see why I shall have to send you back to where you came from. Tell your superiors that your failure is no reflection on you. A better man would have returned no less empty-handed."

Rammen ground out his cigar. Strid, still prevented from enjoying his, put it down beside his cup.

"I appreciate the call," Rammen said. "My daughter will see you to the door. I suggest you get out of the village before dark. No telling what might happen if you don't."

I left Gunnar Strid pacing in the courtyard. The coachman, a young farmer, was still in the kitchen. I told him to have another cup of coffee and take his time since no one was going anywhere without him.

When I returned to the parlor, Rammen was still there. "Sit down. We need to talk."

I did as he said. He never liked to show his cards, and he would surely reproach me for telling Strid that Ramm was not for sale.

"I visited with your Aunt Hedvig," he said. "She says you're secretly engaged."

I kept my gaze on Ulrika's runner. Hedvig must have made inquiries and had been as baffled as Rammen.

"Needless to say, I was surprised," Rammen said. "Hedvig seems to think that this engagement has lasted well over a year. Unless you know something I don't, you'd be wise to turn talk into action."

"I lied to spare his feelings."

Rammen leaned back and tipped his fingers as if only now the conversation began to gain interest. "I'm sure Rikard Lilja knows how to look after himself. Which is more than I can say about you."

Disa came in to clear the table. Rammen told her I would join her shortly. She returned to the kitchen, slamming the door behind her.

"You don't know this but I didn't want to be a farmer," Rammen said. "After Adolf left for America, I was next in line to inherit Ramm. I was eighteen years old. It hasn't always been easy, not for me and certainly not for Ulrika. But the scepter was passed and unlike Adolf I didn't want to shirk my duty."

I tried to grasp the magnitude of his words. That he should have taken over Ramm because of his sense of duty seemed absurd. The farm was so much part of him that he was even known by its name. As for Adolf, I only knew him through his letters, and there had been very few. Now and then he had sent presents to us children, if only to show how successful he was. He had never married. His explanation was that no one would have him, inveterate bachelor that he was.

"What would you have done?" I finally asked. "If you could have chosen?"

"I didn't have a choice. You do. You can have a husband and a life of your own. I've talked to Tekla. Holger Danell, the young lawyer, has been asking about you. She says he sat next to you at the wedding. I want you to travel to Stockholm and let him have a second look. Whatever he saw at the wedding, you'd better make sure he sees again."

A FEW DAYS later, Björn and I walked over to the lake. We sat with our backs against a rock, looking out over the placid water. It was April and only the day before it had been snowing.

"Life in Stockholm could be interesting," Björn said.

"Did you know that Rammen didn't want to be a farmer?"

"What gave you that idea?"

"He told me."

Björn buttoned his thick corduroy vest and folded up his jacket collar. "Well, he got his way."

"What do you mean?"

"He isn't much of a farmer, is he? I bet he can hardly find his way around his own farm unless he can drive there in a carriage."

Almost imperceptibly the clouds had shifted and the sky turned blue. Neither one of us wanted to go back to the house.

I told Björn how I used to come to the lake with Rammen when I was a child. Rammen walked barefoot, with a lightness that seemed remarkable for so large a man. Deer tracks crisscrossed the path as if for a moment the animals had lost their sense of direction. I tried to walk barefoot too, but it hurt too much. Rammen leaned over, my back against his legs, as he brushed the pine needles off the soles of my feet and put my clogs back on.

Björn rose and skipped stones off the surface of the water.

"He used to stand where you stand now," I said, "turning his back as he shed his clothes. His hands and feet were tanned but the rest of his body was a rosy pink. He walked out into the lake, pushing his hips this way and that way, scooping up water and splashing it onto his chest and shoulders."

Björn kept skipping stones, some of them bouncing four or five times before they finally sank.

"I can still see him," I said. "When the water reached his armpits he turned over on his back and began to float. It seemed he lay there for hours. All I could see was his toes and the tip of his nose. Once there was a rainbow, spanning over him like a halo. I thought I was witnessing a miracle, like the parting of the sea or the burning bush. Never went into the water myself. All I could do was stare at Rammen."

Björn returned to my side, brushing sand off his hands. "You were always easy to fool. I guess he never told you he wiggled his fingers."

Chapter Twenty-Two

THE HEAVY OAK door closed soundlessly behind us. I admired the marble that covered the entry walls. Tekla said it was quarried in Sweden and therefore not as white as the kind used for our sister Helga's grave.

While the driver carried the luggage upstairs, Tekla and I rode the lift. Tekla, so attractive in her blue spring suit, said again how glad she was that I had come. On reaching the fifth floor, the lift came to a smooth stop, and Tekla folded back the door. I had never been that high and tried to act as unconcerned as Tekla.

The apartment was vast and airy with views of ships' masts and copper roofs. There were seven rooms, with servants' quarters behind the kitchen. I walked over to one of the windows, holding my cup of coffee as I looked out. The whole city was built on islands, and everywhere I looked, grand facades reflected in the water, vibrating yellow and red. White steamers carried passengers out to the archipelago, while sea gulls circled and dove for scraps. Below, on Strandvägen, motorcars and trams moved at a stately pace, as if they already knew they were at the heart of everything and could think of no other place to go.

The next morning I joined Tekla and Erling in the breakfast room. All I could hear from the street were the bells of the trams and the occasional horn of a motorcar. Encouraged by Tekla, I had taken a bath and my skin still tingled from the hot water that streamed out of brass faucets.

The maid entered the breakfast room to make sure that everything was on the table. Erling, who was fifteen years older than Tekla, helped himself to a second egg, breaking the shell with a precise tap of his spoon. His fingers were long and slender, with clean, well-shaped nails. Tekla had noticed them right away when she met him at the ball. "You can tell a great deal about a man by studying his hands," she had told me. "If he cares for his hands, he cares for his other parts too. I've let him know in no uncertain terms that I'll be his for the asking."

After yet another cup of coffee, Erling folded his newspaper and excused himself. His patients were waiting.

"Another day a little warmer than the last," he said. "Most of the snow disappeared about a week ago. Won't be long now and we'll be able to buy rhubarbs and radishes at the market." He bent down and kissed the back of Tekla's neck. "Thank God for the Swedish farmer," he added with a smile. "Don't know what we'd do without him."

Later that morning Tekla and I took a cab to the city center. On our way we stopped at a tobacconist's shop to buy a postcard for Gustafa. It showed the royal palace, massive and severe, with a lone soldier standing guard. I also bought a box of cigarillos for Ulrika, who always kept some in the drawer of a small table in the upstairs *sal*. She would light one and aim the smoke at the houseplants on the windowsill, claiming she did it to kill the aphids, although surely she also took pleasure in the act itself.

The quiet of the apartment had been an illusion. On Hamngatan, traffic was so dense that the street seemed unable to contain it. Varnished carriages with coachmen wearing tall hats and solemn expressions made way for motorcars that moved through the throng, polished car horns blaring. After one of the motorcars drew up sharply beside me, a man jumped out of the driver's seat and hurried into a store. His passenger, a young woman, remained in the car. Her short hair was as black and glossy as her patent leather collar, which stood up and almost hid her painted lips. I tried not to stare. From her elevated seat, the young woman appeared supremely indifferent to everything around her. Her small dog, secure in her lap, yapped at Tekla and me. The woman did nothing to hush it. This must be the new woman the world was breeding.

At *Nordiska Kompaniet,* cash registers rang as store assistants hurried from one customer to the next. I found a nightgown, made of thin Swiss cotton cambric, for Ulrika. It would hardly keep her warm, but it would cater to her constant delight in things that were of no practical use whatsoever.

Tekla pointed to the label of a perfume bottle that I had selected for Disa. "Do you know what it means?"

I shook my head.

"*Pour être aimé,*" Tekla read aloud. "It's French for wanting to be loved. You might want to reconsider."

Tekla was right. Ever since Disa had met the man from the creamery, she had been in a bad mood. She said she had no idea what Alfrida had been thinking. Instead of the perfume I settled for a tortoise-shell comb with insets of mother of pearl.

"And now you should buy something for yourself," Tekla said and motioned me toward one of the dressing rooms.

A store assistant, already waiting with a box in her hands, followed us behind the heavy curtain, where the mirrors were arranged so that I could see my own back.

The store assistant unfolded the tissue paper and took out a corset the color of cream.

"These just arrived," she said. "I notice *Mademoiselle* is wearing a more traditional corset, but once *Mademoiselle* tries this on, I'm sure *Mademoiselle* will feel quite undressed without it."

Both Tekla and the store assistant looked at me.

"You'll have to take off your clothes," Tekla said. "Everything except your underthings."

It seemed a long time before Tekla understood.

"From here on we'll try to manage on our own," she said to the store assistant. "We'll let you know if we need help."

The woman shrugged as Tekla smiled and stepped aside to let her pass.

"I hope we didn't offend her," I said and began to unbutton my dress.

Tekla laced me from behind, my body yielding to the lustrous satin panels.

"The store assistant is right," she said. "It's not at all like the kind of corsets we're used to. It doesn't restrict your stomach, it only supports it."

"It tugs under my arms."

"The seamstress will take care of that."

I bent over to touch my toes, an exercise I still remembered from my school days, and the corset chafed not just under my arms but also at my chest.

Tekla sighed.

"I just don't see the point," I said.

"The point?"

"From what I read in the newspapers, more and more women wear no corsets at all."

"Nothing wrong with giving nature a helping hand. I dare say most of us can use it."

The store assistant returned, now accompanied by a seamstress. Tekla watched as the store assistant pulled and tucked and the seamstress marked the changes using pins with heads of red porcelain. In addition to some letting out at the top, Tekla suggested some tightening around the hips. "Why not show off the slenderness of the figure?" she said, looking at the store assistant, not at me.

I ran my hand down my side. The back mirror showed the curve of my hips and the long slope of my bottom, red porcelain traversing the satin like mosquito bites in spring.

"You'll get used to it," Tekla said when we left. "Even the doctors recommend it. Easy to wash, too. Just remove the stays."

The corset was delivered at Strandvägen the following day. I never wore it. It is still in my bureau drawer.

THAT EVENING I accompanied Tekla to a meeting. I had always wondered what they were like, these meetings Tekla wrote about. Several women greeted us as we arrived. Only a few seats were still free, and we sat in the back.

The chairwoman introduced the speaker, a woman who looked much older than the others, probably in her late sixties. The topic of her talk was, "Will the war delay the vote?"

"Women believe in peace, not war," she began. "While men glorify war, women see the horror. There's nothing heroic about men killing each other. There's nothing heroic about men killing women and children. If there's any heroism at all, you see it in the nurses who walk the fields after the battles, as they try to help the wounded, whether they're the enemy or one of their own."

The women in the audience focused intently on the speaker. One of them, a tall, thin woman, caught my attention, perhaps because she was taking notes.

"Look at the nurses of France. They volunteer for the front, risking their own lives to save those of the soldiers. We've all heard that French women tend to be vain and superficial. These nurses have once and for all proved such accusations to be wrong. No sooner are they sent home to rest than they're back at their posts at the makeshift hospitals. Who can doubt that their sense of duty will not also manifest itself in times of peace, when they will cast their votes as strong, autonomous citizens of their country?"

Afterward more women came up to greet us. The woman who had taken notes introduced herself as Mrs. Falk and suggested that the women of Hult might want to work for suffrage too. Local groups were being formed all over the country.

I said I did not think the village women would be interested.

"Someone has to go first," Mrs. Falk insisted.

"You don't seem to understand," I said. "How would any of them have time to read and keep informed? Or even attend a meeting? Unlike my mother, most of them don't have help. Their days start no later than five every morning, and they stay up until midnight, baking, weaving, mending. As soon as their daughters are old enough to hire out, they do. They're just as strong as those nurses in France, only they don't talk about it."

"Anna," Tekla said and touched my back.

Still, I thought it important to make Mrs. Falk understand. "I once saw a crofter's wife pull a calf out of the cow. The birth was taking too long, and I watched her slide her hand into the cow and tie a rope around the calf and start pulling. I don't think a woman like that wants to hear about voting. She has quite enough as it is."

"It's late," Tekla said. "We'll have to continue this some other time."

Rather than taking a cab, we walked back to the apartment.

"I think you shocked them," Tekla said as we linked arms. "Mrs. Falk comes from a small town in the north. She's a journalist and has a child of four."

Tekla said the vote would radically transform the social order. "If things were as they should be, a woman should be proud to be a mother, regardless of the circumstances. As society is today, it's not possible. Mrs. Falk never married but she calls herself a widow nonetheless. Even here in Stockholm she has to resort to lies. "

It was still light and we could not bring ourselves to go inside. Back and forth we walked under the linden trees along the water, the way Ulrika and Alfrida used to walk between Ramm and Bergvik, both claiming they were walking each other home.

I asked Tekla if she was happy.

She said she was. "Older men understand their worth and are not so easily threatened. They don't expect women to be all virtue and no fault."

"Older men have a past," I said.

"That's also an advantage. It means their worst mistakes are behind them."

The smell of tar was sharp as boats were being readied for the summer. On the quay men were unloading firewood and herring.

"What's it like?" I asked. It seemed safer to ask this question away from Ramm.

Tekla knew right away what I meant. "It's good, Anna. It's all good. You'll come to want it as much as he."

A woman rode past on a sidesaddle, her blue skirt draping the side of her silver gray horse.

"All I ask is that you keep an open mind," Tekla said while we waited for the lift. "We have to get you out of Hult."

Chapter Twenty-Three

THE FOLLOWING MORNING, at nine o'clock sharp, the doorbell rang and the maid opened the door.

Holger Danell, in a stylish redingote, greeted me with a formal bow. His left hand held an ivory walking stick with a silver handle.

"I've taken time off from the office," he said. "We must make the most of it. Is there anything in particular you'd like to see?"

I said I wanted to see everything except Skansen. From Tekla's descriptions, it sounded too much like home. I did not need to go to Stockholm to see milk cans. And yes, I added, I was very glad to see him. Had it really been three years?

During the next few days Holger showed me buildings and places I had heard of but never seen. I found the new House of the *Riksdag* rather too ponderous and could not help but think that the city would have been more appealing without it. The House of the Nobles pleased me. Built in the seventeenth century, it seemed so light and refined with its curiously curved roof.

"Could it be that they knew more about beauty back then?" I said.

Holger said that buildings were like people. Some would seem out of place regardless of their location. A few, like the House of the Nobles, would shine like stars wherever they were. I felt myself blush for I did suspect he might be talking about me, and I wished he would not.

We stood in front of the statue of Gustaf Adolf, who died in the battle of Lützen in 1632. The statue, on a tall plinth, showed the king on horseback. He looked just as stately as I had imagined, riding high above our heads.

"Those were the days," Holger said.

I did not like his tone. "What do you mean?"

"We were one of the great military powers of Europe."

"My teacher used to say that the victory at Lützen saved the cause of the Protestants."

"Indeed," Holger said, tapping the pavement with his ivory walking stick.

"She told us how the king lost his way in the fog."

"I've heard he was nearsighted too."

"If that's true," I said, "it would only make him braver. He must have known that his eyesight was poor."

"All I'm saying is that Gustaf Adolf was a better statesman than he was a warrior. He would have done the world a greater favor by staying alive."

I had always liked the idea of the king charging ahead of his soldiers, even though the Catholic army was much larger and better equipped. Karolina used to tell us how he was shot after he crossed enemy lines. His horse came galloping back, mane flying, the saddle bloody and empty, and his soldiers were seized with such rage that the Catholic army took fright and fled.

"We owe him gratitude, not scorn," I said. "He valued the lives of his soldiers more than his own. My teacher said we must recognize greatness when we see it."

By now Holger was looking at me and not at the king.

He nodded. "I'm sorry. Please understand. Deriding the past is much in vogue these days. From now on I shall speak with more care. If I fail, please let me know."

I took his arm as we walked on to Norrbro, the arched stone bridge the farmers had crossed on their march to the palace. Tekla was right. Holger was a good man. I should be proud to be his wife.

"This is one of my favorite spots," he said as we stood looking down on the water that soughed and surged toward the Baltic.

"I often come here on my way home from the club," he said. "I like to watch the sunrise. The city is so quiet I can hear the birds. The red light spreads above the ridges, slowly, as if to give the eye a chance to adjust. By the time it reaches Skeppsholmen, it's no longer holding back. The old citadel and the barracks look as if they're touched by fire. And then I smell the cigar smoke in my clothes and hurry home to change. Some mornings I don't bother to sleep but go straight to the office."

We walked over to the other side and looked west. At Södra Bergen, houses clung to the steep hillsides all the way down to the water.

"That's Långholmen," Holger said, pointing at a large island known for its prison. "A hundred years ago most of the inmates were prostitutes. It was a combination of hospital and jail. Those with venereal disease were punished and treated both. Very efficient."

"And now?" I asked.

"We make our prostitutes submit to physical exams to make sure that they're not infected. Should they resist, we still send them to prison. Erling and his colleagues consider the system unfair. Once a woman's name is entered on the police lists it's almost impossible to have it removed. Her customers, on the other hand, remain anonymous, even though they may well have been the ones who carried the contagion."

I had read about syphilis in the Varberg newspaper. The disease, the article warned, pervaded every rank of society. Still, that some women should make their living as prostitutes was widely seen as a matter of course. The Varberg newspaper called it "a necessary evil." In one of her letters, Tekla had written that not even Erling questioned prostitution as such, only the forms under which it was practiced.

The next few days Holger and I continued our walks. Once we stopped to see an exhibition of paintings. The subject was mostly twilight forest glades but the artist also painted cherry trees. One painting showed white blossoms against a pale sky, and the sense of recognition stopped me. I stood before it for so long that the gallery owner rose from his desk and approached me. I told him it looked just like my mother's cherry tree at Ramm. Holger talked about truth in art, but I said it existed in life as well, only we did not always see it.

One day we crossed the bridge to Djurgården, a three-span iron bridge wide enough to accommodate the trams, with statues of the Old Norse gods on high granite columns.

In just a few minutes the noise of the city was behind us and nature was all around. An island unto itself, Djurgården had once been a royal game park, some of the old oaks still standing. Rain had fallen during the night, the earth was wet, and I took long, deep breaths. Holger said you could sometimes hear a nightingale from the dense foliage, but mostly at dusk.

Some boys played soccer in a meadow, and I winced at the smack when they kicked the leather ball. Even in Stockholm, when I was far from the village, it did not take much to bring the memory back. To this day it continues to haunt me, the sight of Erik curled up on the schoolyard ground, covering his head with his arms and his hands. I have tried to explain it to Ella, but she still seems more concerned about me than she is about herself. The worst was not the fury I saw in Johannes and the other boys, although their kicks and their blows were frightening enough. The worst was the blackness that rose inside me and goaded them on.

Holger must have noticed my sudden distress, for he bought me a red balloon from a man with a monkey on his shoulder. I gave the balloon to a girl with a yellow bicycle, and she tied it to her handlebar and rang her bell.

That evening we attended a concert at the Oscar Church with its golden altar and large stained-glass window. Men and women sat together on both sides of the granite colonnade, not apart as in Hult.

Holger seemed surprised when I said I had never heard of Palestrina. He promised me a moment of great power and beauty. He was right. Anyone needing proof of God should only hear such music. The reverberations of the organ filled the church. Then, unaccompanied by the organ, the voices sang the same melody over and over, independently, at their own pace and pitch. The men's voices moved slowly, each syllable drawn out over several beats. The women's moved faster, like the jackdaws in the old graveyard, winding around the men's, rising and tumbling before they caught themselves and could begin anew. Just as I was wondering how all this would end, the music resolved itself into perfect clarity and balance, the whole as dazzling as the parts, not at all like real life.

"I'M SURE HE'LL ask you tonight," Tekla said on the day before I was to travel back to Hult.

The cook and the maid were preparing the evening's dinner. I stayed in my room the better part of the afternoon. If this, as Tekla said, was to be one of the most important evenings of my life, I had better rest up.

At seven o'clock Holger rang the bell, punctual as ever, wearing a gray suit with a striped blue and white handkerchief smartly arranged in his breast pocket.

Erling's two colleagues, Arvid and Urban, arrived with their wives a few minutes later. Arvid's wife Elise smiled warmly, while Kerstin, married to Urban, seemed to appraise me from all sides.

We sat in the drawing room with its richly colored throws and carpets. On a table stood a large bowl of chased silver, overflowing with yellow roses. I recognized it as Aunt Hedvig's wedding present to Tekla. Hedvig and Tekla had always had a special connection. Before Tekla married, and after the captain died, Tekla would often visit Hedvig, returning with gossip about Gothenburg society, passed on by Hedvig over apples baked in the tile stove.

Erling congratulated Holger. "Has he told you?" he asked me as he poured the sherry.

I shook my head.

"I didn't think so," Erling said. "Never one to boast. We've all been reading about it in the newspaper. The owner of a large grocery store sued a charwoman for taking some bruised fruit to her bedridden husband. Holger heard about it and visited the charwoman in her small apartment in the southern part of the city. He interviewed witnesses and contacted reporters. Soon the charwoman made headlines, and everyone discussed her case. Finally, after the labor unions threatened to boycott the store and all its branches, the owner withdrew the charges, and the charwoman has now returned to work."

Erling lifted his glass. "To Holger," he said, echoed by the others. "I predict a great future."

We moved into the dining room, separated from the drawing room by mahogany sliding doors. The curtains were tasseled and fringed, and a mural with fruit and flowers filled one of the walls.

Tekla and Erling presided at each end of the large table. Erling toasted Kerstin to his right, then Elise to his left, and finally me. I raised my glass and returned his "*Skål!*" Even then I was thinking about Fredrik.

The maid spooned consommé into dishes of Sevres china. By the time the salmon was served, the toasting had begun in earnest, now with *Liebfraumilch* from Erling's cellar. Arvid and Urban asked questions about my stay in Stockholm, and I tried to give a thorough account.

"They amuse themselves in Berlin," Kerstin said. "Soldiers' wives gather at the taverns in search of lovers. From what I've read, there's no shortage of handsome young men who for one reason or another have been deemed unfit for war."

"This must be one of the great advancements of our times," Erling said, smiling at Tekla. "The acknowledgment that women have physical needs, just like men."

"What if they become pregnant?" I asked.

"There's certainly no need for that," Kerstin said. "Surely by now we all know how to take precautions."

Tekla had told me about condoms, rubber sheaths that protected not just against disease but also against conception. Even so, I was taken aback by Kerstin's words.

"But contraception is against the law," I insisted.

"You're right," Erling said. "Contraception is indeed against the law. But, as Kerstin says, I don't think anyone here feels restrained by it."

Holger did not join in the laughter, and my gaze met his over the rim of his glass in another toast.

Tekla came to my aid as well. "The law against contraception is certainly enforced in Hult. Our grandmother died when she was thirty-six. She had just given birth to her seventh. And of those, she had already buried three."

The maid served more hollandaise. Would she tell the cook about the scandalous talk at the doctor's table?

"Even today village women go through one pregnancy after another," Tekla continued. "In general they give birth to as many children as they can, usually every two or three years. Should a child be stillborn or die before it's weaned, the next child comes even sooner. It's not just God's order but man's order too. Children remain the best defense against old age."

Elise brought up the old-age pension, introduced a few years earlier.

Tekla shook her head. "It's too small and too new to be trusted. I recall having old people staying at Ramm when I grew up. Most of them were childless. They were too strong for the poorhouse and too weak to be hired out at auction. You'd see them wander from farm to farm, staying no more than a month in each place. Some still had enough strength to help with light chores, but the rest just tried to stay out of our way and not be a bother."

After port wine and crème caramel, we returned to the drawing room. Tekla reclined in the chair opposite mine, draping her shapely body against the rich brocade as if she considered herself part of the decoration. Had she assumed a position like that at Ramm, I would have thought it improper. Here she looked splendid, her eyebrows plucked into fine arches, and her lips made to look even fuller with a touch of rouge. Erling stood behind her, pulling out a cigarette from a monogrammed silver case.

When Holger asked me if I would like some fresh air, the others looked at each other and smiled. Surely everyone knew, perhaps even the cook and the maid.

We stood on the balcony. The sun was setting and the lights of the city grew brighter. I already knew my answer.

"Marry me," he said.

"I can't."

"Is there someone else?"

"There was."

A low hum rose from below, as if the city wanted to remind me of its presence.

"Put two young people together and nature will take care of the rest," I said. "That's what they'd tell you in the village. I just don't think it's enough. We have to ask for more."

The white steamers were making their last runs for the day, their decks lit by red, green, and yellow lanterns. Distant voices, talking and singing drinking songs, traveled across the water.

"I'm sorry," I said. "I shouldn't have come."

"No, Anna, don't say that. Each time I stop on Norrbro I'll remember."

Tram bells rang from Strandvägen. Holger leaned against the railing and asked about Fredrik. I told him he was set to marry someone else. Holger turned to me and touched my cheek with the side of his thumb. I held very still. Having never been kissed, I took note of everything, the softness of his lips, the slight scent of tobacco on his breath, but most of all, my wish that I could have said yes.

"Come back," he said.

I shook my head.

"We'll spend more time," he said. "You don't have to answer me now."

"It's no use. You'd always be second best."

When we rejoined the others, Tekla was serving bonbons and seltzer. We were like participants in a game of charades, having just agreed on how to baffle the others. There would be no cradling of infants, no family meals, no Sunday promenades, no nodding to acquaintances and friends. At least for now Holger would remain the carefree bachelor, the odd man out, and every married woman's charge, always introduced to potential brides, afterward escaping to his club and those early mornings on Norrbro.

Tekla asked if we had something to say, and Holger shook his head.

"Afraid not," he said. "Erling always told me there's something sobering about a woman who grows up on a farm. Must be all that milk."

There was silence and then some awkward laughter. Holger winked at me and handed me a glass of seltzer.

The following morning Tekla said I had made a mistake. We sat at the breakfast table long after Erling left for the clinic.

"Do you think Ulrika knew?" I asked.

"Knew?"

"Hedvig seems to think that Ulrika knew about her father's finances."

"I doubt it very much. If she did, she wouldn't have been able to hide it."

I could have left it at that but pressed on. "Without Rammen, she would have had nothing."

"She was never much of a mother. Let's just hope she's a better wife."

"I can hear the love in his voice," I said. "I can hear it when he walks through the house calling her name."

Tekla rolled her eyes. "Love? Is that what this is all about? Let me tell you about love. There's no one yet who seems to know what it really is, least of all Rammen. At some point we all try to grasp it and get a good look. But the moment we think we have our fingers wrapped around it, it changes into something else. I agree with Hedvig. Best try to manage without it. She once told me that love is God's ultimate revenge. Clouds our vision when we need it the most. What makes so many marriages unhappy is precisely all this talk about love, this idea that we must submit to a force greater than reason. Rammen married the wrong person, even though he won't admit it, not even to himself. Ulrika must have known it all along."

When I asked for the condoms, she did not seem to understand.

"The village women need to know how to limit the number of children," I said. "It's more important than the vote."

Tekla started calling on the telephone. All morning long the women kept coming, putting their envelopes on the dining room table. Tekla said she would let them know when I needed more.

In Håstad, the stationmaster hung on to Caesar's head while I took the reins. Wilhelm stuffed my luggage under the seat, the condoms keeping company with my satin corset. As soon as he sat down beside me, I drew the reins shorter and told the stationmaster to let go. Caesar charged forward and Wilhelm winced and touched his right temple. He said he had been helping Lina Lind in the washhouse, when he slipped and hit his head against the wooden tub.

Caesar moved at a good, steady trot. I could feel the tug of his mouth through the reins as my hands kept restraining and yielding. The men cheered as we flew past the inn. "Let him go, Anna!" one of them shouted. "Let him go!"

Kristina grinned when I showed her the condoms. I told her I had brought them from Stockholm and asked if she knew how to use them.

Her grin grew even broader. "Ah yes, my beauty, I can help you there."

Chapter Twenty-Four

SAMUEL SITS IN my garden chair and looks toward Ramm. Even while seated, he seems large. His broad shoulders, slightly rounded, look as if they could encompass the world.

He lost his wife to the camp. He does not talk about it, any more than I talk about the child.

"Varberg?" he asks, lifting his cup.

I nod. "Only the best for you."

Now and then I take the bus to Varberg. After I buy the coffee, I walk over to the bank, an impressive building with marble pillars and a parquet floor. It is just an excuse, but I bring a bill for a hundred crowns and ask for change. Later I stop by the hospital, for almost always one or two of the patients are from around here, and so I bring them flowers and fruit.

I top his waffle with strawberries and whipped cream. He smiles.

Even with Samuel, I am sometimes afraid. Is that good? "Walk towards danger," Fredrik once said. "Don't turn your back."

Samuel takes very small bites. He does not want our afternoon to be over.

He says, "No man, no woman, no heart is entirely good or evil."

"I wonder," I say. "I really do."

Across the field, Greta steps out on the kitchen steps. Johan's border collie nips at her heels as it tries to herd her back into the house.

"That's where Disa used to stand," I say. "Taking off her apron when the church bells rang."

Samuel sighs, a long, contented sigh, and stretches out his legs. Silence, for us, was never awkward.

"Nietzsche wrote that we must want our life to be just as it is," I say. "We must want it so much that we would live it all over again, the sorrow as well as the joy. There will always be regrets, but there will also be the sense that we did what we had to do, as hard as it was, and that none of it could have happened any other way."

Samuel bows and closes his eyes. He takes a deep breath, his big chest heaving, and then he looks up again.

"Now that would really be something."

KRISTINA MET ME outside the inn. We ran a wash line between the two oak trees on the other side of the road. Kristina used clothes pegs to fasten the condoms to the line. Men, women, and children gathered, with Elias watching in the back, much as the artist painted him in the altarpiece.

The children pointed at the condoms and asked their mothers what they were.

"Step right up," Kristina said as she pulled a condom out of her pocket and waved it over her head. "It won't bite."

She showed how the condom could be washed and hung to dry and used again. Someone asked about sizes, and she said each condom could be stretched to fit all. "Large enough even for Elias," she said and grinned, and just for a moment I imagined her in her younger days, when her body was still supple and light, and men came from far and wide to avail themselves of her service.

Elias told her to watch her mouth and left.

Next she brought out her broomstick, pulled the condom on and off, and filled it with water to make sure there were no holes. She then passed the broomstick around and invited her audience to practice. More women than men took her up on it. She said the condoms could be had for free, but she could promise no such generosity in the future. Since I was the one who gave them out, the villagers must have known that I was also the one who had brought them.

An hour or so later Elias returned, elbowing people aside, a bottle in his hand. Before I had a chance to stop him, he threw the bottle to the ground and grabbed the broomstick from Kristina. Brandishing the stick, he chased the people away, like Jesus in the temple, the villagers said, although in his sermon that Sunday, Wikander would compare it to Sodom and Gomorrah, upsetting Gustafa so much that she hid in her cabin for three whole days.

When Elias finally lowered the stick, Kristina sighed and asked, "Now what was the point of all that?"

The constable took both Kristina and me to the county jail in another village, where we shared a cell. Kristina enjoyed herself greatly, calling the constable by his first name. She told him that from then on she would have to charge him her regular fee, even though in the past she had always been willing to give law enforcement a cut.

When Rammen turned up, he praised the constable for his diligence and said he would personally make sure that this sort of conduct would not be repeated, at least not where his daughter was concerned. Kristina said she could hardly remember a better day, riding back to Hult next to Rammen, waving and smiling to the masses.

As soon as I returned to Ramm, Disa told me that Elias was waiting in Gustafa's cabin.

"It's bad," she said. "Better hurry."

I did not even bother to change clothes.

"Close the door!" Gustafa said as soon as I arrived.

Elias lay on his cot, groaning. His shoes were on the floor beside the cot. A candle burned on the small table.

"The *mara* is trying to get in," Gustafa said. "I've plugged the keyhole but there's always the cracks in the walls."

I pulled a chair to Elias' cot and sat. Elias groaned again. The *mara*, I knew through Gustafa, was an evil presence that would assume the guise of an old hag and ride Elias in his sleep, straddling his chest and clutching his throat.

Gustafa kept watching Elias' clogs. The *mara* would have to step into them to get to Elias. To make it more difficult, Gustafa had turned them so that the toes pointed out.

I never could bear it, seeing him like that. Now and then he would tear at his throat and start to shout. Gustafa got to her feet and checked the rag in the keyhole to make sure it was still there.

"He says you set Kristina up," she said. "Them things fluttering in the wind."

She hauled out a trunk from under her cot and began to place the contents on the floor—an old last, cobbler's thread, jars of nails, and other objects that the shoemaker no longer needed. At the very bottom, wrapped in a piece of cloth, was the small tin box that contained my caul. She always feared that it would fall into the wrong hands and give someone the power to harm me.

"This is where I keep it," she said. "I won't be around forever. Some day you'll have to hide it yourself."

She made sure Elias' clogs had not moved, looked out the window, and peered into the shadowy corners of the cabin. "He wants to tell you to stay away from Kristina."

"Did he say why?"

"There are connections. Connections you don't know."

After covering Elias with an extra blanket, she sat down on her cot and began to darn one of Rammen's socks. A small creature scurried among the rafters, sharp claws rasping against the wood. Elias began to snore.

"Erik is Elias' son," she said. "All those times when Elias was gone, when you kept asking me where he was, he was with Kristina. But not even Kristina would let him stay. Everything in moderation, she told him. Even whoring."

"Does Rammen know?" I asked.

"Remember when he had Erik stuff the new hay up in the loft? Erik was no more than six or seven and the only boy small enough to push it all the way under the eaves. Elias told Rammen that Erik needed rest but Rammen said no. He said Erik needed to learn to fend for himself, seeing he was without a father. I think he was hoping Elias would confess. Don't think he ever did."

She looked up from her darning, her eyes bleary. "Not your fault. Elias loves you all."

"And what about Erik? Has he been told?"

Gustafa shook her head.

"Someone should tell him," I said.

"Elias says no. He says there's no one who deserves to have a drunkard for a father. Bad enough to have a mother who's a whore."

Gustafa held the candle as I stepped outside. Ramm lay in darkness at the far side of the field, and I was relieved to see that everyone had gone to bed. There was a crash from among the trees and a large roebuck bounded across the moonlit path. Behind me, Gustafa quickly closed the door.

Chapter Twenty-Five

IN MAY ALFRIDA brought the news. Agnes had left Prästgården and her marriage to Fredrik Otter had been called off. No one seemed to know why, and neither Agnes nor Fredrik was talking. Agnes now lived in a cabin at Bergvik, and she had given birth to a girl. Wikander had christened her Ella. Some clergymen would refuse to christen an illegitimate child, but at least in this one respect Wikander was lenient.

"Can't say I'm looking forward to housing an unwed mother," Alfrida said. "Still, couldn't very well turn her away. She says she'll make her living as a seamstress. She has fixed up the cabin, and Otter bought her a sewing machine."

A few days later Fredrik's new housekeeper was helping Ulrika and me with the kitchen garden. Marit came from Halland, the province to the south. I could see why the villagers called her looks "unfortunate." Her nose was almost flat and yet it seemed to dominate her face. She was only in her early thirties, but her hair was dry and frizzled with streaks of gray. Fredrik, the rumor went, kept the door to his bedroom locked but Marit would not stop knocking.

"Not too many people grow vegetables around here," I said.

"Where I come from women don't spend all their time weaving," Marit answered. "They know the value of vegetables, especially now with the war and all. I've already helped Mrs. Holmberg at the inn, and we'll be setting an example for the other women too."

As the day warmed, the three of us kept working. Disa was needed in the kitchen. Gustafa said she was needed there too. We all knew that Gustafa found outdoors work degrading, and each time she was asked to lend a hand, she feared it would take her one step closer to the poorhouse. Besides, she told us, she did not consider vegetables proper food for people. Ulrika had enough ideas as it was, and she should not be encouraged.

Marit kept asking Ulrika questions about the soil, receiving vague answers at best. Ulrika had long grown vegetables, but over the years she had planted more and more flowers and now she could no longer remember what she had planted where and much less why. Her use of hen manure had at least been constant, and for this Marit gave her praise.

"Wouldn't hurt to add some artificial fertilizer too," Marit said. "It's good not just in the fields but also in the garden."

"I hardly think it justifies the cost, " I said.

"Have you read Otter's article?" Marit asked.

I had. A successful farmer, Fredrik wrote, must keep abreast of the latest in agricultural research. His most important capital was the soil. If exhausted, it would no longer yield a profit. Fertilizing with manure alone was wasteful. While it did supply nitrogen and potassium, it contained relatively small amounts of phosphoric acid, and therefore it made sense to add the latter artificially.

"Don't let me stop you," Rammen had told the other farmers outside the inn. "If you want to waste your money, place an order right now. Holmberg will be only too eager to fill it. Trouble is, Otter's methods will push your soil too far. You may have great crops today, but tomorrow your land will turn barren."

One of the farmers pointed out that a world at war would need food.

"Just keep rotating your crops," Rammen said. "Barnyard manure will take care of the rest. I, for one, don't foresee a shortage." Here he had the laughers on his side, always a sign that he was winning. "Links the animals to the fields, allows the soil to do its work, as it always has, unless, of course, you now choose to destroy it."

Under Marit's supervision, Ulrika and I raked and leveled the earth. The cows lowed from the barn. The longer days bolstered their memory of summer, when they would finally be let out. Elias was tired of waiting on them, foddering and cleaning and worrying about hay running low.

On the rise behind the barn the wind moved through the forest, making a soft rushing sound. A pair of starlings was building a nest under the eaves of the tool shed.

Stoj loped back and forth in front of his doghouse, and the ring squeaked as it dragged along the wire. I walked over to check on Stella. She had mated with Stoj, and she was now the mother of five. She made way as I reached into the doghouse, all darkness and warmth, moist straw and soft puppy bellies. The puppies whimpered, as one of them pushed its nose against my hand and tried to suck. Stella licked my cheek with her smooth, wet tongue, and I could smell the urine and the sour milk.

"Soon," I murmured. "Soon you and I will hunt again."

When I returned to the kitchen garden, Ulrika was humming. The autumn before, when she dug up the beds, she had let the soil lie as it fell. Marit approved. In Marit's estimation, many "so-called" gardeners packed down the soil too firmly, blocking both water and air. She said it was a mistake to think that nothing happened in the ground during the winter.

But with everything else, Marit found fault. The perennial crops, not just the rhubarbs, should be grouped on one side of the garden, the annuals on the other.

"Vary crops from year to year," she said. "Start with cabbage, onion, spinach, and cucumbers. Follow with carrots, parsnips, and red beets. Third year try peas and beans."

She stopped to reconsider. "Too late now. Perhaps next year."

Ulrika had this effect on people. Not even Marit could stay annoyed with her for long.

And so we worked with what we had, planting the same crop as last year, even though Marit kept telling us that the turnips ought to be planted out in the fields and not take up space in the garden.

Ulrika wanted to know about the flowers.

"*What* flowers?" Marit's voice sharpened.

"I thought perhaps some larkspur and sweet peas, even some nasturtium and phlox? And there must be violets. That's what we use for the graves."

Marit stood broad-legged with her fleshy hands on her hips. "Is this a kitchen garden or is it not? If it isn't, I might as well go home. You'll have to make up your mind."

I tried not to smile. Marit was too new to the village to know that Ulrika already had.

Ulrika kept humming, as Marit strung cords with knots above the beds to keep the planting straight and even. In the field between our house and Gustafa's cabin, Björn was plowing. Now and then I could hear him dismount the plow to smack the horse flies that made the Ardenners stop and stomp. Johannes groomed the horses, the villagers said, and Björn drove them. Even the horses seemed to prefer it that way. When Björn drove them, their huge buttocks tightened as they lowered their heads and pulled. With Johannes holding the reins, they became restless, backing up rather than advancing, rattling their bits and showing the white of their eyes.

Marit lined up shallow furrows into which Ulrika and I dropped the seeds, one under each knot. She told us we would thank her later, when there would be no need to thin the seedlings but lots of room to hoe and weed. Normally the water coming down from the forest would collect in the ditch that ran behind the doghouses, but this year spring had been dry and Marit sent me to fetch water at the well.

By the time Marit rose and pressed her hands against her lower back, the garden had been planted and watered. The soil lay dark and moist, teeming with unseen life. She had shoveled ridges for the cucumbers and planted the seeds close to the top, so the sun would warm them faster. Of the herbs, only the parsley had been allowed to stay with the vegetables, and only in a border around the outer edge. The dill and the chives had been moved to a bed of their own.

"Time to go home," Marit said. "The men will be getting hungry."

"We thank Fredrik Otter for letting you come," Ulrika said. "Be sure to tell him. We know there are many men to feed."

Marit shook out her skirt. "Say what you will about Agnes, but she left the kitchen in good order. It practically runs itself. The pantry is full of compotes and pickled pears. She must have gathered at least fifty liters of lingonberries, not to mention the rose hip and the blueberries. Her canned meat is as good as fresh, if not better. Fricassees, sausages, pigs' feet, oxtails, and mutton, you name it. I heard she went to some fancy cooking school in Gothenburg. All I can say is I like the results."

"And Agnes herself?" I asked. "Any news of her?"

"I wouldn't know. Otter will have nothing to do with her. She'll have to do penance this Sunday."

That evening Rammen returned from Gothenburg, where he had attended the launching of *Sweden*, the new armored cruiser. The hotels, he said, were full. The sun shone from a high, clear sky. The hills, the roofs, all places with any kind of view, were dense with spectators. The king, looking cheerful and rested, arrived by special train from Stockholm. Surrounding ships fired their cannons as the royal cutter crossed the Göta River to the shipyard, where the towering hull of *Sweden* rested on a gigantic cradle. Rammen, as a member of the Provincial Council, had been on the bridge of a large tanker lying next to the cruiser. The last mooring undone, *Sweden* moved, slowly at first, then faster, taking the water with unexpected grace.

Perhaps Erik was right. I had begun to see it too. All that pomp and circumstance only served to disguise the horror. It was like talking to yourself in the dark just to make believe someone else was there. A few days earlier the newspapers had reported on the sinking of the *Lusitania* off the coast of Ireland. More than a thousand men, women, and children had perished. At the fronts the murdering continued, the bottoms of the trenches spongy with rotting flesh.

Where was the glory of that?

SUNDAY WAS WINDY and cold. I saw Fredrik standing with Agnes outside the church. Agnes had crossed her arms and thrust her hands into her armpits for warmth. Kristina curtsied before her, which did not go unnoticed, for Kristina was known to curtsy for no one, not even for Rammen, who avoided her as much as he could.

The rest of the villagers passed them without greetings, looking down at the ground as if sharing in the shame. Fredrik, his large black hat partly shielding his face, spoke to Agnes now and then, but I could not hear what he said. Whatever it was, Agnes appeared to agree, for she nodded and straightened her back. At least Fredrik had come, even though, like Agnes, he would not be allowed inside the church itself. I found myself wondering who would stir his coffee now.

There was the usual coughing and scraping of feet as Wikander climbed the stairs to the pulpit. He read the text of the day and we all sang. I hoped that Agnes and Fredrik had walked into the church porch to get out of the cold. Perhaps Fredrik would take off his jacket and hang it over Agnes' shoulders.

Björn played sharply that day. Not even Karolina could follow as he kept changing the rhythm and embellishing passages we all thought we knew. The night before Disa had caught him in the kitchen with Sara, who had finished with the milking and should have been asleep in her bed in the attic. Björn himself had been sitting at the kitchen table, wearing only his underwear, while Sara had been cleaning the grass spots from the knees of his trousers, singing to herself in a voice that Disa found offensive, "certainly not the kind of voice one would expect to hear in a kitchen."

We all watched as two farmers' wives knelt and bowed their heads at the altar. Many parishes had abandoned this practice, but Wikander followed the Old Testament, which stated that childbirth made women impure. Even with Wikander, the churchings were more of an honoring than a purification, but they still served to atone for the pleasure the women may have felt when they conceived.

The woman to the right had born a boy, the woman to the left, a girl. For the past few weeks they had remained secluded in their homes. Wikander took their hands and welcomed them back to the congregation. "*In sorrow thou shalt bring forth children, and thy desire shall be to thy husband, and he shall rule over thee.*"

Wikander walked down the aisle to church Agnes, who was kneeling on the threshold.

I shuddered as I listened to his words. "*Marriage is honorable in all, and the bed undefiled, but whoremongers and adulterers God will judge. Walk in peace and sin no more.*" This was no longer an honoring but a condemnation, not a welcoming but an expulsion.

After church, Ulrika and Disa went to pay their respect to the two farmers' wives, who would serve coffee and show their babies. I did not join them but turned off on the road toward Bergvik.

Agnes opened the door almost as soon as I knocked. She must have hoped it was Fredrik, for her entire face seemed to slacken and withdraw.

My courage failing, I apologized for bothering her on a Sunday. "I need a new dress," I said, trying to steady my voice.

She asked me to come inside, and I took off my boots and left them by the door. At about eight by five meters, with windows on three walls, the room was rather large for a cabin. It was bright and smelled of hot iron and starch. A crib, covered with cotton lace, stood near the door.

We sat down by the table, and Agnes began leafing through a book of patterns. She moved a small box with buttons out of the way so that she could spread the patterns for a better view.

"Perhaps something like that?" I pointed to a dress that hung loosely on the model's body and reached barely below her knees.

Agnes walked over to a shelf to fetch a bolt of silk. A brand new Husqvarna sewing machine stood at the wall.

"It would look very sophisticated," Agnes said as she draped the silk, a soft mauve, across my chest.

Touching it was like touching water.

"Think about it while I take your measurements," Agnes said. "I'd have to charge you more. Stitching on silk takes longer."

Agnes rolled back the fabric and returned it to the shelf. Bending at my side, one knee against the floor, she measured my hips. Her hair, the color of copper, was gathered in a knot at the back of her head. I was keenly aware that she had known Fredrik Otter in ways I had not.

She stood, pulled out a small note pad from her pocket, and wrote down the numbers. Next she measured my bust, keeping the tape somewhat loose. "I read an article about silkworms. Families keep them in Japan. They feed them mulberry leaves. You can hear them gnawing, like crumpling paper. They look up as the people enter the room. Only a few are allowed to further the species. The others are killed in their cocoons so the silk can be harvested without being broken."

"Seems we must be careful what we wish for."

"I'm not sure I understand," she said, her dark eyes briefly meeting mine.

I always had this habit of thinking as I talked, being just as curious as everyone else to hear what I might say next, but I was nervous that day, and this particular thought was much too tangled. "All I'm saying is that most of us would like to live in comfort. Perhaps we should ask to struggle instead."

Agnes put away her measuring tape and invited me to stay for coffee. While she was in the kitchen, I approached the crib and lifted the lace. Ella was asleep, her eyelids fluttering.

"You're here because of Otter, aren't you?" Agnes stood in the doorway holding a tray. I quickly let down the lace.

I nodded, noting that she called Fredrik by his last name. In spite of the intimacy of their past, they must have resumed a certain distance.

We sat down and Agnes poured the coffee.

"I hear Marit is an excellent housekeeper," she said and held out a plate of almond rings. "I was the one who hired her. She may have hopes for more. She told me she grew up on a large estate. Her father was the estate blacksmith, her mother a cook."

"And your marriage to Fredrik Otter was called off?" I said.

She tensed and returned the plate to the table. "Has he told you why?"

"We haven't talked since the day he reprimanded the farmhand for bringing out the horses."

"All I can tell you is that I was dishonest. That's all you need to know."

Ella began to fuss. Agnes walked over to the crib, wrapped her in a flannel blanket, and brought her to the table. I had seen women nurse children before, and yet I tried not to stare as Agnes unbuttoned her blouse and tickled Ella's lip with her nipple.

"Is there a chance that you might reconcile?" I asked as Ella kneaded Agnes' breast with her tiny fists.

Agnes shook her head. "When he took me home today, he asked to see the child. He stepped inside for a moment but then he was gone. From now on I'm to collect the money from Wikander."

I held Ella while Agnes arranged the bedding. Ella gurgled and cooed, bubbles of milk forming and bursting around her mouth. Unlike Disa, I was never at ease with babies. Disa would burp and check for wet napkins and dispense advice to the mothers, although for the life of me I never understood how she could know.

"It won't be easy for the child," I said.

"Otter says the laws are changing. Children will no longer be called illegitimate. Born out of wedlock, yes, but never illegitimate. He says we write new laws in response to our failings. Injustices become apparent and sooner or later we have to address them."

Ella kept cooing, and I burrowed my face into the flannel, the smell of her close and sweet. Her little arms thrashing, she let out a shriek of delight, so sudden that it seemed to startle even her.

"Let's forget about the dress," Agnes said as I bent to put my boots back on. "It will be easier for us both if we do."

I started down the cabin path, when she spoke again. "It seemed only natural to join him in his bed. We both needed the company." She lifted her hands, only to let them fall, and for a moment I wished we could have been friends.

"He always used condoms," she said. "But even those can break."

"Yes," I murmured, heat rising in my cheeks. "Of course."

As I walked back to Ramm, Alfrida hailed me from the other side of the road and signaled me to cross.

"You'd better go talk to Disa," she said, not even bothering to ask where I had been.

Alfrida had joined Ulrika and Disa when they went to visit the two farmers'
wives. As was the tradition, the hostesses kept asking their guests to step up
to the table and serve themselves coffee and cake. After much coaxing, Ulrika
would go first, then Mrs. Holmberg, followed by the rest of the married
women and their daughters, all of whom were expected to marry in due time.
The spinsters, except for Karolina, would go last. It was the same rigid sense
of order you would see among cows returning to the barn to be milked.

That day, however, several young women, from farms much smaller than
Ramm, had gone before Disa, a sure sign that her standing had changed.

"This is what happens when young women are no longer so young,"
Alfrida said. "When they keep turning up their noses."

As I entered the kitchen at Ramm, Disa had already put on her apron and
was telling Rammen about surprising Björn and Sara the night before. "Never
mind what he does away from Ramm, but in my own kitchen! I ought to
dismiss Sara on the spot, but it's impossible to find good help these days, and
even if I could, nothing would stop him from having his way with the new
one as well. Nobody goes safe, not even my maids!"

Rammen was quiet while Disa fought back her tears. "Now, now," he said,
his voice tender, as if he already knew about her loss of status at the coffee
table. "He's a young man with a young man's needs. As long as the women
are willing and no harm is done, he might as well get it out of his system."

Chapter Twenty-Six

I STILL HAVE not heard from Karin. Not even Lars' letter stirred a response. I tell myself that she will be able to take care of herself, but then I see her before me, the way she lights her Gauloise and picks a fleck of tobacco from the tip of her tongue. I hope Olof is looking after her. I really do.

Ragnar and his wife used to drive her to Ramm for her summer vacations. They themselves never stayed, at least not that I can remember. Björn worked hard in those years. He was always among the first to finish sowing in the spring or get the grain under roof by early autumn. Every day, beginning at dawn, he and his farmhands were out in the fields, clearing stones, draining, spreading manure, and mending fences. His only social life consisted of sessions with agricultural consultants who traveled around the parishes disclosing the latest findings about seeds, crop rotation, fertilizers, and weed control.

When Björn hired Johan, Karin followed Johan around, much as I had once followed Elias. Disa sat by her bed and made her recite her evening prayer. I cannot remember ever joining her myself. I do remember the time a stray dog bit her, a small puncture wound on her left calf. She never told us about it, because she feared we would send her home. Every evening she hid it from Disa, pulling the sheets up to her chin. By the time Disa became suspicious, the wound was blooming blue and red. I was the one who carried her to the ambulance. She still did not want to leave Ramm, so I promised to bring her back myself, just as long as she got well.

When the day came, we walked straight from the hospital to a *konditori*, where I let her have as many pastries as she liked—she only managed two— before we took the bus back to Hult.

I DID NOT tell Disa that Fredrik might be on the train. All I said was that I would like to spend a day in Varberg. With her usual reluctance, she agreed to come along.

It was in the lull between the haying and the grain harvest, and I was hoping that Fredrik would have resumed his habit of taking Saturdays off to go to the bookstore in Varberg. Just as I had hoped, he stood on the platform in Håstad.

He raised his black hat and bowed. I smoothed my white linen dress over my hips. When he put his hat back on, he stroked the broad rim with the palm of his hand, and although I was much too inexperienced to read much into the gesture, I knew enough to realize that it was aimed at me.

After my talk to Agnes, I was determined to take her by her word. She had no claims on Fredrik. Whatever drove them apart, she had admitted that she was the one to blame, and I carried her admission the way you would carry a passport, as if it gave me the right to cross into a foreign land.

Fredrik accepted my invitation to join us in our compartment. He sat down next to Disa, who placed her handbag firmly between them.

As the train traveled west, the landscape became more level, the sky higher. Tethered cows grazed along the embankment, undisturbed by the engine and the smoke-mixed steam. When I pushed down the window, I could already smell the seaweed and the sun-baked rocks.

"Perhaps you might have time for a walk," I asked Fredrik as Disa shot me a disapproving glance. He said he would be pleased.

While Disa and Fredrik walked along the beach, I waded in the warm shallow water, holding my shoes in one hand and lifting the hem of my dress with the other. Small flatfish burrowed on the rippled bottom, stirring up clouds of sand as they scattered and fled.

From a distance Disa and Fredrik looked like any respectable couple taking a stroll by the sea. Disa wore a tailored suit, no belts or frills, only a nosegay of sweet peas in her breast pocket. If I left the two of them on their own, it would be easier for them to get to know each other. Should Disa decide to approve of Fredrik, the rest of the family might be inclined to think well of him too.

When I returned to the beach, Disa and Fredrik were discussing fruit trees and hares. The previous winter the hares had chewed the bark off Ulrika's cherry tree and two of the newly planted pear trees.

"I tie branches of juniper around the trunks but they gnaw straight through them," Disa said. "I've applied both limestone and cow's urine. Just don't know what to do next."

We walked past a boy who was building a sand castle. On the lee side of a low, oblong island, the water glistened and bobbed.

"Have you tried leaving turnips and twigs of aspen nearby?" Fredrik asked. "It might distract them."

Disa shook her head. "I doubt it would do much good. Perhaps Wikander's solution is the best. I'll rig up Rammen's rifle in the parlor window. If Wikander can shoot them, I can too."

I smiled. It was so like Disa to ask for advice and then not take it.

The three of us kept walking. A medieval fortress, built by the Danes, jutted out into the sea, eroding black walls against embankments of green.

Farther out, sailboats appeared to be suspended in a shimmering, seamless void.

We walked over to *Societétshuset*, a fashionable hotel and restaurant, situated in a lush park sheltered from the sea. Fredrik must have abandoned his plans for the bookstore, for his stride was unrushed, as if walking with Rammen's daughters was all he had ever meant to do.

Painted pink, *Societétshuset* was grand and fanciful, a Nordic Alhambra with cornices and arches. We walked up the stairs to the veranda with its iron pilasters and green roof. Potted geraniums hung from the eaves, shaded from the afternoon sun.

A man folded his newspaper, bowed, and relinquished his table. Disa blushed. The table was next to the railing and overlooked the park, where elegant couples wandered arm-in-arm among the trees. The members of a military band were setting up their instruments in an open-air pavilion.

Disa blushed again when Fredrik pulled out her chair and waited for her to sit. The other men wore straw hats and white linen suits, but Fredrik's black trousers and vest, his shirt unbuttoned at the collar, made him seem more real than out-of-place.

A waiter appeared without delay, his shirtfront starched, a napkin draped over his arm.

"Was the pastry made today?" Disa asked.

"Certainly. All our pastries are baked daily."

Disa studied him as if to detect whether he was honest or not. Unnerved by her wandering eye, he kept fussing with his napkin.

"I'll have a Swiss roll and a cup of coffee," I said. "Such a pretty day. I can see you're very busy."

Evidently finding the waiter untrustworthy, Disa rose to pursue her inquiries inside, where pastries were displayed behind the glass of a marble-topped counter.

"I suspect your sister rather disapproves of my presence," Fredrik said with a smile. "She's not putting on airs. You know where you stand with her, even if it's not in your favor."

"It's difficult for Disa to relax and enjoy herself. She works so hard at Ramm. She's in charge of everything in the kitchen."

Fredrik nodded. Most likely he had heard about Disa's strictness. Working for Disa, Sara had told the villagers, was more like serfdom than employment. Should she need the day off, as the time when her mother was sick, she not only had to find her own replacement but she had to pay her too.

The orchestra played a piece from *The Merry Widow* and the waiter arrived with coffee and rolls. Two girls were jumping hopscotch in the park. Everything was festive and light and far away from the war.

"There," Disa said when she returned with a piece of chocolate torte, and I made room for it on the table. "I told them I was perfectly able to bring it here myself."

As soon as she sat down, she turned to Fredrik. "And what, pray, happened between Agnes Hansson and you?"

I held my breath. Disa was nothing if not direct.

"Private matter," Fredrik said, rather too abruptly.

Disa shook her head. "No such thing as private. Not in Hult. Anyone who says that something is no one's concern but his own is bound to have done something he's not too proud of."

"A system of error is always one of complexity," Fredrik said. "Truth alone is simple."

Disa looked at me, as if I were somehow to blame.

Fredrik was smiling now. "It's the established axiom in natural philosophy. Applies to us all." It was the first time I noticed the small scar on his upper lip.

The orchestra struck up the King's Anthem, a signal for us all to rise and sing. Disa's voice soared high and clear above the others. Once having been told by Karolina that I could not hold a tune, I formed the words with my lips but made no sound.

At the table next to ours a young student remained seated and continued to read his book. A dragoon lieutenant walked up to him and lifted him by the collar. Looking him straight in the eye, the student did not resist. The lieutenant slapped his left ear, knocking off his wire-rimmed eyeglasses, which landed on the floor close to the lieutenant's boots.

The student rubbed his eyes and blinked. He went down on his knees and ran his hands across the floorboards. Each time he came close to his glasses, the lieutenant nudged them farther away with the point of his boot. Soon the student followed the lieutenant's boot as if it brought him deliverance rather than torment.

Unable to watch, I picked up the eyeglasses, wiped them off, and held them out to the student. He took them but did not thank me. Disa sang louder and louder, staying with the orchestra until the end, refusing to acknowledge that anything noteworthy had occurred.

The headwaiter emerged from the shadows and told the student to leave. Some people applauded the lieutenant as he returned to his table. For a moment I was afraid that Disa might join in.

"He should have risen," Disa said as a sparrow landed on our table.

"Even so there was no call for violence," I said.

In the park, the members of the orchestra began to put away their instruments. The game of hopscotch was over and the two girls were now tossing a ball. The sparrow kept fluffing its feathers and dipped its beak into our creamer.

Disa turned to Fredrik. "We know what Anna thinks. What about you? Or is this a private matter too?"

"Anna may have offered help where none was wanted."

"The student was irreverent," Disa said. "No respect for law and order."

"I suspect he knew what he was doing," Fredrik said and signaled to the waiter to bring a new creamer. "He wanted a reaction. The lieutenant played right into his hands."

"He should have risen, " Disa persisted.

Fredrik nodded. "I'm not saying I agree with what he did. I'm only defending his right to do it."

"Last I heard it's a crime to hit another," I said. "The man who was guilty of wrong was the lieutenant, not the student."

On Disa's insistence we took the early train home. I sat by the window, next to Disa. Opposite, Fredrik was reading a newspaper, his hat on the seat beside him. Disa kept conversing with one of the other passengers, a squat woman from a village north of Hult. She was constantly changing the subject. The incident with the student had clearly upset her too.

At one of the stations, cattle were being loaded on to railway cars bound for Germany. Because of the war, no cow was too old to be turned into sausage or goulash. The farmers were paid good money, some turned greedy, and soon young animals were exported as well. Tied behind wagons, they trudged along the country roads, worn-out cows and healthy bullocks, all on their way to the stations. No one paid much attention. A quick head count, that was all, and some of those animals were not even watered or fed.

I could read the headlines on Fredrik's newspaper. The Germans and the Austrians were pushing farther and farther into Russia, the Russians burning everything as they fled. I recognized names that a few weeks earlier I would not have known: Kurschany, Zjechanow, Narew, and Njemen. Prisoners of war had been taken, twenty thousand in two days.

The train lurched, and the conductor swung as he checked our tickets. Bells rang at railroad crossings, where men and women stood holding their bicycles. One of the women waved. To prevent her skirts from being caught, she had stretched colorful cotton netting over the rear wheel. For some reason, I found it reassuring, as if even in the midst of a war, the practical could still prevail.

Disa stopped talking, perhaps numbed by the headlines too. My lips tasted of salt. On the wall a decanter with tepid water clinked against a metal rack, hopelessly out of rhythm with the thunking of the rails.

Chapter Twenty-Seven

THAT SUMMER I gathered the pieces from Fredrik's life the way Ulrika would gather flowers in the meadows. We sat at the edge of the forest and talked. Past the field, the old graveyard was almost hidden by trees.

He was born in Uppsala, where his father had been a professor. An only child, he did not remember his mother, who was an artist and died shortly after his birth. She came from a well-known line of clergymen and merchants, all prominent members of the upper middle class. From what he had been told, she was outspoken and unconventional. His memories of his childhood seemed confined to his father's study, long silent days, curtains closed, the musty smell of the carpet, his father writing at a heavy desk, and Fredrik himself reading on the floor, his mother's sketches pinned to the wall, mostly nudes.

He had studied philosophy at the university, intending to become a professor like his father. While spending a summer as a private tutor at a large farm, he realized his true interest lay elsewhere. Everything that had to do with the farm, from grain varieties to dairy cows and fertilizers, intrigued him. Animals responded to him too. Dogs and cats followed him around. He had, as they said, found his calling, picturing himself on early morning walks, inspecting the fields, talking to his neighbors. Reality turned out to be different, with little time for walks. He still could not think of a better life.

He told me he was against organizations of all kinds. In this, he considered himself an anarchist, much more so than Erik. But Disa need not worry. His interest was in agriculture, not politics. He said he had few friends, certainly in the village, where he could count only two, Holmberg and Emilia, who came to Prästgården for milk and often stayed to talk.

I think he had more, only he did not know it. During his time in Hult, people came to respect him. Johannes certainly did. Once, in the forest, Fredrik surprised him with Konrad. Johannes had already moved to the cabin behind the main house, but as far as I know, no one had questioned it, for Johannes had always been more at home with the farmhands than he was with his family. "Love seeks its own," Fredrik said and tipped his hat. Years later Johannes told me.

I asked him about his late night discussions with Wikander. He smiled and said his uncle was concerned about his eternal soul but that he himself preferred to focus on the present. As he saw it, the chasm between God and man was so vast that neither science nor theology could bridge it. In the end there would be just one question left and death alone held the answer.

Wikander, he said, had once been the natural center of the drawing room, charming, entertaining, even brilliant. He had moved among ideas, not among flesh and blood.

"I suppose he misses the debates at the seminary," Fredrik said. "Perhaps I make up for some of that."

From Ramm came the rattle of milk cans as Elias let the cows into the barn, and from the village we could hear the hollow rumble of a horse's hooves against the wooden bridge. If the air grew chill, he covered my shoulders with his jacket, the one that smelled of earth.

"So, Anna, who are you?" he once asked, his gray eyes appraising the entire length of me, as if staking out new land. "Why are you here? Do tell."

If I heard the mockery behind his words—that slightly higher pitch and singsong quality of his voice—I chose to ignore it.

"I'm Anna," I said. "Isn't that enough?"

"Good start," he said, leaning back, his face half in shadow now. "But no. Not enough. You'll have to do better than that."

And so I told him about the time when Rammen sat me down—I was no more than ten years old—and said he wished I were the one to take over Ramm, but it was not in his power to change it. This was when I realized that even Rammen had his limitations, and I began to develop a hardness of my own.

Fredrik nodded, said he understood. His voice was back to normal now, that strong, clipped voice that drew me from the start.

But when I told him a young man had once kissed me, he said that he himself was no longer a young man and that he would want more.

IN AUGUST, RAMMEN made arrangements for me to work at the village bank.

"You don't need a man," he said. "This is your chance to prove it."

He must have known that Fredrik and I were meeting. I was hardly ever home for supper, and when I did come home, I would go upstairs as soon as I could.

Miss Rydelius trained me. She was from Varberg and had run the village bank since it opened a few months earlier. She stayed at the inn and took her meals by herself in a corner. Saturdays and Sundays, she spent in Varberg.

Soon Miss Rydelius stayed only for the day, and with longer and longer intervals. She said I had caught on fast and should have no problem managing on my own. In her estimation I knew more about farming than did many of the farmers. Should I need help, there was always the telephone. She hired Susanna, Holmberg's daughter, as my assistant. I kept a box of condoms under the counter, and Susanna always turned her head when the farmwomen came to collect them.

One evening I was working late. Three farmers had come to the bank to ask for loans that day. Two of them wanted to take on more than they should. The problem was, farmers signed for farmers, and when the day of reckoning finally came, many lost it all.

The clock struck seven and Susanna had left. The store, like the bank, was closed, and the evening traffic at the inn had yet to begin.

Someone knocked on the door. It was Lovisa, my friend from school, the mill worker I no longer talked to. Her kerchief was tied in a hard knot under her chin and the smell of lubricating oil stood thick around her.

"I need to borrow money."

"You'll have to come back tomorrow. The bank is closed."

Her voice was firm, as if she had thought about something for a long time and finally made her decision. "It has to be today."

"What do you need the money for?"

She did not answer, just fingered her kerchief, her cuticles shredded and chewed.

"How much do you need?" I asked.

She stared at the floor. "A hundred crowns."

I could only assume that she needed the money for food. Because of the war, prices kept rising. While the farmers were stocking up, the mill workers could barely afford the basics.

"You're asking for a great deal of money," I said. "But even for a smaller sum, the bank requires some form of security. Something you agree to give up if for some reason you can't repay the loan."

She clenched her lips, her skin sallow and taut. Sven, her husband, had joined Erik in his efforts to spread the socialist creed. From what I had heard, Lovisa was very much against it. She was not the only one. Many of the workers in Hult were hostile to the new ideas. Wikander had taught them well. In sermon after sermon he told them they must carry out their God-given tasks, no matter how lowly or hard. To join a labor union was to align themselves with the Antichrist. Life on this earth was not meant to be joyous. Its only purpose was to prepare them for death.

"Is there someone who can sign for you?" I asked. "Someone who will pay back the money in case you can't?"

Lovisa clenched her lips even tighter.

"It's often done that way," I explained. "It's no reflection on you."

"I know of no such person."

Fredrik and I were to meet at the edge of the forest, and she must have caught me looking at the clock.

"Come back tomorrow," I said. "I'll have the money for you then. We'll make it a personal loan. No rush to repay."

She never returned. Once I saw her on the road, and she crossed to the other side. I crossed too. When I asked her if she still needed the loan, she shook her head. I have often thought of this moment and cursed myself for letting her walk away. There are times when we need to leave people alone. There are other times when we must not. How do we make the call?

Chapter Twenty-Eight

WHEN I RETURN from the grave, Karin sits at my door. Without a word she picks up her suitcase and follows me into the cabin.

"Thanks for the letter," she murmurs after she settles on the sofa. Her eyelids are slightly swollen, and she seems even thinner than when I saw her last.

"I called you but you weren't home," I say.

"I was jogging. Sorry, I should have called you back."

I sit in the Gustavian armchair that used to belong to Ulrika. "No, no, I did not mean to accuse you. I was worried, that's all."

After what seems like an hour, she finally looks up. "I just can't manage."

"Manage what?"

"Life. I just can't manage life."

I watch her for a while before I speak again. I fully expect her to reach for her cigarette pack and shake out another Gauloise.

"And Olof?" I ask.

"He tries to help. He puts the children to bed. I get them to daycare in the morning. He cooks breakfast and I get them dressed."

"Does he love you?"

Her eyes widen in what seems to be disbelief. "Oh, Anna. How very strange you are."

"But does he?"

"Does he what?"

"Does he love you?

She scowls. "He says he does."

"And you?"

"Me?"

"Do you love him back?"

She slides down on the floor, leans her back against the sofa, and buries her face in her hands.

"You're pregnant, aren't you," I say.

She looks at me with narrowed eyes. "I forgot to take my pill."

She reaches into her pocket but withdraws her hand as if she just remembers. So it is true. She no longer smokes.

"We used to make love all night," she says. "But then the children came."

When I do not answer, she pleads. "Isn't that the way it's supposed to be? I mean, aren't we supposed to be there for our children? Who has time for love?"

"I'm hardly the one to ask."

I rise to make tea. Not moving, she does not even seem aware that I am here. Still, there is life in her now, and for some reason the knowledge gives me joy.

It is getting darker and the cabin is cold. I build a fire in the tile stove and leave the brass doors open. Karin still does not move.

"I can't go on like this," she says. "Resenting those I ought to love."

"You're going to need food. You're going to have to eat for two."

"I took the children to the park," she says. "The girl wouldn't leave my side, and even the boy seemed to want to keep an eye on me, as if to make sure I wouldn't disappear. He sat on one of the swings, dutifully pumping his legs. My brave little boy, still trying to please."

I pour the hot water into the teapot.

"Was my great grandmother mad?" she says.

It takes me a while to recover. Still, I should have known. Sooner or later she was bound to ask.

"I don't know what Ragnar has told you," I say. "But I would say no."

"So what was wrong with her?"

I put out the teacups on the kitchen table along with bread and cheese. "If you ask me, I think she used her condition as a refuge, a way to distance herself from the lies."

"The lies?"

"The rest of us became quite good at keeping up appearances."

Karin moves to the table and sips her tea. "So you're saying she wasn't ill at all?"

"We all find ways to cope, Ulrika found hers in solitude. From there, perhaps, the descent into madness seemed natural, and I suspect the temptation was strong, but I don't believe she ever gave in to it, I really don't."

She nibbles on a piece of bread. "I only saw her once."

I push the cheese toward her plate but she ignores it.

"Dad took me. I had just started school so I guess I was no more than seven. She sat in her bed, all wrinkled and sweet. She must have been at least a hundred years."

"Not quite. Almost."

"Her lips were very red, not from lipstick, I don't think. Perhaps they seemed so red because everything else about her was pale."

"Yes."

"What did the doctors say? They must have had some kind of diagnosis."

"I believe they called it neurasthenia. As far as I'm concerned, that's only a word."

I too can see Ulrika, leaning back against her pillows, in her lavender bed jacket and her white lace cap. She never left the sanitarium. Her death should not have shocked me but it did. It was as if I had lost a limb, which seemed curious, because a limb would have been of some use, and even now I cannot say that Ulrika ever was.

I pour Karin a second cup of tea.

"It does run in families, doesn't it?" she says.

Only now do I truly understand why she is here.

"You want me to promise that all will be well," I say. "I can't."

Chapter Twenty-Nine

ONE SEPTEMBER EVENING, Fredrik did not come to the edge of the forest. By then his search for a farm took him farther and farther. Two of his offers had fallen through.

Normally I would have walked back to Ramm, knowing that he would leave a note at the bank, apologizing and telling me when to expect him next. But that day I was not content to wait. Instead I walked over to Prästgården.

I found him in the barn. When he saw me, he leaned the pitchfork against the wall and frowned. His farmhand was spreading straw for the bull.

Marit, his new housekeeper, descended the ladder to the hayloft carrying eggs in her apron. The rabbits rustled over by the window. Agnes had started them, claiming that rabbit meat was nutritious and flavorful both, and Marit must have agreed, for now there were no less than five old herring barrels stacked and converted into hutches.

The farmhand yelled. The hornless bull had cornered him in the pen and was turning his side to show off his size. I had seen bulls do that before, a warning before they attack.

Fredrik ran up to the pen, threw his jacket over the head of the bull, and shouted to the farmhand to jump out. Disoriented, the bull swayed and snorted. The farmhand squeezed past and escaped. A dark stain spread on his trousers where they covered his crotch.

Fredrik reached to retrieve his jacket. "Don't ever approach him from behind. You play by his rules or you're dead."

Marit called from the door, "That animal should be sent back where he came from. He's making everyone nervous. Don't like to come in here myself."

In the pen, the bull butted his head against the wall.

Marit glared at me and left.

"Take the rest of the day off," Fredrik said to the farmhand, whose face was as white as the lime-washed wall behind him.

The farmhand gone, Fredrik turned to me. His jaw muscles tensed. If he had a reason for not coming to the forest, he did not say. He merely nodded toward the loft. Now, in retrospect, I suspect he never meant to come at all.

He followed me as I climbed the ladder. The loft was almost dark. Without a word he closed the hatch.

Light squeezed between the wallboards. The new hay smelled earthy and sweet. A hen, unnoticed by Marit, cackled and flew up, exposing two large eggs. Fredrik still did not speak but seized my shoulders and pinned me against a post. When he wedged his leg between my thighs, I lifted my skirt and slumped, just enough for him to push inside me. The searing pain made me gasp.

He said he was sorry, although I was not sure for what. I had known what to do, and I could not have been the first woman to receive a man like that. Still holding me against the post, he reached down with one hand, seeking and stroking, until my pleasure took over and I pressed my face into his jacket to stifle my cry. When he pulled me back by my hair and put his hand to my mouth, I tasted the blood.

"This is who you are," he said, his voice rough. "Now you know."

Without another word he buttoned his trousers and left. Staying for a while, I gathered myself together in more ways than one.

The bull lowed from below. The hen had returned to her eggs and clucked and tilted her head. A beam of light struck her eye, and her stiff, icy stare bored straight through me.

SUPPER DRAGGED ON. Rammen talked about the new thresher. He kept talking even after Gustafa began to clear the table and Wilhelm left to play at a dance. Farmhands and day laborers would follow the thresher around, until it had been used at all the farms. Barring rain, the work would continue from sunrise to sundown. It would be a sight to see, he said, all those people out in the field, tending to that great machine.

Gustafa, by the sink, kept sighing. "And who's going to feed all these hungry men?"

"We'll find a way," Ulrika said. "We always do."

Rammen watched me as he talked. I had no doubt that he kept me late on purpose. Since that day in the loft, Fredrik and I had begun to meet again, but by the time Rammen stopped talking and I arrived at the edge of the forest, Fredrik was no longer there.

I walked over to Prästgården and knocked on the front door.

This time he did not frown but appeared relieved to see me. "Please come in. We're looking for some papers. Won't be long."

A paraffin lamp burned in his office, where Marit was rummaging through the wastepaper basket.

"It's a manuscript," Fredrik said as he examined the papers on his desk. "It's due at the newspaper next week." He crushed one of the papers into a ball and tossed it to the floor.

He saw me studying the sketch pinned to the wall above his desk. It was a study of a female nude, sketched from behind, the groove down her back softly shaded in.

When his eyes met mine, the light had gone out of them entirely and only emptiness remained.

"A month before she died," he said. "She still worked."

Marit kept searching the wastepaper basket, all the while muttering to herself. When I tried to help, she pushed me aside, saying she was in no need of assistance. Presently she pulled some sheets out of the basket and gave them to Fredrik. She said she must have thrown them out when she was cleaning.

Her voice shook. "I may just be the housekeeper. Don't mean I have no feelings." She blew her nose and stalked off to the kitchen.

"I apologize for Marit," Fredrik said, checking to make sure that the pages were all there. "Altogether uncalled for."

"What is it about?" I asked.

"A new kind of seed. Much hardier than the old. Or so it seems. We don't know enough yet."

We could hear Wilhelm's fiddle through the open window. When I explained why I was late, Fredrik said that Rammen and he should talk.

The fiddle music grew louder and I could hear clapping and laughter.

Fredrik kissed the back of my hand. Something rang false and I pulled back.

"Shall we dance?" he said, his eyes still void of life. "Shall we feed the village tongues?"

In a clearing, lit by torches, Wilhelm sat on a large stone, his fiddle across his lap. Young women crowded together, glad to be finished with their chores. Standing apart, a group of farmhands took quick drinks out of their hip flasks. Konrad saw me and nodded. Johannes was off to the side, talking to Lisa Lind, Nils and Lina's eldest, who worked as a maid at one of the village farms.

Wilhelm played a schottische and couple after couple started to dance. Something happened to Wilhelm when he played. He retreated into himself, and yet it was as if all those who listened felt that he played only for them. I was a child when the stranger gave him his fiddle. I watched them through the kitchen window, the man teaching Wilhelm how to rub the rosin on to the bow, and how to bend his wrist and position his fingers. No one asked where the man came from. All Rammen cared about was that he was strong and worked hard. He was gone right after the harvest. Gustafa said that Wilhelm was wrong to keep the fiddle. She had lived long enough to know that nothing in this world was free.

"Sister!" Björn came up from behind with Emma at his side.

Being Rammen's daughter, I had never attended one of these dances before. Even so, I wished Björn had not been so quick to show his surprise.

Fredrik asked Emma about the mill library.

"The catalogue is done," Emma said. "We're still hoping for more donations."

Some of the other women had gathered close, clearly hoping to gain Björn's attention. Björn, however, was wholly occupied with Emma, whose beauty still waged war with her modesty, no matter how high-necked her blouse.

"Emma has begun to join Emilia on her calls," he said. "Sounds like quite an adventure, walking through the woods and braving the dark."

"I wish they wouldn't call us last minute," Emma said. "Seems women around here feel they ought to be able to manage on their own, as if it's a shame to ask for help. And their husbands apparently agree."

Two farmhands wrestled. A dance without a fight or two was unusual. Björn once told me that two women had come to blows, the younger one even pulling a knife. He said that he was the one they fought over, and when he saw that the two of them were temporarily engaged, he took the opportunity to wander off with a third.

"No harm done," he said, eyes laughing, and even I found it hard not to smile.

Wilhelm tucked his fiddle under his chin and launched into a hambo. The clearing filled with dancers, Björn and Emma among them. Robbed of spectators, the two farmhands held out their hip flasks to each other and slapped each other's backs.

"Your brother is in love," Fredrik said.

I could see it too. Björn still would not take his gaze off of Emma, who danced much as she talked, with great consideration and care.

When Wilhelm played a polska, dissonant and slow, Fredrik and I joined in the dance. He put his hand behind my neck, and I leaned back into his hold.

The torches waned and flared. Wilhelm's bow lashed at the strings as the music grew faster, sliding from major to minor. The women's skin glistened and the men whooped and stamped. Couples disappeared among the trees, ducking under branches. Both Fredrik's hands were now on my waist, and I leaned back even farther, my hips against his, rocking and dipping. Then, his forehead touching mine, he held me with just one hand, and so I let go of him too, swaying and bending, the music pulling me under and down. That was when I heard the women, not the living but the dead. I heard them in the wind that blew through Rammen's forest, and in the strains of Wilhelm's fiddle, the crescendos and the sudden stops. "This life, as you live it now, we have lived before you. As it was for us, so it will be for you, and every pain and joy will be repeated."

They stayed with me long into the night. I never spoke of them, not even to Gustafa, for even though she might not question their existence, she would surely question their intent.

Just before dawn Wilhelm put away his fiddle, shook hands with Fredrik, and said he would walk me home.

THE NEXT DAY all of Hult was talking. I heard about it through Disa, who had heard about it through Sara, who had gone down to Holmberg's store for yeast.

"Shouldn't a woman be free to do what she wants?" I asked Disa when we took out a rug to be shaken. "They're already gossiping about Björn. Why not let them gossip about me?"

Disa, holding on to the other end of the rug, shook fast and hard. "Björn has nothing to lose. You do. You can't afford to be seen at a common dance, certainly not with a man like Otter. And Marit telling everyone that you came to his door isn't helping."

I mirrored Disa's movements as we folded the rug.

"I've done nothing wrong," I said. "Fredrik will talk to Rammen this afternoon. They'll work things out."

Disa shrugged and carried the rug back into the house.

I was not nearly as confident as I let on.

Rammen had said he would receive Fredrik in his office. "Tell him to come this afternoon. Tell him I look forward to it."

This would not be a conversation suitable for the parlor.

Rammen did not rise as Fredrik and I came through the door. With a sweeping movement of his hand, he pointed to two wooden chairs facing his large oak desk, which was covered with letters and reports.

I held my breath as Rammen offered Fredrik a cigar. Fredrik turned it down.

"I understand you keep company with my daughter," Rammen said.

Fredrik nodded. "We do meet, yes."

We waited while Rammen held the match to the cigar and puffed. A fly buzzed against the window.

"Your reputation as a farmer may be solid," Rammen said, "but your reputation with women is not. It's well known that your travels to Gothenburg have included visits to a woman of a less respectable class. How can my daughter be sure that such habits, well established, will not be kept up?"

A branch of the linden tree scraped the window and the fly wheeled back.

"That's all in Fredrik's past," I said, even though we had never discussed it.

Fredrik took my hand. No doubt Rammen saw it, for his knuckles turned white as he gripped his armrest.

"My doctor assures me that I'm healthy," Fredrik said. "But since you bring it up, I'd like to let you know where I stand. I believe it's more honorable to visit a prostitute than to have relations with a woman who entertains false hopes of marriage. A prostitute has no illusions. I see no reason to treat her with disrespect."

Rammen nodded. "If this is indeed your position, and I must say you state your case well, I'm even more at a loss to understand. Why did you share your bed with Agnes Hansson, only to send her away when she was with child?"

Fredrik let go of my hand. "I'm not here to talk about Agnes. I'm sorry, but on this I must stay firm."

"There's only one explanation," Rammen said. "You thought you could do better. There's something you should know about me too. I only ask once. And I'm asking you now. Stay away from Anna. Put an end to this foolishness now. Should she marry against my will, she'll no longer be welcome at Ramm."

For a minute none of us spoke. The fly struck the window and fell to the sill, momentarily stunned.

Rammen knocked the ashes off his cigar. "Clearly Anna thinks she loves you and that her feelings are returned. Your interest, I fear, is more material. Let me level with you right away. Wilhelm will be in no position to buy her out. All you can expect is her dowry, and even that will be modest. Your best bet is to go back to Agnes. She's a handsome woman, of good moral standing, at least until you came around. For heaven's sake, man, if you've got an ounce of decency left, admit your mistake, marry Agnes Hansson and do right by your child."

"Anna will no doubt make up her own mind," Fredrik said. "I believe she already has."

Rammen shuffled the papers on his desk. Looking up again, he arched an eyebrow, as if surprised we were still there.

Through the window we saw Fredrik walk stiffly across the courtyard, his hands jammed into his jacket pockets.

"His place is with Agnes, not with you," Rammen said. "A man who sleeps with his housekeeper has no right to abandon her when she's pregnant with his child. I'd be a poor father indeed if I didn't prevent you from seeking your own ruin. Otter is a coward. In times past we'd put him in the stocks as well, right next to Agnes."

Marit told everyone that she had to mend the linings of Fredrik's pockets. "Both pockets. That's how hard he must have shoved."

Chapter Thirty

THE PARISH COUNCIL was about to convene. I was the first to arrive at the schoolhouse and Karolina greeted me at the door. While I kept minutes, she herself would listen from the upstairs landing.

The men sat on top of the children's desks, their heavy bottoms knocking the slates off their hooks. Gavel in hand, Wikander faced them. Behind him hung a large map of Sweden, with the names of the towns in red.

I sat in the back and was just as surprised as everyone else when Fredrik arrived, stomping the mud from his boots and unraveling his woolen muffler.

"Holmberg is on his way," he said. "He asked me to represent him until he's here."

One or two men objected. Rammen said nothing but stiffened and raised his head.

Wikander decided to carry on. "You're all acquainted with the matter before us. Holmberg wishes to buy more land to expand the mill. The land he wants is next to the warehouse and belongs to the parish. He's prepared to pay in cash."

The first man to speak owned a small farm down by the river. "The mill takes workers away from the farms. My wife just lost another maid. Barely had time to train her."

Another farmer concurred. "The temperance group is up to no good. Before we know it, they'll rally the farm workers too. If we don't stop this now, we're surely aiming for disaster. Crops rotting in the fields, cows not getting milked, the poor beasts staggering around with their teats leaking."

More members shared his concerns. Erik, who now called himself *Ombudsman*, was said to be getting too big for his breeches. I often saw him outside the inn on his way to visit labor unions in other parts. He would wear a black suit and shiny leather shoes. Holmberg once suggested that Erik and he address each other as *du*, implying that the two of them might be on friendly terms. Erik, however, smiled his wry smile and said he was looking for justice, not friends. Kristina, while buying herring at the store, told Holmberg he was welcome to say *du* to her. She would gladly stand in for her son, who nowadays was far too busy standing in for everyone else, but Holmberg did not take her up on it.

Theodor, Augusta's husband, rarely spoke, but when he did, the men would take notice.

"No one can deny that the mill has done good for the village as a whole. The mill is heated. The large skylights make the place seem less oppressive. Weavers make about three times as much as they did in the past. My only question, and it's an important one, is how come Holmberg all of a sudden is able to buy this land. As I recall, he's always been short of cash. Always made sure we didn't forget."

Fredrik's voice came from the back, as he stood leaning against the cabinet where Karolina kept her supplies.

"Whether you're for it or not, industrialism is here to stay. I see no reason why you shouldn't sell Holmberg the land. Erik's brand of socialism is hardly dangerous. Even Holmberg has begun to agree. He would actually welcome a union, rather than have one worker after another traipsing through his office asking for a raise. Told me so himself."

The men, confined to the children's desks, tried to turn. One of them, his hands thrust under his suspenders, swung, and tumbled to the floor. Rammen did not move.

I kept my eyes on my note pad, wishing Fredrik had not come. What gave him the right to show up at will and unsettle the council, outsider that he was? And yet, as soon as he spoke again, all I could think of was his voice, the heat burning through me, like a horseshoe emerging orange from the blacksmith's forge.

"What will happen if you don't sell Holmberg the land?" he said. "Most likely the mill will close. Holmberg will leave, hardly the worse for the wear. The workers will have to find other ways to feed their children. For all your complaining, there's not enough work at the farms. Most of them would be forced to move. I'm sure you've read about the city slums. That's the kind of place where socialism grows, where women turn bitter, and men learn to curse."

Karolina sneezed from the top of the stairs. In the silence that ensued, all that could be heard was the muted snap of Rammen's watchcase. Fredrik wished Karolina good health.

More stomping came from the door. Holmberg entered, followed by Klas. Holmberg, as dapper as always, escorted Klas to the front of the room. He apologized for the delay and nodded to Klas to speak.

Like Wikander in the pulpit, Klas made everyone wait while he laid in snuff. "Won't come as no surprise," he said, his voice raspy with concern. "I've told you before, and I'm telling you now. The new cemetery is too small. Got to remove the old coffins to make room for the new. I collect whatever's left, a skull here, a plait of hair there, some loose teeth. Pour it all into a small hole in the bottom of the grave and cover it with soil. Pat it down as best I can. When they lower the new coffin on top, no one knows the difference. But mind you, I lie awake at night thinking about Judgment Day. For too long I've been pouring new leftovers on top of the old. It can't go on forever. When the day comes for the dead to rise, as the vicar says it will, they'll have a hard time finding their own bones. Not even Jesus will know who's who."

A drop of spit dribbled down Klas' vest, already speckled brown. "If you don't believe me, come see for yourselves. In one hole, I've seen as many as two or three skulls, a big toe next to a nose, thighbones and kneecaps all mixed together. A man bound for hell may easily get confused with a woman bound for heaven. For all I know, some people may end up in heaven and hell both, being just as happy or miserable as they were on this earth, which ought to be punishment enough but might not meet with our Lord's approval. Holmberg here says he's come up with a solution. I say you ought to hear him out."

Holmberg stepped up and patted Klas on the back. "Thank you, Klas. You may leave."

Klas sat down on the floor by the stairs. "Seeing that this is a matter that concerns us all, I'd just as soon stay." Arms around his knees, he grinned up at Karolina.

Holmberg turned to the council members. "Gentlemen, I just returned from a meeting with Wikstrand at Brunnsdal. I won't bore you with the details. Suffice it to say that we had a most pleasant visit, made only more so by Wikstrand's charming wife and daughters."

The mention of Wikstrand did nothing to alleviate the tension. He was the current owner of Brunnsdal, the farm where Ulrika grew up, the one that Rammen had held up to Gunnar Strid as an example of exploitation and neglect.

"Before I left, Wikstrand insisted on a toast," Holmberg said. "I couldn't very well rush off and not oblige him. Say what you will about the man, but he knows he isn't a farmer. He believes, as do I, that the good of the country can also be furthered through industry and commerce. He's already lost both his sons to America. That, to him, is the greatest danger, emigration robbing us of our young and our best. We must provide the same opportunities here in Sweden, which is why he's prepared to help."

Holmberg pulled out a piece of paper from his pocket and held it high for all of us to see. "This, gentlemen, is proof of Wikstrand's convictions. He allowed me to purchase some of his land, a large chunk that borders on the cemetery. It's of little use to me, but I happen to know that it would be highly valuable to the parish. I suggest an exchange. I offer my new land to the parish, and in return I get the land adjacent to the mill. The new cemetery won't run out of gravesites, and I won't be forced to close the mill."

Moments later Wikander's gavel struck the desk. The meeting was over and Holmberg had his land.

The following day Holmberg was greeting travelers outside the inn, pulling his handkerchief out of his breast pocket to give their boots a few well-intended swipes. Soon it was common knowledge that Fredrik was the one who had come up with the plan. Even Wikstrand would admit it. Fredrik and Holmberg had come to see him a few nights before. Fredrik had outlined everything right there in the parlor and it did not take long for Wikstrand to see the brilliance of his proposition. When I confronted Fredrik, he said he would never have sided with Holmberg, had he not believed in the cause.

A few weeks later, construction on the new wing began. Carpenters arrived from Varberg, a boisterous lot but skilled at their craft. Holmberg put them up at the inn.

"My brother-in-law is right," Rammen said. "Josefsson's money is involved. This will not end well."

Chapter Thirty-One

WINTER CAME ON slowly. From my bedroom window I saw the fog thicken over the ditches. Elias stacked wood in the courtyard and made new perches for Ulrika's henhouse, while the shoemaker set up shop in our kitchen and fitted clogs for us all. In one of the fields hopped a hare with white tufts of hair amidst the brown, and from deep within the forest the wood grouse drummed their wings. Pictures in the newspaper showed soldiers in trenches, hiding like foxes below ground.

Fredrik and I began to meet in the wise woman's old cabin. This was where Gustafa had taken me after I witnessed the killing of the pig. I had lost my appetite and Gustafa said the wise woman could restore it. Since then the wise woman had died and the small cabin with the peat-covered roof had stood unoccupied for years. Her spirit still lingered, and no one had dared remove the furniture. Fredrik brought a mattress and a bearskin pelt. He tore the tarpaper off the inside walls, cleaned out the stove, and carried large supplies of firewood through Rammen's forest.

I came to think of myself as two—the woman who worked at the bank and the woman who rushed to meet her lover. The two of them had very little to say to each other, the one so respectful of rules, the other daring enough to go up against everything she had been taught to believe in.

I rarely had supper but walked straight to the cabin, following the path that wound through the meadow and in among the trees where large boulders made it all but impassable. More often than not Fredrik would already be there, his jacket hung over the back of one of the chairs.

His lovemaking was not always gentle, nor always rough. I was attentive and malleable under his hands, learning when to give and when to take. But often, when my caresses became too bold, he stopped me.

He talked about the farm he was going to buy. I would trace the straight line of his nose with my finger, and kiss the thin purple scar across his upper lip, a memory of a fall from a horse. Now and then a gust of wind blew smoke from the fire into the cabin, and he leapt to his feet and shielded his face as he closed the doors to the stove. Even in the midst of winter, he smelled faintly of clover, and when I walked back to Ramm, the scent of him was still on my skin, like the moon that shone on the snow and colored it blue.

He never tired of sifting through all the agricultural information that came his way, gleaning what he felt might be of use. Nor was he afraid to change his mind. One day he might consider the benefits of a new kind of seed, the next, based on more recent evidence, he might denounce it. For all his faith in science, he saw the potential harm of it too. There were already people, not just in Germany, who said we should breed people the way we bred livestock and grain.

Once, as we lay naked under the bearskin, I told him I could still see myself standing by the door, a small girl in a striped cotton dress, a ribbon bow tied to my hair. Gustafa whispered something in the wise woman's ear and showed her the tin box with my caul.

The villagers said that the wise woman was a troll, one of those craggy, spiteful creatures who took pleasure in wreaking havoc with the minds of men. Gustafa said the wise woman knew the trolls, living as she did out in the forest, but the wise woman herself was a good doctor, just as human as everyone else, and she never shunned the light of day. I still tried to get a look at her back to see if it was hollow, or to catch a glimpse of her tail, even though it would have been well hidden under all those skirts.

After she studied my caul, the wise woman pulled out a skein of yellow yarn from her cabinet, the one where she kept vipers' tongues and sand from the parish graveyards. She made knots on the yarn, marking the distance between my joints, shoulder to elbow, elbow to wrist, and wrist to fingers, muttering words I did not understand.

Fredrik paid close attention as I spoke, his knuckles grazing the inside of my arm.

"She dipped three lumps of sugar in greenish-black coffee and strung them onto the yarn like pearls, don't ask me how. As best as I can recall, she slid them back and forth, and then she hung the yarn around my neck and told Gustafa I was cured."

"Did it work?"

"It must have. I began to eat again. Gustafa made me promise not to tell Ulrika or anyone else. Most villagers feared the wise woman, perhaps for good reason."

"These stories should be written down," he said. "The sooner the better, before they're altered or lost."

"So, you do believe in trolls?"

"The anthropologists will tell you that trolls were entirely natural manifestations of primitive thought, although I'm sure Gustafa would beg to differ. I side with Gustafa. I say they're still around. We fear what we can't control and so we banish it to the forest."

That night the lake froze over. On our way back to the village, before he took the path to Prästgården and I the path to Ramm, he talked again about his farm. This was what drove him, his desire to farm his own land. It was something I could understand, for I too was propelled by the notion that the two of us would build something lasting and solid, something having to do with the soil. Farming, he said, had to be a business like any other. It was not just a matter of husbanding existing resources, but also a matter of future expansion, and carefully weighing the cost and return on machinery and labor. Still, land prices kept soaring, and so far none of his offers had met with success. For all his determination, he was too good a farmer to do anything rash, and because of his pride, he would never settle for a farm that was not at least as large as Ramm.

"It's only natural that you should be impatient," he said. "But Prästgården is no place for you. It's much too small."

A few weeks later Elias found a woman in the lake, her body imbedded in the ice, her hands pressing upward and her mouth frozen in a scream. Because she was so well preserved by the ice, a young tenant farmer was able to identify her as his wife. He said her mind had been dark for months. One Sunday before the morning service, she had simply disappeared. He said his only comfort was that the church bells had been ringing, and he had been told that the reverberations would have penetrated to the bottom of the lake.

The doctor confirmed it over a game of cards at Ramm. "The husband is probably right. Time after time, when we question people who almost drowned, they tell us that the pealing of bells, whether real or not, was the last sound they heard."

Part of me already knew that Fredrik was not the man I thought he was. One night I woke to find him standing by the cabin window, looking out. He kept thrusting his fingers through his hair, until he sensed my gaze and turned. His eyes were hard and calculating, like those of a bird of prey. I pushed up in fright and hid my nakedness under the pelt.

"Don't," he said, shaking his head. "Much too late for that."

I never did forget those eyes, and yet I kept returning to the cabin, evening after evening, because by then my need for him was greater than my fear.

When he called me Ariadne, I did not ask him why.

IN THE SPRING of 1916, the constable's wagon passed outside the bank window. Susanna, my assistant, thought it turned down by the mill. A while later a customer told us the constable had arrested Lovisa, the young mill woman who came to see me at the bank. No one knew what for, but there had been a great deal of commotion around the outhouses and the workers were not allowed to use them.

The telephone rang. Emilia wanted to know if I could drive her to the county jail. Lovisa was accused of killing her newborn child.

On the road to the jail Caesar kept shying. I was not driving him as much as I used to and it showed. As we approached a farm where two dogs barked and pulled at their chains, he slowed down, weaving from one side of the road to the other. When I flicked him with the whip, he stopped altogether, and Emilia had to lead him past. A horse will read you like that. He knew I was dreading the worst.

The constable showed us to Lovisa's cell. "The doctor has examined her," he said and stroked his jowl. "Her husband is with her now."

The cell window was small and too high for a view. On the plastered wall, a sampler warned that life was short and death was sure. A corner shelf held a copy of the Bible.

Sven sat on the iron bed next to Lovisa, his shoulders slumped. "Didn't even know she was pregnant."

Lovisa kept staring at the newly scoured cement floor. Sven rose and said he had to go home and look after the children. He knocked on the cell door and the constable let him out.

Gently, Emilia began to ask questions. Lovisa was surprisingly cooperative, her voice flat.

"I was at my loom when the water broke. And then the cramps kept coming, much sharper than any cramps I've ever known. I hurried to the outhouse, barely had time to sit down. It fell into the hole."

"Was it crying?" Emilia asked.

"It was. I think it stopped when I reached down and tore the cord. I must have fainted. Next thing I knew, I was sprawling on the floor but then I got back on my feet and lifted it out."

"Was it a boy or a girl?"

Lovisa pressed her fists against her chest and rocked. "Don't know. I took care not to look. It lay face down, arms moving. All I remember is wrapping my hand around its neck. It jerked a few times but then it stopped."

"How long before it died?"

"Can't say. No more than a minute, I wouldn't think. Can't be sure. I rolled it up in my apron and put it back in the barrel. Tried to push it out of sight, all the way into the corner. When I returned to my loom, I was so weak I could barely stand."

"What happened then?"

"All I remember is a lot of shouting. Perhaps I fainted again. When they led me outside, my eyes hurt."

"Why?" Emilia finally asked. "Why did you kill it?"

Lovisa, still staring at the floor, now kept her hands in her lap, as if all their work had been done and they could finally rest.

"Sven is a good man," she said. "He's kind and considerate. Never drinks. Gets along well with the children. Only problem is he wants to lie with me at night. We couldn't feed another child."

Emilia pushed Lovisa's stringy hair away from her cheeks. "I need to look you over. The way I always do. Just to make sure all is in order. Everything else we can deal with later."

I excused myself and said I would go call a lawyer.

The constable let me use the telephone in his office. Tekla's voice sounded brisk and busy, and she hardly had time to find out why I called. She said that Holger would have left his office by then and gave me the number to his apartment. She also reminded me that he had married, just in case his wife should answer when I rang.

Holger answered himself. He sounded glad to hear me but said he could not talk long since they were on their way to the opera. He had heard that I was working at a bank. When I told him about Lovisa, he said he could not possibly take the case himself. Surely there was someone closer.

"We really need you. Lovisa is a friend of mine."

"I'm sorry, Anna, but I simply couldn't take the time. Besides, I'm no longer a trial lawyer. My other clients would disapprove."

"What about the charwoman?"

"That was different. I needed to make a name for myself. She came along at the right time. She may well have been guilty all along. Actually, she seems to have made a career of it. Pilfering from her employers."

"But Lovisa is not a criminal. She never thought of the child as a child, only something to get rid of."

"Did she keep her pregnancy a secret?"

"Women around here wear layers of loose clothing and large aprons on top. It's often hard to tell. Not even her husband knew."

"She never made preparations for the arrival of the child? Never alerted the midwife?"

"Not as far as I know. She once tried to borrow money at the bank. I was in a hurry and rushed her. At the time I thought she needed the money for food, but now I suspect it was for an abortion. I told her I would lend her the money myself but she didn't take me up on it. I'm afraid she must have felt she had no choice."

There was a click on the line.

"Someone's listening," I said.

Another click. The operator was a frequent guest at local coffee tables. The subject of abortion would have made her even more the center of attention, as abortions were illegal and often dangerous. Some doctors defied the law and performed the procedures in their offices, but Lovisa would surely have had to travel far to find one who would.

"The prosecution is going to try to prove that it was premeditated," Holger said, ignoring the operator. "She has to plead insanity. If not, no one can help her. The birth itself could have been so traumatic that she literally didn't know what she was doing. It's a murky area, but it has been fairly well documented. Biology and psychology both. More and more judges tend to listen. If not actually acquitted, she should at least receive a lighter sentence."

A woman called out Holger's name.

"Have to go," he said. "Cab's waiting. You must come see us the next time you visit Stockholm. I'm sure you've heard. Tekla and my wife have taken on the entire establishment. Speeches and rallies and tea parties that go on until dawn. All they talk about is the vote and contraceptives."

He laughed, and I thought he must have fallen back on his old ways.

By the time the constable let me back into the cell, Emilia was combing Lovisa's hair. The floor was still wet, the cement so porous that I doubted it would ever really dry. A while later the constable brought some herring and oatmeal porridge. Lovisa refused to eat but asked Emilia to take the food to her children.

"I'll make sure that Sven and the children are looked after," I said.

She bent her head to the side while Emilia disentangled her hair. I was not at all sure that she had heard me.

"I talked to the lawyer," I said. "You must tell the judge that you didn't know what you were doing."

For the first time she looked up. Her mouth tightened as she straightened her back.

"I may be a murderess but I'm not a liar," she said. "I've already told you. I did it so my other children could eat. It happened just as I planned. Only the child came too early. Anything else, and I'd be lying."

I asked her why she never came back to the bank.

"Never did ask for handouts," she said. "Besides, it's not just Sven. I wake up in the middle of the night and I want him too. It's best for us all if I go to prison."

I waited outside until Emilia finished.

"I saw the child," she said. "It had both hair and nails. Its little hands were open, not clenched as in stillbirth. The coroner will examine the lungs, but I've no doubt that the child was breathing."

The sermon that Sunday did not offer comfort.

"One of you lost faith," Wikander began. "While the rest of you went about your daily lives, working, talking, perhaps even laughing, a mother killed her child. When the child did not want to die, she pressed harder. This morning she's alone in her cell. May she repent and see the horror of her ways. The child is forever damned. Born in sin, it died in sin. Denied the rite of baptism, it now belongs to the Devil. The angels may cry, and so may we, but God makes no exceptions."

I stopped listening. All I could think of was the small body on the coroner's table, prodded and poked, the lungs spread out like linen bleaching in the grass.

Chapter Thirty-Two

IN JUNE THE war came closer. British and German ships clashed in the North Sea off the Danish coast. The firing, the Varberg newspaper reported, lasted through the night, so loud that the people of Denmark left their houses and gathered on the beach. The German fleet had been the first to retreat, but heavy losses had been incurred on both sides.

More articles followed. The crew of a Danish steamer had seen several large warships sink. The sky filled with smoke, and even though the steamer was several miles away, the cannonading was so violent that the men could not stand erect on the deck. Bodies floated ashore in Sweden, bodies of young men in their prime, or not yet having reached it, rolling and pitching with the swells, tied to each other by seaweed, arms in the air as if waving.

In Hult, the smell of scouring soap was everywhere. Agnes, of course, took the brunt of it. At church, she sat with Ella in the very last pew, even behind the women from the poorhouse. Word was she pinned the dresses all wrong when any of her customers mentioned Fredrik's name.

Some said that Fredrik was not Ella's father. The farmhand, who had been cornered by the bull, claimed that Agnes Hansson would "spread her legs for just about anybody, and she still wouldn't get enough."

Björn laughed. "All you have to do is look at the girl's eyes. Anyone can see that Otter was the pollinator."

Marit was a target too. The village was never kind to its spinsters. Should they fall ill, the reason was almost always believed to be repressed physical longings and their failure to attract a husband. Marit, or so the rumor went, suffered from strange convulsions during the nights and Fredrik had to get in bed with her to calm her.

One evening, when Fredrik was away looking for farms, Marit was carving up meat in Prästgården's kitchen. The farmhands were bantering at the kitchen table, half cautiously, the way men would banter amongst themselves when a woman was present.

"If any woman can hold Otter's interest," one of the farmhands said, "it should be Anna of Ramm. And not just because of her looks either."

A knife shot across the room and lodged in the wall. "That's enough!" Marit hissed. "Another word and I'll cut your throats." After that she went to her room, and the meal was finished in silence.

As Alfrida told me, her rotund body shook with indignation.

"I'm glad Marit stood up for me," I said.

"She did nothing of the sort! Marit, in case you didn't know it, is telling everyone that Otter could do better."

"She's a hard worker. Fredrik has no complaints and neither do I. She's entitled to her opinion."

"All I'm saying is that Marit isn't your friend."

"I have more faith in the villagers than you do. I doubt Marit will be able to sway them one way or the other."

"Well, I declare!" Alfrida said. "More ears willing to listen than you think."

Ulrika returned from her henhouse, her basket full of eggs, and told Alfrida she would walk her home.

"And when, pray, will you stand bride?" Alfrida asked, while Ulrika waited at the door. "The sooner the better, or we'll never see the end of it."

A wind had come in from the west that morning and rain had begun to fall, a light drizzle at first, but by the time I reached the cabin, I was wet from top to toe.

As I lay under the bear pelt, Fredrik hung my clothes to dry. He added more wood to the stove and blew on it until it caught. He said he did not believe in gossip. "It seldom lets the facts get in the way, does it? Rarely gives people a chance to defend themselves."

He held me longer that night, repeating my name as if only then he had begun to know it. I caught him watching me out of the corner of his eye. He seemed to want to say something and then decide against it. He spoke of his mother, whom he missed, even though she had left him with no memories other than her sketches. As was the custom in those days, she had stayed in bed for weeks after giving birth. When she finally rose, she had complained about a pain in her leg, or so he had been told. She was dead within minutes.

"When your turn comes," he said, "we'll make sure you get up and walk right away. Too dangerous not to."

I must have known we were running out of time, for I fixed it all in my mind: the curve of his back, the muscles of his thighs, the way his damp hair clung to the nape of his neck, where his skin was as smooth as mine. But more than anything it was his scent—that dark, sweet scent of clover that went to my head like wine, for death did not come as itself but as a promise of life.

He no longer held me back but welcomed my boldness. When I touched him, he moaned with pleasure. Each time he reached for a condom, I felt the emptiness, however fleeting. Even at the peak of passion, when I bit down on his shoulder and almost drew blood, more than anything I longed for a child.

He walked with me all the way back to Ramm. The rain had stopped. It was one of those misty summer nights, when the light still lingered, as if radiating from the earth itself. He stood by the barn until I opened my bedroom window. Then he walked back into the shadow-less woods, winding in and out among the trees, his shirt glinting white.

Chapter Thirty-Three

OLOF TELEPHONES.

"I don't know where she is."

"What's happening?"

"They won't ask the father," he says. "Not even now."

It takes me a few moments to realize what he is saying. Could Karin have gone for an abortion? Next year abortions will be legal. It has taken the committee ten years to decide. But even now there are ways. Seems there always were.

I promise to call him if she comes.

"She talks about you," he says, just as I am about to hang up.

"Oh?"

"She says you had a child."

I do not answer.

"I'm sorry it died," he says.

"Wasn't meant to live. Suffered too long as it was."

He seems to hesitate. "She never speaks about the father."

"Neither do I."

SUNDAY MORNING, AS we prepared to leave for church, we all took solace in the familiar. The day was warming, garden paths were raked, and farm machinery stood idle. Wilhelm had hoisted the flag, and Ulrika had covered her loom with two white sheets. The windows in the parlor were open and the curtains swelled in the breeze. Elias went out to the barn to feed a calf that had been born in the night and taken away from its mother.

In the middle of the sermon Ulrika's calfskin boots scraped against the floor. Gathering her skirts, she rose and made her way past me. She stepped out into the aisle and curtsied as she faced the altar. It happened just as the sun struck the altarpiece, where it mingled with the painted sun and sought out Ulrika's likeness, the young woman in blue.

Wikander stopped preaching, took off his glasses, and looked down on Ulrika. As Björn played "Chief of sinners though I be," Ulrika turned and walked toward the door. Her step as soft as ever, she glided past the farmers and the crofters, past the tradespeople and the mill workers, past the people from the poorhouse, and past Agnes and Ella in the very last row.

I followed her to Ramm. She walked as if nothing uncommon had happened, but she must have noticed that she was alone on the road, with the exception of one of her daughters walking a few steps behind her. From the church I could still hear Björn playing. Wikander, Alfrida would tell me, never did regain the villagers' attention.

In the barn the new-born calf was bleating for the cow. Ulrika let it suck her fingers. She found the cow as well, caressing its neck, using words that made no sense.

At the house she walked straight upstairs, where she sat down in her chair and started nipping dead leaves off a fuchsia on the windowsill.

"You're tired," I said and removed her shawl. "It's all right."

An hour later Rammen walked into the room and kissed Ulrika on the forehead. "Are you well?"

She nodded. He did not say a word about her walking out in the middle of the sermon.

I sat with Ulrika while Rammen telephoned the doctor. She pulled out a cigarillo from the table drawer and lit it with short, rapid drafts. Elias was straightening nails in the shed, his hammer ringing against the anvil. Gustafa had tried to get him to stop, this being a Sunday, but Elias just struck harder and harder until even Gustafa left him alone.

Disa and I waited in the parlor while Rammen and the doctor tended to Ulrika. Through the window I could see Wilhelm, Björn, and Johannes standing in the courtyard, Johannes kicking at the ground. How rare to see the three brothers together, and how sad that it would take something like this to draw them close.

Disa said, "The villagers will be talking."

"Gustafa has already begun. She says that Jesus shook his head and wept."

The doctor's voice reached us from upstairs, low and monotonous. Now and then came a few words by Ulrika, who, as I left the room, had kept blowing smoke on the fuchsia, her face void of feelings of any kind. Rammen did not say much, but when he did, his voice was as low as the doctor's, the kind of voice one would use in a sickroom.

After the doctor left, Disa took a tray with soup for Ulrika. Rammen asked me to step into his office.

He sat holding a photograph. I knew it well for he kept it on his desk. It showed Ulrika on the day of their betrothal. The two of them had walked arm-in-arm in the Gothenburg harbor, Rammen pointing out the passenger ships, the Mediterranean trading vessels, the deep-sea trawlers, and the fishing smacks. The sound of the different languages had mixed with the cries of the sea gulls, and the longshoremen had stepped aside and called Ulrika ma'am. She was twenty-two years old and her pregnancy did not yet show. Her black hair was styled high with a fringe and a small hat on top, and the front of her white dress was almost flat, most of the material pulled back and piled into folds over her bustle.

"Wilhelm has proposed to Emilia's Emma," Rammen said. "Emma will bring nothing to the marriage. No money. No land. If Wilhelm insists on marrying her, I must tell him to leave Ramm."

"I thought it was Björn—"

"Be that as it may. The fact remains that Wilhelm is the one proposing. With Wilhelm gone, Björn will inherit Ramm. I'm not sure he has what it takes. Farmers need enthusiasm and dedication. As far as I can tell he's lacking in both."

Rammen ran his thumb over the photograph of Ulrika. "All this has opened old wounds for Ulrika. She's been sleeping poorly and I was afraid she was building up to something like this."

"What did the doctor say?"

"Nothing new. He wants to take her to the hospital but I told him no."

Rammen pulled out a document hidden among the pages of one of the studbooks on the shelf beside him. "There's something you should know. Your uncle Adolf is Wilhelm's father. He was going to marry Ulrika, but when he learned about her father's finances, he changed his mind. Ulrika's father threatened with court procedures to force him to acknowledge the child."

He handed me the document. Signed by both brothers, it stated that Rammen, not Adolf, would take over Ramm. In return, Rammen would marry Ulrika and bring up Adolf's child as his own.

"He couldn't leave soon enough," Rammen said. "Alfrida was too young and Hedvig had already moved, so none of them knows. At some point Wilhelm must be told. His inheritance from Adolf might be substantial."

As I gave the document back to Rammen, Wikander's carriage pulled into the courtyard. Unless one of his parishioners was deadly ill, Wikander was not in the habit of making house calls, but with Ulrika he always made an exception.

"Now you see why I can't let you marry Otter," Rammen said. "He's no better than Adolf, abandoning a woman pregnant with his child. I used to think that the Bible had it wrong. We're independent people, I told myself. All that talk about punishment has no foundation. But I can tell you this, if God is busy elsewhere, which all too often seems to be the case, we learn to punish ourselves. Take my word, Anna, you want no part of it." With that he walked out to greet Wikander.

Johannes at long last persuaded Ulrika to come down for the mid-day meal. She entered the kitchen holding his arm, hesitating as she saw us all around the table. Rammen pulled out her chair and nodded to the rest of us to go ahead as if nothing were the matter. Elias filled his plate with sausages while Gustafa picked at her food and blew her nose with a handkerchief she stuffed up her sleeve.

"Saw one of the queen's trains when I was in Gothenburg," Björn said to Gustafa.

The queen was back in her native Germany and large quantities of food were being shipped to her and her entourage while shortages in Sweden grew.

"Ten trainloads a week," Björn said. "Or so the stationmaster told me. Her appetite must be greater than yours."

Gustafa continued to pick at her food, sucking at her upper gum. Not even criticism of the queen could rouse her. When Rammen asked her to bring him more potatoes, she seemed glad to have something to do.

"Ulrika and I are going for a ride," Rammen said. "The day is still warm and Ulrika is entitled to a little relaxation."

Rammen himself harnessed his warmbloods and steadied Ulrika as she stepped up to her carriage seat. The sun was lower now and the sky a darker blue. Disa had packed a basket with coffee and fresh rolls, and Johannes had stuffed a blanket under the carriage seat. Gustafa was not the only one seeing things that day. I thought I could see Adolf sitting between Rammen and Ulrika, no stranger to either one.

Chapter Thirty-Four

ONE EVENING IN early autumn, I came home from the bank to find the house all lit up. Arne Karlsson, Emilia's husband, had come to measure the milk yield of our cows. A large wooden chest with a handle at each end served as his traveling laboratory. It was so heavy that it took two men to lift it down from the wagon. Karlsson expected a good dinner and no holding back on the liquor. He was never disappointed at Ramm and he showed his gratitude by raising the milk fat by a few percent in his report.

Björn played the organ in the parlor. Of late he had been leaving for Gothenburg, sputtering through the countryside on his lightweight motorcycle, his goggles strapped over his brown leather helmet. Earlier that day he had returned to Ramm, irritable and unshaven, the heels of his shoes worn out from negotiating the rough gravel roads.

Elias sat by the kitchen table, his hip flask before him. He stared at Rammen's pocket watch, which Rammen was in the habit of leaving on a shelf by the stove. Gustafa wiped off her chair and sat.

"Engineer Moberg is here," Disa said the moment she saw me. "They're playing cards."

Even her bad eye was now focused on me. Knowing that Moberg would come, she had rubbed Tekla's rouge on to her cheeks, too freely, for it colored her face an angry red.

"We can use your help," she said. "Ulrika had to go to Bergvik to borrow a sausage."

Elias took a swig from his flask. "Never thought the day would come when Ulrika herself would have to go begging."

"He should go back to the cabin," Gustafa said as Elias burped. "Shameful to see him carry on like this."

"It's been at least an hour," Disa said, ignoring Gustafa and Elias. "Had I known she'd be so long, I'd gone myself."

Every time Ulrika went to Bergvik, whether she needed to borrow something or not, she and Alfrida would walk each other home, arm-in-arm, back and forth between Ramm and Bergvik, until they had exhausted all the topics of the day. At some point, Alfrida would stop half way and declare that it was time to part.

Björn played one melody after another, some of which I did not recognize. When in Gothenburg, he spent most of his evenings at the opera, where he was one of the few admitted to the private dressing room of a celebrated soprano. He stayed with Hedvig, who most likely enjoyed having a young man in her apartment, even though her efforts to bar him from the maid's quarters were bound to fail.

Sara, still our maid, despite her misdeeds with Björn, came back from the cellar to tell us that potatoes were missing. Gaining access to the cellar did not require great stealth, for the only door was on the side of the house and was hardly ever locked. Still, that someone had entered at all was disturbing.

"I saw Andrasson behind the barn," Elias said, slurring his words. "Last I heard he was hauling timber for Otter. He's got no business at Ramm." Gustafa, still on her chair, pinched at her apron.

Elias took another drink and glared at me. "*Thou shalt not steal.* Says so in the Bible." I knew he was not just talking about Andrasson, for like many of the villagers, he was convinced that I was the one who had lured Fredrik away from Agnes.

The door to the parlor swung open and Moberg strode into the kitchen, his hair slick with pomade, the organ music sweeping in behind him. He took hold of Sara and waltzed with her as Elias stomped off beat. Disa removed her glasses, wiped her eyes with her sleeve, and turned her face to the wall. I could not help but feel that she ought to be above it.

Moberg finally let Sara go and picked up some wood from beside the stove. Elias staggered to his feet, seized Rammen's watch from the shelf, and followed Moberg into the parlor. I tried to grab his arm, but it was too late and all I could do was stand in the doorway and watch.

Björn stopped playing. The cigar smoke hung thick around the beams in the ceiling. Moberg took his seat and Rammen rippled the cards. Karlsson pulled at his nose. Wilhelm and I exchanged glances.

Elias stared at Rammen and snarled. "*The crown has fallen from thy head.*"

Rammen cut the deck and began to deal. "If you have something to say, come see me in the morning."

"Won't be here in the morning."

Without looking at Elias, Rammen held out his hand, palm up. "Better give me back my watch. Wouldn't want you to forget."

Elias raised his fist, clutching Rammen's watch. "*And thou shalt be like dung on the earth,*" he shouted, "*and all thy land shall be laid to waste and thy carcass shall be meat for the fowls.*"

He raised his fist even higher, his sleeve pulling down and exposing his slack, blotchy skin. "Andrasson is stealing your potatoes and all you do is play cards!" I felt as powerless as a spectator in a theater.

Rammen withdrew his hand. "These are difficult times. Some men would rather steal than beg. Can't say I blame them."

I gasped as Elias flung the watch on the floor. Glass shattered, gears and springs flew all over Disa's runners.

Björn and Rammen wrestled Elias to the floor. With Björn kneeling on Elias' shoulders, Rammen used his belt to tie Elias' hands behind his back. By the time he pulled him up on his feet, Elias was no longer resisting.

"I'll go with you," Björn said.

Rammen raised his free hand. "You stay here. This is between Elias and me."

"Be careful," I said as Rammen pushed Elias past me. "He's an old man."

"Tell Disa to fill our glasses," Rammen said. "I won't be long."

Even though Björn played "Where God the Lord not by us stands," we could hear the cracks of lashes coming from the barn. Gustafa flinched at every one, her bony hands pressed to her mouth.

By the time Ulrika returned from Bergvik, the card game had begun anew. On my way to the cabin, I stopped by the barn. The pigs snuffled and grunted in their stall. Slumped in a corner of the empty stall beside them, Elias snored. He smelled of stale sweat, and his long beard spread like a bib over his chest. One of the pigs had reached in and pulled off his sock, which now lay shredded in the trough. I could not bring myself to leave, so I covered him with a horse blanket and sat with him until dawn.

THE FOLLOWING MORNING, when I left to go to Enebacken, Elias was still asleep in the barn. He had threatened to leave us before, but he always changed his mind, telling us we could not manage without him, which was likely true.

Björn was washing milk cans in the courtyard. Using a brush with a long wooden handle, he whirled the cold soapy water around and around inside the can, spinning the can itself in the opposite direction, the water spurting up the rim. I walked toward him, wanting to ask him about Elias. He tipped the can slightly and aimed the water my way. I had to jump to avoid getting wet. I could tell he meant it. He did not want me near him.

At Enebacken I found Emilia eating breakfast. She was already in her midwife uniform, a crisp cotton dress with white and blue stripes. Emma was putting away the ironing board.

"I'm concerned about Edit Andrasson," I said after Emma poured me coffee. "I've heard she's pregnant and they may not have enough food."

Emilia admitted she was worried too. "I was over there the other day." She dabbed her mouth with a napkin and raised her hand when Emma brought more porridge. "She's worn out by six children already. Andrasson comes home and throws the mucky tackle on the floor and then he sits down and eats. When she asks him to wash, he ignores her. She's been reading the newspapers but I explained to her that she can't get syphilis from dirt alone. But what she has is bad enough, a nasty infection, most certainly caused by Andrasson's lack of hygiene."

"They need to know there are ways to avoid having more children," I said. "We could show Andrasson how to use condoms."

Emma stood behind Emilia and shook her head. "Aunt Emilia is supposed to assist birth, not prevent it. All she can do is answer questions. Anything else and she'll be risking her livelihood."

"You surprise me, Emma," I said. "You once told me you don't believe that knowledge can ever do harm."

Even in the rush of the morning, Emma's skin was luminous, her brown eyes as clear as ever. "I still believe that's true. Women should be taught about their bodies. I certainly intend to teach my own daughters, simply and truthfully, not just vague allusions that alarm rather than help. But I don't believe in forcing information on people who don't want it."

"Emma is right," Emilia said. "We'd be breaking the law. Still, no one can fault us for answering questions. As long as that's all we do. It's a fine line, but I do believe it can be drawn."

Rapid knocks came on the door.

Emilia reached for her bag. "It's Pettersson. We have to go."

I followed Emilia and Emma out. The young farmer barely waited for them to get up on the wagon. Emma sat very straight. Now that she was about to marry Wilhelm, she wanted no part in my campaign.

Emilia, however, nodded and said, "We'll talk."

A few weeks later Emilia came to the bank. She said that Edit had given birth. We sat in the back room while Susanna, my assistant, helped the customers.

"It was a difficult birth," Emilia said. "She was anxious from the start. Don't push too hard, I said. All in good time. I told her to scream, said it would help. But she wouldn't utter a sound, and all along Andrasson was cussing and drinking in the kitchen. At first, when I held up the child, she was afraid to look at it. I assured her it was healthy, but she kept searching for blisters and counting fingers and toes."

Later that day Emilia and I walked over to Andrasson's cabin.

"Don't forget," Emilia said. "All we can do is answer questions. Anything else, and we'll be breaking the law."

A boy saw us coming and ran into the cabin.

"He's warning his parents. One little girl actually thought I brought the new child in my bag. Another closed the damper because she thought the child came with the stork. It's a sad situation when you have to rely on fairytales to hide the truth."

Andrasson was in his undershirt when he cracked the door open.

The children were lined up on the kitchen bench, all six of them, the eldest around twelve or so, the youngest not much older than a year. Emilia built a fire in the stove to heat water for me to do the washing. Meanwhile, she had brought her own clean sheets and towels. As the children watched, I found some turnips in a bucket and placed them in a pan to boil. One of the boys was crying, and the eldest girl tried to make him hush. Andrasson said he had to go outside to tend to his horse.

The children watched my every move, one girl chewing on a strand of her hair, another crossing her thin arms above her bloated stomach. When I tried to talk to them they did not answer. As soon as I put out the cooked turnips, they grabbed them as if they might disappear.

Next I went to work at the washtub beside the stove. I was hanging towels on the line outside when Andrasson came by on his way back to the house.

"Bring in the laundry before nightfall," I said.

He grunted and kept walking, his eyes avoiding mine.

"And hang it up again in the morning," I called out after him. I had checked the barometer. The good weather was supposed to last.

Later I sat with Emilia and Edit in the bedroom. The new child, a boy, was nursing.

"You asked about Kristina's rubbers," Emilia said as she closed her bag.

Edit bit her lip and did not answer.

"It would be up to Andrasson himself to learn to use them," Emilia said.

Edit grimaced as she shifted in her bed. "Can't rely on him. He would get drunk and forget. Please go talk to him. Scare him. Scare him good. Tell him he can't come near me."

A while later Emilia and I joined Andrasson in the kitchen. Emilia sent the children outside.

"Edit is going to need her rest," Emilia began.

Andrasson scratched the side of his neck. "Damned if I know how I ended up with a woman who's with child every time I look at her."

"It's amazing she lets you close at all," I said. "Haven't you heard about bathing?"

"Quiet, Anna," Emilia said.

Andrasson glared in my direction but said nothing.

Emilia faced Andrasson. "You must control yourself. If you don't, you'll have more children than you have the means to provide for."

"Money is no problem."

Emilia looked around. The cabin walls showed signs of mold, caused by moisture that crept up from the ground, turning to frost in the winter.

"I see no signs of abundance," she said. "But the one I really worry about is Edit. She never has a chance to build back her strength. Unless you leave her alone, I fear she won't be long for this world."

Edit called and Emilia went back to the bedroom. Finally alone with Andrasson, I was not about to waste more time.

"Abstinence may not be the only solution," I said.

He sat by the table, staring out the window. He did not ask what I meant.

"Have you heard about condoms?" I said.

He took out his pipe and began to stuff it.

"I brought some," I said.

The tobacco glowed as he lit the pipe. When he spoke, I could barely hear him.

"You'd better leave or I'll fetch the constable. Or would you rather I talk to Wikander? Either way is fine with me. You may be Rammen's daughter but that don't give you the right to come here and tell me what to do."

I placed the envelope in front of him. "Here. Just in case you change your mind."

He slammed his fist down on the table. "Take your wares and get out of here!" he said, wagging a black-nailed finger so close to my eyes I feared he might poke them.

Emilia stopped short when she returned from the bedroom.

Andrasson rose and pointed at me. "Everyone knows she's Otter's whore. I don't want her near my children."

We walked back in silence. I had spoken out of turn, but Emilia did not reproach me. When we said goodbye outside Enebacken, I saw Wilhelm twirling his mustache in the parlor.

The following day I sent Sara with cheese and eggs to Andrasson's cabin. She said no one opened when she knocked, so she left the basket by the door. Fredrik said he would send Marit too.

As it turned out, Andrasson told both the constable and Wikander. Rammen dealt with the constable. He said it would be Andrasson's word against mine, and the constable did not take action.

"Can't help you with Wikander," Rammen said. "Best go see him yourself."

That evening I heard the faint ticking of beetles inside the parlor wall— the clock of death, Gustafa called it, for it meant that someone in the house was about to die.

WIKANDER'S HOUSEKEEPER LOOKED tired, her hairnet torn and her stockings crumpled at her ankles. Wikander had been called to the poorhouse but would soon be back.

I sat on the bench in the narrow hall. Through the window I could see the birches that had already turned. Past them lay Prästgården's barn, dark red behind that burst of yellow. Fredrik was away looking at farms.

The hall looked much like the one at Ramm. The door to the right opened into Wikander's office. The stairs ahead led to the bedrooms, where the window shades were hardly ever pulled and the villagers could see Wikander pacing long into the nights. Fredrik had told me he still wrestled with the angel although you would never know it when you heard him preach.

Horses' hooves struck the gravel. From where I sat I could see one of Fredrik's farmhands lead away Wikander's mare, her left eye socket empty. Wikander had always been unclear on how she came to lose her eye. He had been on his way home after a card game, and he cracked his whip to make her trot faster. The eye was still there when they reached the vicarage, but it was too mangled to be of use. The doctor, who tended to animals and people both, had been forced to remove it.

Wikander told me to join him in his office, where I sat on a ladder-back chair, waiting as he wrote in his register. The stubble shadowed his chin, his sideburns were untrimmed, and gray hair sprouted out of his ears.

At long last he put away his pen and peered at me behind his black-rimmed glasses. "I've talked to Fredrik. You must set a date for your wedding."

"As soon as he finds his farm."

"There can be no more stalling. Think what harm might come to your children if your marriage begins in sin."

At this he turned his attention back to his register, apparently copying something from one page to the next.

After what seemed like an hour, Wikander cleared his throat. "Andrasson came to see me. Said you had harassed him in the sanctity of his home."

I held my tongue.

"Well, Anna, I'm interested in hearing what you have to say."

The steadiness in my voice surprised me. "We have to let the villagers know how to limit the number of children."

Wikander rose, walked over to the bookcase, took down a copy of the Bible, and placed it before me. "Find Matthew 6:33," he said and sat back in his chair.

I found the page.

"Read it aloud."

My voice kept steady as I read: "*But seek first his kingdom and his righteousness, and all these things will be added unto you.*"

"These things," he said. "What are they?"

"They are everything we think we need," I said, repeating words I had known since I prepared for the house examinations. "They are food, drink, shelter, and clothing."

"Go on."

"We must thank God with full hearts when we receive them, but we must be equally grateful when we do not. For it is then that we shall know if we truly love him, it is then that we must learn to chastise and discipline our sinful selves."

Perhaps it pleased him that I remembered the answer for he spoke more gently now. "I was once young myself. Just like you, I thought I was invincible. At the seminary there was so much wit and laughter. But when I came here, I saw my limitations. So if I preach with harshness, it's because too much is at stake. I can't afford to be lenient. The Word of God is not open to interpretation."

"It seems to me we're guilty of sin if we see suffering and don't attempt to relieve it."

He stood, blocking the light from the window. "You tell them there are ways to circumvent God's will. And because the truth of God is contrary to their sinful hearts, they listen. What will you say on the Day of Judgment, when the trumpet sounds and you shall have to answer for your deeds?"

"I shall have to say that I followed my conscience. If God saw fit to give me a brain, he must also expect me to use it."

"Conscience! Your conscience may serve you in matters of the world, but it has absolutely nothing to do with religion." He blew noisily into a large handkerchief and stuffed it back into his pocket. "Can your conscience tell you that Jesus rose from the dead? Can your conscience tell you that he died for your sins? Can your conscience tell you that he will return again to judge you? No, Anna, a thousand times no. If we couldn't read it in the Bible, none of us would ever know."

Before I left, he made me kneel and recite the Lord's Prayer.

"Thy Kingdom come, thy will be done, on earth as it is in heaven."

There was dust on the floor. The housekeeper was too old. The vicarage was too large for her to manage. Perhaps some of the other women in the village could come and help her. Take turns. Write their names on a list and assign the days. I promised myself I would mention it to Alfrida. Dismissing the housekeeper would of course be out of the question, at least not unless Wikander chose to do so himself. Yes, the whole village would be outraged at such a suggestion, for the housekeeper had waited on Wikander since he first arrived in Hult. And yes, there was her loyalty too. That certainly ought to be factored into the calculation. Every Sunday, when he returned from his sermons, she was waiting with his supper, putting aside her knitting as she heard him walk up the front steps.

That was when I noticed that Wikander was kneeling beside me. His voice was steady and calm.

"And forgive our trespasses, as we forgive those who trespass against us. And lead us not into temptation, but deliver us from evil. For thine is the kingdom, the power and the glory, for ever and ever. Amen."

I heard the strength of his conviction, and bowed my head.

Chapter Thirty-Five

I GO DOWN to the church office to pay for the maintenance of the family graves. On my way, I stop at the store to see if there is a letter from Karin. There is not. More and more I begin to think that Olof may be right. She could have gone to Poland for an abortion. If she has, she is going to need him more than ever.

I rarely visit the new cemetery. Only now and then, after a service, will I linger at the family gravesite, which is close to the church. A white marble dove perches on the headstone and the inscription speaks of peace and the glory of God. Farther away, next to the cemetery wall, are the graves of Gustafa and Elias. Gustafa's stone has a chiseled olive sprig.

Wikander's grave is to the right as you approach the church. He called me to his deathbed in 1933. The cancer was eating him alive, and he had to rest between words. "Bend, Anna. Bend before God and he will make you whole again." The schoolchildren filed by his coffin. The headmaster insisted that the lid should be off, but I had a talk with the bishop, who saw my point—the children ought to remember him as the forceful man he was, not as a corpse. Björn delivered a eulogy at the funeral. He said Wikander did not share his taste in music. I think this must have been the first time I ever heard laughter in that church, subdued though it was. He also said that Wikander's love for his parishioners had never flagged, and I had to fight back my tears, even though I knew that Wikander had chastised and wounded more than he had healed.

After paying the woman in the church office, I cross the road to the old church. The walls, or what is left of them, are almost hidden by wild chervil and nettles. A slender birch grows in what was once the vestry.

The child was buried in the midst of winter. The ground was hard and Klas had to use a pickax to dig the grave. I often wonder what is left in that small white coffin that was covered with earth. Of course I know what Fredrik would have said. Except for the tin box that held my caul, there would be nothing but decay, the only transfiguration he believed in.

That winter, when I buried my child, the women drew together and whispered. I knew what they said in the farmhouses and in the cabins. They said the child was conceived in sin and the good Lord took care of the rest.

Fredrik's headstone is of dark gneiss, unpolished, just what he had asked for in his will. Dagmar put up at the inn when they came to bury him. She stopped at the bank to say hallo. Fortunately it was a quiet day and Susanna made some excuse to leave.

"So why did he want to be buried here?" I asked.

She shook her head, her pallor stark against the black half moons under her eyes. "He never got over the death of the child. You were always the woman he loved. How can you forget?"

I once met with Fredrik in the doctor's office. A new law required that all infected persons, regardless of gender and social status, must submit to treatment. Fredrik, however, refused to be treated for a disease he claimed he never had.

The wise woman's cabin burned in 1922. Lightning struck the tall fir by the door, scaling off the bark down to the root. Elias alerted Björn to the smoke and when the two of them started out for the cabin, it hailed. The pellets forced them to take shelter in the barn, where the cows jerked at their chains and fell over, lowing and bawling, all four legs in the air. When Björn and Elias at long last reached the cabin, it was all but gone. The fire had been explosive, shattering the chimney. If not for the hail, the flames would have spread, but as it was, none of the trees, apart from the fir, had even been scorched.

Word spread all over the parish and people shook their heads. "Odd thing we never heard the thunder here," they said. "Sky in these parts was clear." Old stories about the wise woman were told and retold, memory serving some of the tellers better than others. Few had actually met her, although there were those who claimed her ghost still walked down the by lake, an eerie light before her. Even the constable felt called upon to contribute, recounting the time his predecessor went to arrest her, after accusations of quackery had grown too numerous to ignore, the old troll fixing the horses with her stare and the horses refusing to budge.

This evening I miss his hands, the way they quieted and gripped me. My old body aches. Shame on you, Anna. At your age.

1917 ARRIVED, AND the end of the war was still not in sight. It was as if all of civilization had regressed to the dark ages. Everything we believed in had come undone. Young men committed acts that terrified them, wiping their tears so that the officers would not catch them crying. Yet, for all the bombs and the mines, it was also a war of bayonets, where a man would be close enough to see the whites of the other man's eyes before he stabbed him. Many, even those whose bodies showed no wounds, were harmed forever, mere shells of their former selves.

Sometimes when I walked through the village I thought I could smell the poison gas.

The snow layer was thick that year and Fredrik and I used skis to get to the cabin. He did not ski as well as I, but after a few weeks he took great joy in it, making playful turns as he glided down the path, his jacket billowing around him. We would lean our skis against the cabin wall and dig out the snow so we could open the door. While Fredrik started the fire, I warmed my hands with my breath, for I could not touch him soon enough, running my fingers down his spine, grasping his buttocks, the pleasure building as I arched my body against his. And always—always—I wished for a child. Once, after his condom tore, I marked the days and hours, secretly hoping my monthlies would not come. When they did, I wept.

There is nothing as silent as the forest in winter. All we would hear was the crackle of the fire, the gentle thud of collapsing wood, and the occasional hiss when melted snow dripped down the chimney and struck the embers. One night we heard a lynx mewing and yowling and calling for a male. Her calls were soft at first, like the hooting of an owl, but gained in yearning and strength. We saw her tracks when we left, her fur spreading out over her paws, leaving wispy imprints in the snow. For days she and the male would travel together, crouching on fallen logs, stalking their prey, bellies to the ground. They would mate often, the male biting her neck and holding her down. In the end she would drive him off. She alone would bring up the cubs and teach them to kill.

In February, after the Germans announced their unrestricted submarine campaign, Swedish ships were either torpedoed by the Germans or confiscated by the English. With no coal available, the government resorted to the use of wood. All over Sweden forest owners were told to contribute. As soon as the fuel commission had taken what it wanted, the farmers themselves, spurred by the high prices, continued the felling on their own. Timber was stacked all along the rivers, and our region was no exception. Rammen went from door to door trying to talk sense into the farmers, but since they never lacked for buyers, most of them continued to fell.

Rammen told Elias that if he ever wanted to use his rifles, this might be the time. "I never thought it would come to this. We could use a few socialists, if only to counter the greed."

Wikander preached on the war, the famine, and the plague. This, he said, was the Almighty's way of dealing with those who continued to reject his commandments. One Sunday he came straight to church from playing cards in a nearby parish. Reeking of *brännvin*, he had rigged two cards as a makeshift collar. In the pulpit, he held up a third card to the congregation.

His voice boomed as he flashed the card back and forth. "What is this?"

"Ace of spade," the men's side shouted back.

Wikander lowered his voice so that we all had to strain to hear, his sorrow so audible that it seemed to hover above him. "You know about this. But you don't know about God's word."

Outside the mill Erik spoke about the revolution. The day when the red flags were hoisted at the winter palace in Petrograd had given him hope. He said it was only a matter of time and the Swedish workers would follow, stepping out of the shadows, no longer scraping their feet. Tekla seemed to agree. Breadlines were forming and workers were demonstrating all over Stockholm. She and her women friends had joined them, carrying placards demanding suffrage for all, regardless of income and gender. When Fredrik returned from Gothenburg, he talked about women forcing their way into a bakery. Other women, in different parts of the city, had followed suit. The police and the military had been called in, but by the end of the day there was scarcely a store that had not been looted.

That summer Rammen tore down the cottage that had served as a summerhouse for Sylvia and her husband. In its place he built a larger house with dormer windows and a glassed-in veranda. All day long he stood and watched the men as they worked. Sometimes Ulrika joined him. He said he was not ready to set a date for his retirement yet, but when he was, this was where Ulrika and he would live. I wondered if he really meant it. Björn must have wondered too, for his trips to Gothenburg lasted longer and longer, and when he returned, he muttered hardly a word.

Every week Ulrika and I took food to the poorhouse, where the old men sat on their benches, their chins propped on their canes as they watched us climb down from the carriage. If we saw beggars on the road, Ulrika asked me to stop so she could give them whatever was left in her basket. Alfrida told Ulrika she was much too generous. Those same beggars, Alfrida said, were actually people from the cities, who traveled out into the countryside and changed into much better clothes before they boarded the trains back home. That might well be so, Ulrika answered, but she did not think it should be held against them. Now and then she would search a stranger's face as if looking for someone in particular, but on the whole she seemed well, spending less time at the upstairs window and more time riding around with me.

One day, when Ulrika and I returned, Gustafa had dropped Ulrika's crystal vase, the one that came from Brunnsdal. Rammen took it to Varberg to be mended. He brought it back, expertly repaired, with not the faintest trace of breakage. Even so, we never dared fill it with flowers, only a single peony on some special occasion, for it could never be as strong as it once had been.

EMMA AND WILHELM married in the autumn of 1917. The ceremony took place in the church in Nybo, Emma's home parish. Borrowing money from Wikander, Wilhelm had leased the farm belonging to the Nybo vicarage. He brought Stella and his fiddle, leaving his other possessions behind.

Emma's gown, in keeping with modern times, was white rather than black. Holding a bouquet of roses and wearing a myrtle tiara, she stood next to Wilhelm outside the church with the stubble fields behind them, Wilhelm's mustache freshly waxed. Emma had insisted on myrtle for Wilhelm as well. She said it symbolized prosperity and she herself had fastened a sprig to his black frock coat.

At Emma's home, preparations had been under way for days. The house smelled of scouring powder and newly baked bread. Neighbors had loaned silver, china, and chairs. The hired man joked that not even in this house had he opened so many bottles in one single day. Björn grabbed a pilsner before we sat down.

Over soup, consisting of hen with parsley dumplings, Emma's father wished everyone welcome. Emma's mother fidgeted with her dress and kept sending nervous glances toward the kitchen.

Already Wikander and Hedvig, opposite the bride and groom, were engaged in conversation. Wikander turned down his wine, brushing the servant girl aside, a peremptory gesture that made her leave for the kitchen and not come back. Alfrida sat next to Arne Karlsson, Emilia's husband. She wore a fox stole over her shoulders with buttons of amber for eyes. Karlsson kept grinning and raising his chin, not from amusement, I realized after a while, but in an effort to lessen the restrictions of a collar too well starched. Alfrida, for once utterly dumb, stared at a water stain near the ceiling as if it might attack. From my seat at the short end of the table, I could see it too. I also noticed the small tear in the curtain and the paint peeling around the windowpanes.

The pork roast was served, not by the servant girl but by a sturdier girl, less prone to flight.

Emma's father rose again, this time turning to Emma. "You've always made us proud. We're not surprised that you would choose for a husband a man as worthy as Wilhelm."

Next he lifted his glass to Wilhelm. "I welcome you as my son-in-law. And since a marriage is a union between individuals and families both, I also welcome the Larssons. May you be frequent guests in our home, and may we all continue to thrive. "

Disa huffed. I was sure everyone heard.

Wikander spoke a few minutes later. Holding a glass of water, he reminisced about Wilhelm being a quick study when preparing for his first communion. He praised Emma for her work at the mill library and predicted that the village would miss her. As always on these occasions, he talked about the changing times and the significance of home and family. The bride and groom nodded and smiled.

And so the dinner wore on, seemingly endless minutes, when all that was heard was the scraping of silver on the plates. Johannes was sullen as usual and focused on his food. Emma's brother was talking to Disa, who pursed her mouth and said nothing in return. Emma's sister, tall and awkward, laughed a little too loudly, probably at one of Björn's jokes.

Alfrida, when she finally talked, complained about the shortage of sugar. "Used to take three lumps with my coffee but now I take only two."

While Karlsson tugged at his collar, Alfrida warmed to the sound of her own voice. I thought about Fredrik who once again was off looking at farms. He would spend the night in Gothenburg, putting up at a small hotel. Sometimes he telephoned me at the bank, but just as often I did not hear from him for days. It did not seem unusual, or so I told myself.

I still wanted to believe that all would be well. Rammen and Fredrik would let bygones be bygones, and there would be visits back and forth. I could see them having rum toddy at Ramm, discussing politics and farming. Our children would be darting in and out of the kitchen, snatching meatballs out of the pan while Disa pretended not to notice. Later Fredrik would fetch my coat and tell me it was time. The children would want to stay but Fredrik would be firm. There would be waves and laughter and promises to come again soon.

But on that particular afternoon, with Emma and Wilhelm just having entered into marriage, the light dimming outside the windows, and Alfrida's voice droning on, my spirits were as wizened as an old woman's breasts.

Every now and then Alfrida rested her hand on her purse, which she kept in her lap, as if someone might steal it. "And before the war is over, we'll run out of coffee too. What then? Shoot the jobbers? Or the government? They've got large supplies locked away, not just sugar and coffee but herring and pork and beef, most of it rotting or already dumped in the sea."

The horses neighed from the barn, not the only ones eager to leave.

Just as I began to think that Rammen would not give a speech, he finally tapped his glass. First he turned to Wilhelm. "You told me that without Emma you'd be nothing. You said she's the last in your thoughts when you go to sleep, the first on your mind when you wake up. Well, I say you're a fortunate man. In this I speak from experience, for I feel the same kind of love for your mother."

Ulrika did not seem to hear him. She wore dark green silk, the perfect color for her large ruby broach.

Rammen turned to Emma. "I hope you grow to love him back. Not that way perhaps, but in another."

Emma sat as straight as ever. Wilhelm reached for her hand and twined his fingers with hers.

Did Emma's family know about Björn? If so, they put up a good front, for they raised their glasses too. Rammen sat down and looked at Ulrika, who continued to ignore him. She was young that day, never mind her matronly figure and the fine lines around her eyes. When Emma's father called for more wine, she held up her glass in anticipation.

The girl brought almond cake for dessert. Johannes read a telegram from Tekla and Erling and passed it around the table so everyone could admire the cupid and the garlands.

Björn rose. With one hand resting on the table and the other stretched out before him, he tossed back his hair, filled his lungs, and sang the duke's aria from *Rigoletto*. Mercifully, it was in Italian, or at least Björn said it was. Searching Emma's face for traces of regret, I saw none. Rammen had been wrong to compare her to Ulrika. She was not pregnant and she had not been coerced.

We stood around as the hired man fetched Wikander's carriage. The air was cool and smelled of wet fields and fires smoldering in farmhouse kitchens. Rammen pulled up next, the two chestnut warmbloods arching their necks. Johannes helped Hedvig up into the carriage, where she took her seat between Ulrika and Disa. Johannes rode in the front, next to Rammen. Björn and I would follow in the gig.

Björn drove. Caesar kept his head steady, quietly chomping at the bit, his harness slapping as he trotted down the single-lane road. The moon was out.

Ahead of us the warmbloods moved at a good speed. Hedvig would stay at Ramm, but these days she never stayed long. On her way to the railway station, she would not even ask the driver to stop at Bergvik so she could say goodbye to Alfrida. From what I had heard, the two sisters used to be close, but life took them in separate directions and now they were too far apart to reclaim what they once had.

Björn rested the hard end of the whip on Caesar's rump.

"I know you're hurting," I said. "You'll never find another Emma."

"Never meant to propose. Worked out exactly as I hoped."

Despite his words, I could not help but think that from then on Björn's life would always be lacking. No other woman had touched his heart like Emma. Still, she could not have been expected to wait forever. After she danced with Björn, it was Wilhelm who knocked on her window at dawn, fiddle in hand, barefoot, and too happy to leave.

"You've told me so many times that you didn't want to farm," I said.

He scoffed. "There was always old Lars. Rammen's stories made me feel as if knew him. Whenever I came home, there he was, waiting in the courtyard. Wanted to see past him but never could."

He pulled back his arm and cracked the whip on Caesar's rump. Caesar fired, his ears pinned flat against his neck.

Rammen heard us coming and pulled the warmbloods to the side. There was a rumble like the sound of an approaching train as a herd of horses galloped in the field beside us, moving as one dark shape, widening and narrowing, then veering back and out, dissolving into the night. Caesar never broke his stride. Only when we neared the village did Björn slow him down, using his voice instead of the reins.

When we arrived at Ramm, Caesar was breathing hard. Björn gave him a pat on the neck and Caesar watched him as he disappeared into the house. Elias walked Caesar for a good half hour. I saw them from the bedroom window, man and horse, circling the courtyard in the light of the moon, both with their heads down.

The next day there was a telephone call from Wilhelm. He said that Stella was gone. A few hours later she stood in the courtyard at Ramm. Disa cleaned her paws with equal parts of vinegar, *brännvin* and water, before she let her lie down by the stove.

The last I saw of Stella she was following Björn into the forest, still wagging her tail. Minutes later I heard the shot. When I asked him where she was buried, Björn would not say. All he said was that stray dogs should be shot and Wilhelm's bitch was no exception. An hour later he left for Gothenburg without another word.

From then on, his mood seemed to get worse by the day, until he picked quarrels even with Gustafa, bringing her to tears. Rammen, of course, gave no sign of wanting to retire, and until he did, Björn was no closer to taking over Ramm than before.

Chapter Thirty-Six

OLOF TELEPHONES AGAIN, his voice giddy with relief.

"She's back."

"Let me talk to her."

"She's gone for a run."

What is wrong with this young woman? She cannot hold still long enough to talk to her great aunt?

"She says she wants to buy a farm."

"A farm?"

"She says there's one for sale. She saw it when she was out jogging."

"Do you know the name?"

"Not sure. Brunnsvik? Brunnsberg? Something like that."

Brunnsdal? Ulrika's one-time home. Does Karin know?

"It won't be in very good shape," I say. "It's been sold so many times I can't imagine what it looks like now."

"That's why I'm calling. Why don't we all go and see it? Karin seems to think you need to get out."

"Get out?"

"That's what she says. She says you spend too much time with the dead."

"Well," I say. "She's a fine one to talk."

"We'll pick you up on Sunday, when you're done with church."

"Done with?" I say. "What does that mean?"

He laughs and hangs up.

WITH LOVISA IN prison, I kept going to see Sven and the children. In the houses that Holmberg had built for his workers, families had to share both washhouse and kitchen. The walls between the rooms were so thin that everyone knew everyone's business. Mothers, whose infants would not stop crying in the night, gave them lumps of sugar drenched in *brännvin* to suck on, a practice that Lovisa herself had brought to Holmberg's attention. Holmberg shrugged and told her he had done all he could.

To make up for the loss of Lovisa's wages, Sven had taken in a boarder, a young man who worked in the warehouse. They all slept in the same room. The boarder was the only one who did not share a bed but slept on a rug on the floor, apparently using firewood as a pillow. As Sven and I talked, there was the continual passing of people outside the window, women carrying water, men returning from the mill, the doctor on his way to treat a man whose hand had been caught in one of the machines.

I brought milk and eggs and Sven never ceased to thank me. One evening Erik came as well, snow swirling in when he opened the door. He turned a chair around and straddled it, resting his arms on its back.

"I know you keep rubbers at the bank," he said. "The mill workers could use them too. Can't see them coming to the bank, though. Best leave some here with Sven."

I promised I would.

While I put the children to bed, Erik and Sven were talking. There was more trouble at the mill. The government had begun to seize existing supplies of grains, while rationing flour and bread to the public. The mill had been allotted sufficient oats for the three horses used to transport goods to the station. However, when the allotment was reduced to feed only two, Holmberg persuaded Wikstrand, the owner of Brunnsdal, to sell him enough oats to keep the third. Without Wikstrand's help, he would have been forced to cut back production and some of his workers would have lost their livelihood. When the authorities found out, and they had their methods, inspectors arriving without warning, both Holmberg and Wikstrand incurred heavy fines.

In January 1918, Holmberg announced that he had sold the mill. Word was that he was tired of dealing with all the wartime commissions. The new owner, who also operated other mills in Ramm, hired an efficiency expert, a zealous young man who kept checking his watch, noting how much time the workers spent in the outhouses and how much time they wasted talking. When the workers finally ran out of patience, they carried him outside and tossed him in the snow.

Not that it did them any good. The mill closed in March. The machines were dismantled and removed. The owner offered the workers employment at another mill some thirty miles away. Arne Karlsson took over the store. Unlike Holmberg, he did not give out candy to the children, nor did he put out free snuff for the men. One morning he had simply moved the scales closer to the cash register to make the absence of the snuffbox less conspicuous. That same day he also made it known that the mill workers could no longer buy on credit, something Holmberg had always encouraged since it made them depend on him even more.

I was at the bank when Erik and the other workers confronted Karlsson outside the store. Erik threatened to take what they needed, whether Karlsson would allow them or not. Someone sent for Rammen, who joined Karlsson at the top of the steps.

"Karlsson has a point," Rammen said, looking down on the workers. "He's not in business to give away his goods."

"We're only taking what should already be ours!" Erik shouted, his fellow workers closing rank behind him.

"This isn't Russia," Rammen said. "Change in Sweden will be by law, not by revolution."

Fists shot into the air and Erik spoke again. "So far every one of your laws has been made to protect you and your own. We don't see the farmers go hungry. How do we tell our children there's no food?"

"The war has been hard on us all," Rammen answered. "Mistakes have been made, I'll be the first to admit it. But Karlsson is a reasonable man. He'll give you what you need. Once you start working, be it here or somewhere else, he expects you to pay him back at cost."

He looked at Karlsson, who nodded, even though all of this was probably news to him too. As the workers filed into the store, a small girl lagged behind. She was no more than six or so, not dressed as warmly as she should have been, her hands in her apron pocket and her bootlaces dragging on the wooden floor.

TROTTA WAS EVERYTHING Fredrik had wanted. Not far from Gothenburg, it covered almost four hundred acres of forest, and two hundred acres of pasture and arable land. The purchase price, one hundred eight thousand crowns, included animals, machinery, and growing crops, although some of the crops had already been sold and would be harvested by a neighbor.

To close the transaction, Fredrik offered to take over a mortgage debt of nearly ninety thousand crowns, while paying the remainder in cash. The factor that swayed him was the forest. It was the only part of the farm that had not been exploited, some of the trees more than a hundred feet tall. He should be able to start felling the coming winter, anticipating an initial income of at least forty thousand crowns, and with the right balance between felling and planting, the forest should yield even more in years to come. Now all he needed was someone to co-sign a loan.

No one in Hult was willing to come to his aid, or if they were, Rammen soon made them decide against it.

"I'll find a way," Fredrik said while he rubbed the back of my neck.

Late one afternoon Alfrida came to the bank, waving her arms as if making way, even though no one else was in sight. We talked in the back room. She said they had heard Agnes scream. By the time Theodor arrived at her door, Agnes was crouched in the hallway corner, wielding her scissors at the farmer. Ella was hiding in the cleaning closet, like a mouse still alive in a trap.

Theodor thought the farmer had been too drunk to do much harm. Alfrida disagreed. "Saw him with his trousers down. Like an old warhorse, his member in full attention."

Alfrida was the one who had called the vicarage, telling Wikander to find Fredrik. Legitimate or not, Ella was still Fredrik's daughter, and wherever he was, she was badly in need of his protection.

Wikander found Fredrik in the stable, and by the time the two of them arrived, Theodor had hoisted the drunken farmer up on his wagon and said he would drive him home. Fredrik insisted on taking him to jail. What had happened was clearly a crime and the farmer must be held accountable.

Wikander tried to talk to Agnes, who carried Ella on her hip. Agnes said she was not interested in hearing about God, "not now and not hereafter." Wikander staggered and had to sit down.

"She put her hand on my groin," the farmer slurred in an effort to regain attention. "To see if I was willing."

Fredrik grabbed him by the throat and hauled him down from the wagon, the farmer gurgling and writhing.

"Theodor pulled them apart," Alfrida said, ignoring Susanna who came to sharpen a pencil. "Lucky for us all, or we'd have not just a rapist amongst us but a murderer too."

The rest I heard from Fredrik himself when he came to the cabin. By the time he had delivered the farmer at the county jail, the farmer had been asleep on the wagon floor, his tongue lolling. Like Theodor, the constable pronounced the farmer too drunk to carry out his intentions. Still, he promised Fredrik to keep him overnight, before he drove him back to his wife. "I know him to be a respectable man," the constable said. "Clasps his hands at church like everyone else." At this he rubbed his jowl and studied Fredrik. "Around here we're all entitled to make a mistake, as long as it doesn't turn into habit."

That night, as we lay in the cabin, we heard the shots ring out at the vicarage, reverberating through the dark. Fredrik jumped up from the mattress, dragged on his trousers and jacket, and ran out the door.

Marit spread the news. She had watched from behind the curtain as Wikander, in nothing but his nightshirt, fired at the sky, a human fireball on hairy legs. His old housekeeper stood under one of the lindens holding a box of cartridges in one hand and a bottle of *brännvin* in the other. Sputtering and exploding, he spun around the courtyard, before he stopped to reload and take one more swig. Then off he flew again, stepping high like a rich man's carriage horse, aiming at Andromeda and Cassiopeia and yelling their names. By then the old housekeeper had fallen to her knees and appeared to be praying, the only person left, Marit said, who still believed in God. At long last Otter arrived—no secret where he had been—and managed to coax Wikander back to the house. As for Marit, she was merely thankful for still being alive, but now she was going back to Halland, for this was not what she had hired herself out for, a near-naked clergyman shooting at the stars.

A few days later Fredrik telephoned the bank. Axel Persson, who owned the farm east of Trotta, had offered to co-sign his loan. Persson had read Fredrik's articles and said he was exactly the kind of farmer he wanted for a neighbor. Persson was also the man who had bought some of the growing crops.

I heard Fredrik laugh at the other end.

"We can get married now."

"Let's ask Agnes if Ella can come live with us," I said.

There was a click on the line.

"Anna, let it go."

"It would be better for Ella, perhaps for Agnes too."

"Ella belongs with her mother. We've no right to take her away."

AFTER THE MILL closed, the workers needed our help. Employment at the farms was scarce that early in the year, and not even Arne Karlsson could let them buy on credit for more than a few weeks.

Rammen asked me to join him for old times' sake. In a few days I was to become Fredrik's wife. Wikander had agreed to travel to Trotta and marry us there. No one from my family was to be present. Rammen stood by his word that I would no longer be welcome at Ramm.

Together we drove from farm to farm. "Anything you can contribute," Rammen told the farmers and their wives. "Both the workers and I will thank you."

He drove half hunched, the reins loose in his hands, his warmblood geldings at an easy walk. Now and then he pointed at the bedrock that lay exposed in some of the fields.

"Imagine," he said. "Earthquakes ripping apart entire mountains."

He talked a great deal about Lars. "He was hard. Even harder on himself than he was on others."

He said his death had not been an accident. Lars knew how to handle dynamite, that day when they broke ground for the new church. "He and his farmhand tamped the hole full of powder and set the fuse. The men found his brain splattered on the farmhand who survived but was never quite the same. Scraped up what they could and poured it into the coffin."

He clucked his tongue against the roof of his mouth, and the warmbloods broke into a trot.

"They talked about his death for miles around. Sermon that Sunday was on the Book of Proverbs, which states that pride goes before destruction, and a haughty spirit before a fall."

As we turned a corner, yet another farmhouse lay before us, smoke rising from the chimney.

Rammen brought the horses to a halt and tied the reins to the carriage before he climbed down. "As for me, I never was one to put much stock in the Bible. He knew his time had come. Can't say I blame him. Can't blame him at all."

For all his distrust of the Bible, Rammen still knew how to put it to use. When the farmer's wife said they had nothing to spare, he quoted from the Book of Revelation: "*And all liars shall have their lot in the lake which burneth with fire and brimstone.*"

Then, as if to soften his words, he added that these were indeed difficult times. "Holmberg is the one to blame, always threatening with shortages. Can't fault you for stocking up. The commissions and the regulations haven't helped either, and most of them are misguided to begin with. The law of man must ultimately yield to the law of nature, which demands that first of all we must feed our own. Still, that goes for the mill workers too. If they can't do it legally, they'll have to find another way."

Two days later Rammen stood at the door to the vicarage, greeting the workers as they arrived, the women curtsying when they walked past him. Agnes was helping in the kitchen. Wikander had insisted that she come, saying God welcomed back all those who repented, and we should too.

I was in the large room, where four years earlier Rammen had talked to the farmers the night before they left to march in Stockholm. The room looked very different now. Carbide lamps and firewood crowded the floor. Eggs, potatoes, and sacks of flour were laid out on the table and clothes were stacked high on the chairs. The workers carried everything away. Only Ulrika's green silk dress was left, too fanciful to be claimed. I noticed that Marit had her eyes on it and told her to take it.

When I left, Rammen was talking to Karlsson outside Prästgården's barn. Ella was playing with the other children. It looked as if they were rolling marbles for they all huddled on the ground.

Ella wore her new red coat. Fredrik had brought her to the store, just before Holmberg turned it over to Karlsson. He had lifted her up on the counter and told Holmberg he wanted the prettiest coat that Holmberg had to offer. When Holmberg suggested he choose one that was a little too large, so that it would last her longer, Fredrik said no. As soon as she outgrew it, he would buy her one that fit.

As I walked toward the road, Ella's scream cut through the air. Rushing back, I saw her run in circles, striking at herself with her fists. The children had formed a wall around her and blocked her as she tried to escape. I squeezed past them, but when I tried to catch her, she screamed even louder, as if terrified of me as well.

A dead rabbit kit fell from under her coat, and others lay on the ground. Like a pack of wolves giving tongue in a chase, the children shouted, "Bastard! Bastard! Bastard." Just as I scooped Ella up, one of the boys tried to force another dead rabbit under her collar. His eyes wild with hate, he kept thrusting the blue and hairless kit at Ella even as I held her high. I felt her heartbeat in my hands, rapid and shallow, like a tiny, snared bird.

That was when I recognized the small girl. Her bootlaces still untied, she was trying to pull the boy away. He knocked her to the ground, but soon she was back on her feet, dragging at his jacket and begging him to stop. The boy shouted more taunts, and like electricity, his words sparked and leapt from child to child.

"The thief on the gallows! The whore's on her back! Bastard! Bastard! Bastard!" Their voices rose and fell in perfect unison, as if they were reciting a nursery rhyme they learned long ago, the savagery of the words as familiar as the milk from their mothers' breasts. The girl kept pulling at the boy, pleading and crying. Dirt streaked her cheeks, mixed with gobs of snot and blood.

Agnes came running from the kitchen and brushed against me as Ella flew into her arms. Carrying Ella, she hurried down the road. When I turned around to find the small girl, she was gone.

The children were silent now, all spent, but the taunts still hung in the air, like dark clouds after a storm. When I bent to pick up the kits, the boy tried to snatch them away. Not until Rammen grabbed him by the scruff of his neck was it truly over.

The kits lay cold and limp in my hands.

"Here," Rammen said. "Give them to me."

Chapter Thirty-Seven

FREDRIK HELD OUT his hand as I stepped down from the train. He wondered about my luggage.

"I've brought all I need," I said.

We rode in a light carriage. His horse was a dun *Nordsvensk* with black mane and tail. Coltsfoot was blooming close to the ground, yellow flowers on stems without leaves. The hoof-shaped leaves would emerge only after the flowers themselves had withered, but for now the sandy embankments were strewn with gold in places where nothing else could take root.

The landscape was open and flat. Well-tended, the soil was generous in return. At the farms, men and women moved about their tasks, their manner dignified and easy.

The road that led up to Trotta was lined with chestnut trees that vaulted and met over our heads.

"Wait until spring," Fredrik said. "Like driving through a tunnel of white."

He smiled, and I smiled back.

The main house, more like a manor house than a farmhouse, was painted yellow. The upper story had no less than ten windows. I wished that Rammen could have been there to see it.

The steward, a quiet man whom I liked at first sight, took the horse to the stable. Fredrik ran up the steps to the house and held the door as I entered.

Inside all was air and light. Built in the late eighteenth century, the house had been added to several times. Yet it felt very much as it must have felt from the beginning. On the ground floor the doors were open so that I could see from one end of the house to the other, with a large room in the middle and smaller rooms to the sides. Paintings had been taken down from the walls, leaving unbleached squares of creamy white wallpaper.

Dagmar, a young woman, had set a table by the large windows and said she was pleased to meet me. The room looked out on a terrace and a lawn with croquet hoops still in the ground. A swing—two ropes and a board—hung from an old maple.

Dagmar told me her father was Axel Persson, the farmer who had co-signed Fredrik's loan. She said she would stay on until we found a permanent housekeeper. "Just let me know when you're ready to start the interviews. I've got several candidates in mind."

The mid-day meal consisted of pike, fresh from the lake and coated with breadcrumbs and baked. The horseradish sauce was lighter and more flavorful than any I had ever tasted.

Dagmar wanted to know what to serve Wikander, who was to arrive the following day.

"The best of everything," Fredrik said, all the while smiling and looking at me. "Considering what we've put him through."

There was something extravagant, almost frivolous, about him that day, such a contrast to his usual restraint. And when I looked into his eyes, those golden flecks danced in his irises, the grayness gone.

How perfect it could have been, the two of us about to marry. What if a tramp had passed through the garden gate and walked across the lawn? Surely he would have seen us through the large window and reflect on the attractiveness of the couple, the woman in her light brown traveling suit, the man in a white shirt and riding breeches. He would judge the man quite a bit older, one might say in the prime of his life, leaning back in his chair, gesturing expansively, his dark hair falling over his eyes. And as the tramp approached, the man would reach out and rest his arm on the woman's shoulders, but the woman would rise, open the French doors, and invite the tramp to go around to the kitchen. The late winter light soft on her face, she would laugh and tell herself that this was now her life.

After the meal Fredrik showed me the upstairs. The previous owner and his family had left in a rush, and in the nursery tin soldiers lay scattered on the floor. Dolls in child-sized chairs were having tea at a small table, the cups as translucent as Ella's eyelids the first time I saw her.

There were no less than six spare bedrooms, one of them set up for Wikander. The main bedroom was ready for Fredrik and me. The walls had stenciled patterns of squares and diamonds, which pleased the eye and gave a sense of continuity and order. Two armchairs were covered with red and green chintz, and the writing desk was inlaid with silver. All this, Fredrik said, came with the farm.

"It's difficult to be happy at someone else's expense," I said.

"How so?"

"Ulrika's parents left in a hurry too. She still talks about some of the furniture they had to leave behind."

"I don't know about Brunnsdal, but the man who owned Trotta almost destroyed it. He's fortunate to come out as well as he did."

In the afternoon, as a light rain was falling, he showed me the rest of the farm. The stable, like the barn and the main house, was lit by electricity, even more valuable now that kerosene was rationed. All in all there were stalls for twelve horses and boxes for mares with foals. At that point, however, all the horses had been sold except for the *Nordsvensk* that Fredrik was driving.

There were more than thirty cows, all Holsteins. Chalk slates hung over their stalls, stating when each cow was expected to calve, the weight of milk she was yielding, and the amount of fodder she was to receive. Two years earlier there had been twice as many, but the previous owner had kept selling them off. The remaining cows, however, were of excellent stock. Now that the war finally seemed to be coming to an end, Fredrik was confident that he could rebuild the herd to its former standard and size.

He drove us through the forest, where the spruce trees stood straight and tall. A lakeside gazebo had been boarded up for the winter. The rain had passed and the clouds were beginning to clear. He tied the horse and we stood on a small stone pier, looking out over the water.

I told him what had happened to Ella.

He kept looking out over the water.

"The children sit in their pews and they hear it all," I said. "They're told they're born in sin. They're told that justice will prevail, but they know it isn't true, not in this life and not in the next. They're frightened out of their wits, and when they see someone like Ella, someone who's even more wretched than they, they fall on her as one. It's as if by punishing her, they think the rest of them can be saved."

A fish jumped, a silver streak against the black. In the distance the roof tiles of the main house glistened red.

"We don't protect them by yielding," he said. "We protect them by showing them a better way."

"You don't know the village. I do. I've seen what can happen in the schoolyard when even Karolina chooses to look away."

We walked back to the house, Fredrik leading the horse. The ground was soft from the rain, and the horse snuffled gently against Fredrik's jacket. He told me he loved me, and although I had longed to hear him say it, my throat burned as I held back the tears.

Dagmar had gone home. The old house was breathing all around us, as if my presence had been well received. We ate some bread and cheese that Dagmar had put out in the kitchen, and Fredrik poured wine from a bottle he found in the cellar.

We walked upstairs and lay down on the bed. Lightly, almost timidly, he stroked the inside of my thighs, all the while speaking words of reassurance, even entreaty.

I stayed awake through the night, listening to his breath as he slept. Whenever I closed my eyes, I saw Agnes' face that day when I came to her cabin and she opened the door. Even I could see that she had hoped it would be Fredrik. Her gaze kept turning to the window, while I chattered on about dresses, when she knew perfectly well that this was not the reason I was there.

Shortly before dawn, I moved on top of him and felt him grow hard underneath me. He smiled and murmured something in his sleep. Perhaps he thought he could look forward to more moments like this, waking up to his wife's caresses. When he reached for a condom, I checked his hand.

"No," I said. "Not this time."

At first light he had fallen asleep again. Dressed and ready to leave, I sat in the green armchair, waiting for him to stir. As soon as he did, I told him I had to go back to Hult.

"Anna?" He rose from the bed and reached for his robe, his eyes still heavy with sleep. "What's going on?"

"It's no good. Don't you see? We can't build right on wrong."

The scar on his lip was almost white. "Please, Anna. Tell me anything, but don't tell me this."

"Change may come, just as you say, but it will be too late. If you love me as you say you do, you must marry Agnes and keep Ella safe."

He did not speak as he drove me to the station. I too had run out of words. Had I touched him, or even looked at him, I would not have been able to leave. He did not return the stationmaster's greeting, nor did he walk with me to the train. By the time I found my seat and pulled down the window, he was gone.

Somewhere between Ljunga and Håstad the train stopped on a sidetrack to let a meeting train pass. As the other train rushed by, I caught a glimpse of Wikander, a massive silhouette against the dim compartment light.

"Golden eyes," I whispered and cradled my womb. "Your eyes will be golden like his."

Chapter Thirty-Eight

"LET'S GO," OLOF says. "We're late."

I have never been to Brunnsdal before and am in no hurry to go there now.

"The children are with my mother," he says with a frown, as if I should have known to ask.

Karin waits for us at the main house, the early autumn wind tugging at her hair. She is wearing a large oilskin jacket so I cannot tell if she is pregnant still.

I keep thinking about Ulrika. Naturally, Brunnsdal does not look the way it did when her father owned it, but even so I can still see her, young and full of hope.

The forest, once gone, is reclaiming the land, the way the forest will, and the fields have long lain fallow. The barn is in decent shape as is the stable, where the current owner keeps three riding horses that belong to his daughter. The machine hall resembles a wrecking yard for everything that is no longer in use. An old harvester stands in the middle of the floor, covered with dust. Rakes and spades and pitchforks have been tossed into the corners, next to carpentry tools and baskets with potatoes, all rotten by now.

The three horses will stay on as boarders and Karin will make room for more, even build an indoor riding arena where valuable show horses can be trained for jumping and dressage. She also intends to run a herd of beef cattle, not as lucrative as dairy cows but much less work. Most of the land will be used for grazing and she also expects to grow her own feed.

"Are you sure you're up to this?" I ask.

Karin and Olof exchange glances, before she speaks. "I've talked to Johan and several other farmers. Johan warned me that modern farming is not at all the way it was when I came to Ramm as a child. Almost everything is done with machines. The loneliness grinds. Still, none of the people I talked to would have chosen a different life."

"What about the children?" I ask.

"They'll spend part of their time with me," she says.

Again she looks at Olof.

"As much as they want," he says. "We'll take turns."

While I try to grasp the meaning of their words, Karin keeps talking about pasture management, crossbreeding, and the advantages of keeping the calves rather than selling them off. Moments later she talks about starting a farm store in one of the buildings where she will sell her own meat. As she visited the various farms she met several weavers, women as well as men, and she will sell their products too. She claims that all those old tools in the machine hall will fetch good prices as soon as she cleans them up and places them on display.

"Perhaps we could even start a small museum," she adds, as if still weighing the thought. "You could show visitors around."

By now I have run out of objections. We watch Olof as he walks down to a small creek. He stops before a flock of grazing sheep, his hands in his pockets, his back turned. He seems elongated, even taller than usual, as if both his body and his feelings have been stretched too far.

"Olof was worried," I say. "And mind you, so was I."

"I was only gone for a few days. Long enough to talk to Johan and the other farmers. I put up at the hotel in Håstad. Needed some time for myself."

I hold my tongue. This is hardly the time to reprimand her for being selfish, even though all the evidence points that way.

She talks fast, not looking at me but at Olof, who still seems to study the sheep. "When I returned, the children were back with Olof's mother. He said we couldn't continue like this. The children missed me. He said he would do anything I wanted him to do, even if it meant a divorce. That night he slept in the children's room and I lay alone in our bed."

Below us, Olof picks up a stone and tosses it into the creek. The sheep turn to face him, their ears folded forward, their muscles tensed.

"The following day his mother brought the children," Karin says. "I expected them to run into my arms, but they didn't. They just stood there, the girl sucking her thumb and the boy eyeing me with suspicion. Olof's mother pushed them toward me, but they still didn't move. That was when I realized I could actually lose them."

Olof wanders on. The sheep spread and bleat. After he has passed, they begin to graze again, their backs like gently rolling hills.

"Olof was late from work that evening, and his supper had long since grown cold. I told him he was right. The best thing for us all would be to end the marriage. And then the children woke up, and when he took me in his arms I started sobbing, damn it, my own children watching, but all he did was rock me, until he slowly let me go, as if afraid I might fall."

I turn and look up at the main house, still grand with its three stories and ivy-trained windows, although like most everything else, it is badly in need of repair. Ulrika was only eighteen when she left. To this day I can see Adolf and Rammen bargaining in the parlor at Ramm. Was she already lost in that inner world? Or did Rammen truly believe that he married a perfectly healthy woman, only so much more beautiful than the rest? Was it only because of the baron's bankruptcy that Adolf no longer wanted to marry his daughter? Or had he caught an early glimpse of her illness, so terrifying that all he could do was flee?

Karin watches Olof, her lips pressed tight.

"Once that door is closed, you can't go back," I say. "He won't let you hurt him twice."

She nods, fishes a handkerchief out of her jacket pocket, and blows her nose. "I'm all out of regrets. Don't know how I could possibly come up with more."

Olof's face breaks into one of his smiles as he ambles up the hill. When Karin smiles back, he starts sidestepping the sheep dung, like a log driver on the river, balancing and swaying, before deciding where to jump.

I hold my cup as she pours coffee from a thermos.

"This is where Ulrika grew up," I say.

"I know."

IT WAS MAY 1918 and Ulrika's cherry tree bloomed. A new man had leased Prästgården, but Agnes and Ella still lived at Bergvik, the disgrace running deep, despite Wikander's words about forgiveness. One after the other, Fredrik's letters kept arriving at the bank. I returned them all unopened. No one, not even Disa, asked me why I had come back to Hult.

Disa was spring-cleaning, moving everything in and out of the cupboards, dusting, scouring, and polishing. Leaving Susanna alone at the bank, I helped with the washing. Lina Lind placed a sack of ashes in the bottom of the oak tub, on top of ox bones so as not to cover the drainage hole. After soaking the laundry overnight—men's shirts and long underwear closest to the ashes, as they were always the hardest to clean—we scooped and drained and scooped again, while Ulrika heated more water in a large iron pot, humming and wiping her brow with her sleeve.

On the third day Elias harnessed one of the Ardenners and drove us to the river. There we scrubbed and pounded and twisted and rinsed, while Elias paced in the meadow above, annoyed because he would miss his midday nap. Distracted by honking geese, flying high on their way to the north, I lost a towel to the current. I raced it down to the river bend, but when I waded out to catch it, the cold water stung my ankles and I let it go. The child was growing inside me although so far I was the only one who knew.

A few days later Disa hung up the newly ironed curtains. From the second story, she looked down at me as I passed on the garden path. She opened the window and called out that this was indeed a fine day, her eyeglasses glinting in the sun. With Wilhelm gone, her position at Ramm was safe. Not until

Björn married would it be threatened again, and so far Rammen was very much in charge.

That afternoon Björn returned from Gothenburg with a phonograph, which he set up in his room. Caruso's voice drew me upstairs and Björn said I could come in and listen as long as I did not talk. The drinking song from *Cavalleria Rusticana* lifted me off the floor. Who would want to talk when someone sang like that?

Gustafa put her head inside the door and asked to be let in as well. She was not so much interested in the music as she was in hearing about what the women wore when they went to the opera and how the talk died down as the conductor took his place in the pit. Time after time Björn told her how the seat would fold on its own each time he stood, Gustafa shaking her head in disbelief. Only with Gustafa would he show such patience.

One morning Fredrik arrived at Ramm. By then it had been two months since my last bleeding. He came down the hill behind the barn, red-eyed and unshaven.

Rammen went out to talk to him, and after a while Björn joined them. Finally I went out myself.

"Marry me," Fredrik said, his voice hoarse.

"I can't," I said.

Björn moved between us. "You heard her. She can't."

Fredrik struck first, a sudden blow to Björn's chin. Björn tumbled backward but did not fall. The fight flared like lamp oil on cinders, and Rammen pulled me out of the way. Björn drove his shoulder into Fredrik's s midriff, almost lifting him off the ground. The two men kept swinging at each other, Fredrik's fury equal to Björn's strength. Elias came running from the barn and managed to hold Fredrik back.

Björn picked up Fredrik's hat, and put it back on Fredrik's head. "Get out of here! Anna doesn't want you."

"It's all right, Elias," Fredrik said and Elias let him go. "I didn't come here to fight. I came to talk to Anna."

Fredrik tried to touch me, but Björn, rubbing his knuckles, blocked him again. This time Fredrik stayed calm.

Rammen, quiet until now, finally spoke. "I warned you before, and I told you I wouldn't do it again. You've got no right to bother us here. Ever since you came to this village, you've caused nothing but dissent. I'm glad to see it's over. Anna has made her decision, and if you're half the gentleman you claim you are, you'll leave her alone."

"Rammen is right," I said. "Please go."

And so I returned to the house, never once looking back.

The following morning I went to the wise woman's cabin. I would always wonder what might have happened had he still been there. Why did I even go? Perhaps I wanted him to hold me one last time, as if it might give me the strength to live on without him. At any rate, he was gone. I could see that he had stayed for days. There was a pot on the stove, and even some potatoes and bread. The cabinet had been pushed over and one of the chairs had been smashed. All around were books, some thrown into the far corners of the cabin, their pages torn and strewn all over the floor. He often read while he waited for me to come through the door but this time even the books had failed him. It was as if he had been up against the trolls themselves.

Chapter Thirty-Nine

IN JUNE, JUST before midsummer, I stood on the steps to the bank and saw the last of the mill workers leave. They had all accepted work at the other mill and Erik had gone ahead. The wagons rattled by, loaded with household goods and mattresses. Children sat dangling their legs from the back. I looked for the small girl but did not see her.

A month later I sat with Aunt Hedvig in her drawing room. The maid was fussing, wanting to know what kind of jam to serve with the scones. Hedvig waved her away.

Rammen had told Hedvig that I had decided not to marry Fredrik Otter after all. She said she could think of at least two or three young men right there in Gothenburg who would be glad to hear it.

"Come live with me," she said. "Disa will have to take care of Rammen and Ulrika, but for you we can still find a husband."

I too had come to believe that Disa would never marry. I sometimes saw her draw in the lavender scent of her linen cupboard, where the sheets and the towels were folded so that her monogram showed. She would run her hand over a stack of pillowcases whose ribbons she had curled with iron thongs. Her feelings, I thought, had been stashed in there as well to prevent them from wreaking havoc with the rest of her life, which she tried so hard to keep in check.

"Please, Hedvig, there's something you should know."

"Such as?"

"I think I'm pregnant. I haven't bled for four months."

Hedvig studied me for a long while, the blue veins on her hands winding around patches of brown. "Does Otter know?"

I shook my head.

"Probably just as well," she said. "I hear he already has a child."

"I went to talk to the mother once. She said she had wronged him but she didn't say how. I still hope they'll marry, if only for the sake of the child."

The maid brought the tea.

"I'll pour," Hedvig said and waved her away again.

"I would like to see a doctor," I said. "I need to make sure that all's well."

The following morning we visited a lying-in hospital in Vasastaden. It had once been a private residence and Hedvig and the captain had been friends with the owner. Large maples shaded the back entrance, which everyone seemed to use.

Hedvig was in the room as the doctor examined me, and for once I found her presence reassuring. I lay on my back with a pillow under my pelvis, knees bent, the whole room smelling faintly of ether. The doctor asked about Hult, the kind of conversation you might have in a drawing room. I tried not to tense, but when I did, he told me to keep my mouth open and take deep breaths. After pulling on a plastic glove, he parted my thighs and entered me with his finger, all the while averting his eyes and reassuring me that it would soon be over. I tried to count the shiny instruments on the table beside me—tongs, scissors, and any number of scalpels, some of the blades triangular, others shaped like crescents—but when I looked at Hedvig, she stood looking out the window, her back rigid against the foliage of a maple. Afterward the nurse drew my blood to test for syphilis. Hedvig still stood with her back turned, the white wall stark against the spiky maple leaves.

Later Hedvig and I talked to the doctor in his private office. He said there was no doubt I was with child. When I said I was glad, he looked at Hedvig, who shrugged. He also said he would inform me about the result of the blood test as soon as he knew. "Meanwhile there's the matter of the father," he said, pen poised.

Both the doctor and Hedvig looked at me now.

When I did not answer, the doctor put down his pen. "Your aunt tells me he's been visiting prostitutes. Should the blood test come back positive, the new law will force him to reveal the names of all the women he's had intercourse with, prostitutes or not."

"He always used protection," I said.

"Still, you'll be wise not to associate with this man in the future," the doctor said. "We try to ascertain the health of the prostitutes but the situation is by no means under control. Condoms are no guarantee. Your child could have been blighted in the womb."

I gripped the armrests of my chair but my hands were still shaking.

Even Hedvig seemed unsteady as we walked out of the doctor's office. "While we're here, we might as well have a look around."

A woman showed us the visitors' rooms on the first floor, and the bedrooms and the nursery on the second. It was not difficult to imagine what the house must once have been like, the closets filled with day dresses and evening gowns, sporting coats and capes and furs. Now young women ran up and down the stairs with bedpans and washing.

In the nursery the curtains were drawn for the children were asleep. Wet-nurses sat in rows by the children's cribs, some reading, some knitting, some staring at the walls. All of them came with good recommendations, and most of them had agreed to offer their services in return for having their own babies housed and adopted. The children, the woman assured us, all went to good homes, and so far there had never been anything but happy endings.

That afternoon I wandered alone through Gothenburg, gathering my thoughts. A sign at one of the livery stables warned that some of the horses had caught the Spanish flu. I had read about it in the newspaper. Several stables had reported cases of high fever and swollen eyes and legs. The veterinarians were at a loss what to do. The symptoms usually lasted five to six days, provided the horses were allowed to rest. Given the hard times and lack of good feed, their resistance was already low. At least one of the articles mentioned that people had begun to catch it too.

In the harbor, men shouted on decks and gangways, while huge cranes swung back and forth. The water was gray and choppy, white spume against the blackened rocks. I thought about Rammen and Ulrika walking along the wharves on the day of their betrothal, Ulrika pregnant with Adolf's child. Rammen used to say that people in Gothenburg were more courageous than others. Every day they looked out over the open sea and something responded inside them. Perhaps that also happened to me.

The shop was squeezed between a haberdashery and a tavern. A bell jingled as I opened the door. The woman behind the counter wore a green dress with a crocodile sash, her straw-colored hair curled tight.

I told her I was pregnant with Fredrik Otter's child.

"Don't know what that has to do with me."

"I'm worried about the child."

"What has he told you?"

"He said he used protection."

"I would have insisted."

I picked up a small porcelain unicorn, white with a gold-trimmed horn.

"I heard he helped to have your name removed from the lists," I said.

"He did."

A man stopped on the sidewalk and stood looking at the figurines on display in the window.

"Those inspections will soon be a thing of the past," she said, running her feather duster over the cups and saucers on the shelf beside her. "The new law will do away with them entirely and that's all to the good. Talk to any of the women whose names are still on the lists. They'll tell you about standing in line at the police station with their skirts hiked up. One woman I know was actually infected during the inspection. I held her hand when she died."

The bell jingled and the man stepped inside. While he looked around, the woman dusted a Dresden ballerina with delicate roses strewn on her skirt.

"More pieces in the back?" he asked.

She nodded and pointed to a door. I caught a whiff of her perfume. Elderberry? Not as strong but almost as sweet.

"I can't marry him but I want to have his child," I said as soon as the man was out of hearing.

For the first time she truly looked me over. "You must be Anna," she said, her eyes not unkind.

All I could do was nod.

"Well, Anna, I can see you're in a difficult situation. I haven't seen him in several months. He came to say goodbye. Said he was going to marry you."

"And before that?"

"On and off, whenever he happened to be in Gothenburg. I gather he was looking for a farm."

I steadied myself against the counter.

She pointed to a chair.

I sat.

"There." She handed me a glass of water. "Shall I send for a doctor?"

I shook my head. Part of me wanted to know more. Where did he leave the money? On the bedside table? Did she count it as he dressed? Did he tell her when she could expect him back? The other part wanted to flee.

I caught her glancing toward the back. She must have known I understood.

"It's the war," she said. "Forced me back to my old occupation. Can't make a living on bric-a-brac when most people don't have enough for food. Fredrik Otter didn't judge me. Not in his nature."

Still unsteady, I bought the unicorn and waited while she wrapped it. As soon as I left, the Closed sign went up in the window. The doctor's words kept ringing in my ears. *Your child could have been blighted in the womb.*

Hastening down the sidewalk, I tried to fight back my sense of doom. I almost collided with a man pushing a wheelbarrow. A policeman blew a whistle when I crossed a street, just in time to stop me from stepping straight in front of a fast-moving horse.

Back in the apartment, Hedvig was waiting. I finally told her that I had become pregnant on purpose and had no intention of giving up my child.

"I plan to move to Stockholm," I said. "I've put away a good amount of money from my salary and it should keep me going until the child is born. I'll introduce myself as a widow. No one has to know."

"And after the child is born?"

"I'm sure I'll find work at one of the banks. Boy or girl, the child will have opportunities I myself could never have dreamed of. Tekla once told me that no one in Stockholm thinks twice about a woman wanting to become a doctor or a lawyer. At some point I'll inform Fredrik but not until I'm settled in every way. I want the child to know its father."

She must have realized that I had thought about all this for a long time for all she did was sigh.

Before she retreated to her bedroom, she placed her hands on either side of my face and kissed the top of my head. "It must run in the family. This proclivity for misery."

That night I could not sleep. For all my plans, I had not planned for this. The prostitute's thoughts must have been the same as mine, for she had certainly not gone out of her way to calm me. What if Fredrik had visited other prostitutes too, women I had never heard of? The doctor was right. Condoms could break. It had happened once in the cabin, had it not? Like so many others, he could carry the contagion without exhibiting any symptoms himself. Syphilis was everywhere, or so the newspapers informed us. Its march was so secret and its attacks so insidious that none of us could be certain to escape. I thought about Edit examining her newborn son, counting his fingers and toes. She had read the newspapers too, harrowing descriptions of children covered with sores, their faces rotting, the stench of the nurseries so revolting that only the mothers would want to stay.

All night long I kept hearing Wikander's voice, gravelly and dark. *Think what harm will come to your children if your marriage begins in sin.*

By dawn I had worked myself into such a state that I could hardly breathe.

LIKE MOST VILLAGES in our region, Ljunga was remote and hidden in the forest. I got off the train and walked over to the small, white church. The sun shone from a cloudless sky, insects were busy with summer, and my shoes had turned brown with dust.

The church itself was plain. The only adornment was a vase of flowers on the altar, grayish green foxtail and ox-eye daisies. I had not been back since I was a small girl and Rammen took me to see Lars' wooden Christ. Now the Christ was freshly varnished. Someone had repainted the blood, dots of red on his temples and brow. The gash in his side was redder too, as if he had begun to bleed anew, but the grotesque angle of his head was just as I recalled.

I bent below the Christ and prayed for my child, but when I looked up, I could not see his eyes.

Afterward I took a seat in the pew. Someone coughed by the door. A tramp entered and sat on the other side of the aisle. His cough was thick and gurgling. A cleaning woman came out of the vestry with a man I took to be the sexton. They spoke to each other in whispers and the man told the tramp to leave.

The tramp struggled to his feet, and I followed him out the door. A lark flew up in song. On reaching the road, the tramp faltered and fell. Thinking it would ease his coughing, I sat beside him and told him to rest his head in my lap. I must have been aware of the risk, but hearing the lark made me lose all fear, a reckless variation of warbles and trills, the high notes climbing higher and higher as the small bird rose and disappeared into the sky. That was when I recognized Rammen's old coat.

He said the devil had followed him to the church and had waited for him to come out.

By now two boys were kicking stones on the other side of the road. A farmer drove past and I hailed him, telling him the tramp needed a blanket to keep him warm. He threw us an empty sack and continued on his way. Soon people were gathering all around, their faces cold and wary. I recognized none of them and they seemed as suspicious of me as they were of the tramp. The tramp kept coughing. When I asked one of the men for a handkerchief, all he did was murmur and back off.

The tramp's beard had turned almost white, and his lichen hair had thinned. He must not have washed for weeks, for the smell of him was foul. Over and over he told me he his soul was bound for hell.

"I met you once," I said. "You came to our farm. You told me to dance and laugh."

His eyes burned with fever and he seized my arm.

"We don't want him," a woman said with a snarl. "He's not one of us. Where are his papers?"

Dark green vomit spilled down the tramp's chin and I used my sleeve to wipe it off.

"Stand back!" one man called out. "He's got the flu!"

The people scuffled to the other side of the road. The tramp's hold was still firm on my arm and blood seeped from the cracks on his callused hand.

"You followed your calling," I said. "You said one step led to the next. Surely God won't punish you for that."

Peace spread across his face. "God bless you," he murmured. He must have heard the heartbeats of the child, for he added, "And God bless your child." His hold on my arm slackened, his throat rattled, and he was gone.

Moving my hand over his eyes, I closed his lids.

I waited as they loaded the body onto a wagon and covered it with two more sacks. By the time I boarded the train, I had gathered his words and saved them.

Chapter Forty

TWO SMALL BICYCLES lean against the house at Brunnsdal. The children are with Olof in Gothenburg. Karin expects them back in a couple of days.

We walk over to the machine hall. The air is high and cool, a perfect autumn day. Down by the creek, leaves cover the ground, a mosaic of red, yellow, and black. Niklas, the hired man, is building fences for five Hereford cows and three calves. Horses are being exercised in the riding ring, elegant warmbloods with powerful strides.

"Don't worry," Karin says. "You and I shall know each other better now."

She slides open the large machine hall doors. The harvester is gone, and the cement floor has been swept.

"Mom and Dad were here. They'll need some time getting used to the divorce. Can't blame them. They never really knew."

By the far wall she has heaped old objects found around the farm. Now she wants me to tell her what some of them are.

She holds up a curved, serrated blade, attached to a short wooden handle.

"A sickle," I say. "They used it for cutting grass and grain. Backbreaking work no doubt."

She puts it aside. "I'll clean off the rust and sell it in the shop."

"Still sure you want a divorce?" I ask.

"We both are. The children smell dishonesty, just like that stray dog smelled fear. Remember? The time I got blood poisoning and almost died."

"I do."

She continues to rummage around, picking up a cowbell, a blacksmith's rounding hammer, a pair of docking shears. The bulge under her sweater has grown. I do not believe she forgot to take her pill.

"You must have made difficult choices too," she says.

"We all do," I say, hoping to leave it at that.

She frowns and examines a wicker basket, shaped like a cone.

"Perhaps some kind of eel trap," I suggest. "Can't be sure."

It goes on her museum pile.

"I know you had to bury your child," she says.

"It was the father's fault. You've probably heard."

"Still."

I take a deep breath. "Still what?"

She finds a flail and starts hitting it against the floor, too hard, I want to say, but bite my tongue.

"Still what, Karin? What do you mean?"

She keeps striking the flail against the floor, as if trying to kill an invisible snake. "Johan has one of these at Ramm," she says in between thwacks. "They used it to separate the grain from the husks."

At long last she stops and designates the flail to the pile of objects to sell.

Next she studies an old horse bit with a missing shank. "Perhaps at some point it's best to bury the memories too."

When I stroke her cheek, she places her own hand over mine and leans in. The moment is over before either one of us has time to cry.

"Is that what you intend to do?" I say. "Bury your memories too?"

"In a way. I want to forget all that was bad. Just remember the good."

I shake my head. "Don't think we can. Without falsifying the whole."

THE RESULT OF the blood test was negative. Nor did I catch the flu from the tramp, a possibility that had come to frighten me more and more, as I read about it spreading north and causing women to miscarry.

After her initial dismay, Tekla developed a plan. "Of course you'll stay with us," she wrote. "When you're ready, we'll find you a place of your own. A friend of mine has just organized a childcare group for working mothers and she says she'll be proud to look after your child."

Whenever I had the opportunity, I left for the forest. It seemed only right that I wanted to spend so much time alone. New life was growing inside me, my blood coursing through its veins.

I was happy then, happier than I had ever been. As my womb grew heavy, my sense of abandon grew wilder too. No one is braver than a woman with child. Voices still call her, but none is as strong as her own.

The paths I walked I had never walked before. They would twist and bend, split into two and meet again on the other side of a boulder or a tree. Some might have fallen out of use. Others might have just begun to form, as the feet of man and animals crushed the twigs and scraped the moss off the stones. From a ridge, I looked down at the narrow valley, as the lawless and the outcasts must have looked down at it too, the river gleaming gray and blue. In a clearing, I passed a ring in the grass, where a roebuck had chased a doe until they had finally mated. Dogs barked at distant farms, warning off strangers.

Once, under gathering clouds, I lost my way. A toppled pine blocked the path and water was filling where the root had been. As I stepped around it, I thought I heard cowbells, but whether real or imagined, they only led me farther astray. I thought I recognized a small lake but was not at all sure. I had heard that when we are lost we tend to walk in circles, so I sat down under a fir, waiting for the sun to break through and guide me. A light rain fell, drops shivering on the tips of the fir needles. The wetness seeped down into the moss, as I remained motionless, complete in myself. From the lake came the snap and the whisper of the reed. Wings beat from above, the earth smelled faintly of mold, and I thought I could hear the crackle of ants from deep down their hill.

Hours later I walked out of the forest. Night was falling and the lights of Ramm glimmered below.

A letter from Tekla had been set on the hall table.

> *The Spanish flu has come to Stockholm. Stay in Hult for now. Wear layers of clothing as you begin to show. Above all, we must keep you safe from the flu.*

IN AUGUST, A man representing the Agrarian Party spoke at Brunnsdal. The party had made little progress in Hult, where most of the farmers were Conservatives. Long planks were laid out on sawhorses outside the barn.

"This won't take long," I heard Rammen say. As usual I was the only woman present.

The speaker argued that the Conservatives were too closely allied with the industrialists to look after the interests of the farmers, particularly those whose farms were small. Farmers should vote for farmers and for themselves as a class. They should stay away from questions with no direct bearing on their own occupations. Other issues would only distract and divide, pitting farmer against farmer and weakening them as a group.

Rammen stood and interrupted the speaker. He said the approach of the Agrarian Party was too narrow. Reforms were only good if they benefitted the country as a whole.

I pulled at Rammen's sleeve to make him sit down. It was unlike him to interrupt, no matter how much he disagreed.

But Rammen was not to be deterred. Belonging to a particular class, he said, should not automatically define your political orientation. More important were certain basic principles and beliefs, which applied to all classes and affected the human condition as a whole. "Uninformed gibberish, as put forth by the speaker today, is of no use to anyone, and certainly not to the people of Hult."

The meeting broke up and Rammen offered to take the speaker to the station. He drove his two warmbloods, claiming he wanted to make sure that the man would not be late for his train. From what I heard, he unloaded the man just outside the village, knowing that no one would dare give him a ride. When the man finally arrived at the station, dragging his suitcase on the road, his train had long since left, and the stationmaster and his wife were forced to put him up for the night. They heard him cough and in the morning he was dead. It was the way of the flu. It gave no warning, and when it killed, it rarely wasted time.

A week or so later Konrad fell over and slumped in Johannes' arms. They were at the inn and several villagers saw it. When I came home from the bank, Disa said she had tried to persuade Johannes to move back to the big house but to no avail. She wanted me to try to make him see reason.

"I should think Johannes is man enough to make his own decisions," I said.

Disa sneered. "*Man*? Fine choice of words. It's just a matter of time and the whole village will be talking."

Disa was right. Sara, as soon as she was done with her chores at Ramm, found eager listeners wherever she went. Konrad, running a high fever, was in and out of restless sleep, always calling for Johannes. Rammen and Johannes had an argument in the parlor, an argument that almost came to fists.

By then even I was beginning to understand. I had heard about the cavalry troopers in Stockholm, but would never have thought that Johannes too was a lover of men.

"I've always known it," he said when I confronted him in the stable. "Even when I was a boy. All those times I wrestled Erik. All I wanted was to hold him."

Konrad recovered but the flu kept spreading. Rammen and Emilia joined to help the sick. Emilia, word was, barely slept, stealing only a few hours now and then, not even bothering to undress. While she examined the patients, Rammen inspected the buildings.

"This will have to do for now," he said, after he secured a floorboard or covered a hole in the ceiling. He would send someone over as soon as the risk of contagion had passed. "Feed the patient a steady diet of cognac and milk and raw eggs," he added. Knowing that cognac was beyond the means of most, he brought some of his own.

The disease seemed to favor the young and the strong. It began like a cold, with a cough and a stuffy nose, followed by a dull pain that pervaded every muscle and joint. Most patients recovered within a week, unless they developed pneumonia, in which case the outlook was bleak. Emilia rubbed their feet with sheep fat, but when she saw their toes turn black, she knew the end was near.

"No point in taking anyone to the hospital," she said. The hospital in Gothenburg was crowded. The patients' names were attached to their beds, but many of them got up in the night and wandered off. If they died in someone else's bed, or in another room, no one knew who they were, and their families had to search through mounds of naked bodies to find them.

Disa and Sara delivered soup and clean laundry to cabins and farmhouses where the flu had struck. They would place the pot and the laundry on the doorstep, give a quick knock and leave. If a cow lowed from a shed, Sara would milk it, leaning her forehead against it flanks. Over supper Disa said they needed my help. Rammen agreed. "Plenty of time before you open the bank."

That evening I joined him in his office.

"I'm pregnant," I said. "I have to think about the child."

If a shadow crossed his face, I did not see it.

"Leave the child with Wilhelm and Emma," he said, his voice as composed as his face. "You wouldn't be the first to rely on relatives in matters such as these."

"I'm not giving up my child. I became pregnant on purpose, even though I knew we couldn't marry. I'm moving to Stockholm. I've already written Tekla."

Our eyes met and neither one of us looked away.

"I'll tell Ulrika myself," he said. "When the time is right."

In the next few weeks the flu was unstoppable. When the warmbloods needed rest, Rammen drove the Ardenners. Sometimes the doctor rode beside him, sometimes Emilia. If it was Wikander, the villagers knew it was too late.

"Stop by Ramm at milking time," Rammen said to those who had no cows. "Elias will give you what you need."

In terms of eggs, he said he had none to spare. Ulrika's henhouse had already been taxed to the limit, not just in terms of eggs but also in terms of old hens that would normally be too tough to eat. Gustafa chopped off their heads and hung them in her cabin for two days. They spent two more days wrapped in paper and buried in the ground, before she plucked and cleaned them and boiled them with a pinch of soda until the flesh loosened from the bones and they were ready for the table.

In the end I caught the flu as suddenly as Konrad. Disa sent for Emilia, who wiped my brow and propped me up when I coughed. She told Disa to cover me with wet sheets to keep the fever down. If she could tell I was pregnant she did not say.

Drifting in and out of consciousness, I saw the women waiting on the shore, like ravens perched on the rocks. Men, blinded by ice, fumbled with their arms stretched out before them, and yet the North Pole was right there, only they could not see it. I heard shouting and glass shattering, and my head was throbbing. Gustafa chased the pig with her bucket, the pig screaming and skidding in the mud. A shot rang out, and I saw a great desert, no less blinding than the ice, and a blue sea beside it. A black motorcar pulled up and stopped by a long yellow wall, and goats jumped out, hitched to small wagons. Soldiers drove the goats into the sea, firing their rifles when the goats tried to run back, all that white and blue and yellow, and the water churning with blood.

When I woke the doctor leaned over me and told me I was out of danger. Disa sat with me for the rest of the day. She said that Konrad and Johannes had left at dawn. During the night a group of villagers had run torches along the walls of the cabin where Konrad and Johannes were asleep. If Elias had not fired his gun, the whole cabin might have burned. Johannes had left a note for Ulrika, telling her not to worry.

As of that day the flu was gone from Hult. There were those who said it disappeared with Konrad and Johannes. In Stockholm, however, it kept spreading. Tekla told me to remain in the village until the danger was over. By then my womb and breasts felt heavy, and it was only a matter of time before my pregnancy would show.

Chapter Forty-One

GRETA INVITES ME to supper at Ramm. She agrees to serve it in the kitchen and not in the parlor, which makes it easier for her. She puts out eggs, sausages, cold cuts, and various leftovers from dinner. She does not say much and neither do I, but her company soothes me and I hope she derives some kind of comfort from mine.

No sooner does Johan join us than the telephone rings. It is Karin. She has bought a young Charolais bull at auction and needs Johan's help to unload it. I leave with Johan but Greta stays at Ramm. I know what she is thinking. The bull will know what it is doing, and so will Johan, but Karin is new to this. She is the one who poses the real danger.

Karin meets us, waif-like in leather boots and her oilcloth jacket. A flock of starlings descend on a poplar as if perching to watch.

She thanks Johan for coming. "I wouldn't have called you but Niklas is done with the fencing and has the day off."

The trailer stands in the middle of the pasture, tailgate down. It rocks dangerously as the bull digs his hooves into the floor. The five cows lumber closer, followed by the calves. The bull has been fitted with a ring earlier in the day and his nose still bleeds. Letting him out of the trailer too soon would have been risky. He is already upset and might be blind to fences and anything else that stands in his way.

Following Johan's instructions, Karin snaps the end of a long rope to the bull's halter and throws the rest of the rope out the trailer rear. Johan fastens it to the trunk of a crabapple tree, which looks scrawny but is the only candidate within reach.

Karin unties the short rope that keeps the bull in the trailer. He starts to back up, his hind legs gauging the lean of the ramp. Once out, he reacts to the pull of the rope and begins to circle the tree. As the rope wraps around the trunk, he walks in smaller and smaller circles. Finally, his head against the tree, he stops.

So far Johan has kept his distance but now he approaches. The bull is only one year old, but is all muscle and nerve. Keeping the tree between him and the bull, Johan reaches out with one hand and loosens the halter. The bull shakes his head and the halter drops to the ground.

With Karin still by the trailer, and me on the far side of the fence, it is now strictly between Johan and the bull. Johan does not move. I imagine Greta sitting in the kitchen at Ramm, immobile as well. The bull shakes his head a second time to make sure he is free. His dark eyes bulging, he rams his pale, short horns against the base of the tree. Then, ignoring Johan, he trots over to the cows. One of them rears and tries to mount him.

"Can't help him there," Johan says as he pushes back his cap and winks.

There is a thunder of wings as the starlings lift, a black formation against the gray evening sky. Karin drives off, the trailer bouncing down the field.

She does not need me anymore. She is writing her own story now. All I have to do is finish mine.

Chapter Forty-Two

RAMMEN CALLED ME to his office. Fall was coming on and the oil lamp burned on his desk. Also on the desk was a photograph of Ulrika. I had the impression that he had stared at it for a long time.

Once the flu was gone, he had begun to lock himself up in his study for hours on end. He still walked down to the inn to fetch the newspaper, but he had lost the spring in his step and he was never gone for long.

"I was the one who made the children toss the rabbits at Ella."

He had to say it twice before I understood.

"Human nature," he said. "They didn't need much coercing. I saw them playing with the dead rabbits and as soon as I made my suggestion, they knew what to do."

At first I could not find the words. "What about Ella?" I finally said. "How could you let her suffer like that?"

"Didn't like to watch myself. Still, you left me with no choice. At some point they would have done it anyway. Without my help."

He picked up the photograph of Ulrika and ran his fingers across her face. Then, as if catching himself, he put it back.

I rose.

"Not yet," he said. "There's more."

When he spoke again, he kept looking at the photograph on the desk. "I always loved her. Taking over Ramm seemed a small price to pay."

Once more I needed time to fully fathom the meaning. "A small price?"

"It was Ulrika I wanted, not Ramm. Adolf never knew. He saw a way out and grabbed it. If it weren't for me, he might have stayed."

My first reaction was one of panic. I wanted to ask him why he was telling me now, but I feared the answer.

"And Ulrika?" I said. "Did she know?"

"I'm sure she did. If it had been Ramm I had wanted, she could at least have felt useful. But love? Her heart was already taken. I knew she couldn't make room for me too."

I rose again, as if being in the same room with him posed a great danger. "I must go talk to her. I must tell her that I know."

Rammen raised his hand. "The night is long. Time for all of that in the morning."

And so we sat on.

"Were her nerves already weak?" I asked.

"Nothing wrong with her nerves back then, no matter what the doctor says. Even now she'd be better off without me."

Only then did I notice that his desk had been cleared. Normally it was stacked with letters and documents of all sorts. He might not have wanted to become a farmer, but his role as the village leader had never been questioned, and many a man, and woman too, would be the first to thank him for all his hard work.

"There was one small girl," he said. "She tried to stop them."

"Yes. I saw her too."

"One small girl," he said. "Perhaps that's all it takes. One small girl who dares say no."

It was as if he found comfort in this, for in the light of the lamp his features softened. He was not a man who saw what did not exist. That small girl was as real to him as she had been to me.

Around midnight a roebuck barked hoarsely up in the forest. It jolted Rammen too, but then he seemed to be back in his thoughts, impenetrable as the dark outside the window. By the time I went to find Ulrika, she had long since gone to bed.

In the early morning hours we heard the gun go off. Rammen, slumped at his desk, had shot himself through the heart, his blood dripping down onto the rug. Björn had to restrain Ulrika, who stood shivering in her thin nightgown and seemed to be the only one who fully understood that Rammen was dead.

An envelope lay in his desk drawer. The note inside was carefully blotted and folded. Even now he told us what to do. The cause of his death must be put down as a heart attack. He did indeed intend to shoot himself in the heart, where the wound could easily be concealed when we placed him in the coffin. The doctor, he wrote, would take care of the death certificate. He could be trusted not to talk.

The doctor was there within the hour.

"I think he tried to tell me," I said. "Perhaps I could have stopped him."

"He had made up his mind," the doctor said. "I doubt you could have done anything to change it. He never learned to accept what the Bible tells us, that we're much lower than the angels and not much higher than the beasts. He always thought he had to be better than that."

And so we performed our tasks, all in accordance with Rammen's wishes. Disa and Gustafa laid out his body, while Alfrida sat with Ulrika. Björn went to the vicarage to make arrangements for the funeral, while Elias took the measurements to the carpenter. I telephoned Wilhelm and Tekla. No one knew how to reach Johannes, as none of us had heard from him since he had left. Sara was sent upstairs to start cleaning. She never knew that Rammen had staged his own death. Perhaps because she slept up in the attic, or because she was simply too exhausted after a long day's work, she never heard the shot.

Björn and I spent the evening in Rammen's office, Björn pacing while I ran the numbers. Rammen had borrowed money in Vänersborg, using Ramm as security. To pay off his debts, he had sold off remote pockets of land, once part of BrittaLena's dowry. Even when his debts grew out of control, he never touched the forest, the one asset that was worth the most.

In his note, Rammen apologized to Björn. The slightest doubt cast upon Rammen's ability to manage his own house would have shaken the confidence of his constituents, and his political career would have been over. But that was not the worst of it. It was the verdict he had pronounced on himself that had brought him to his knees. He had violated the one rule he claimed to hold sacred: Always leave a farm in better shape than you receive it. His loss of self-respect had blackened his days. Like a shabby stranger, the thought of death had followed him around, always at a distance, not yet ready to make itself known. Now that it had actually introduced itself by its proper name, he was relieved.

"No one will blame you if you sell," he wrote to Björn. "There will be enough for Disa and Ulrika. Elias and Gustafa will have to move to the poorhouse. Elias may actually come to enjoy it. Gustafa can look after him and make sure his coffee is hot."

Just before midnight Disa joined us. She closed the door and stood with her back pressed against it. Her voice was hurried and strained. "Ulrika doesn't make sense. We've tried to make her come upstairs and get some sleep but she keeps saying she has to wait for Adolf. Not even Alfrida can get her to move."

I took the studbook down from the shelf and pulled out the document that Rammen and Adolf had signed.

After Björn read it, he handed it to Disa.

"I'll telephone the doctor," he said. "Ulrika needs more help than we can offer her here."

I went to the bedroom to check on Ulrika. Rammen's body lay on the bed, dressed and covered with a sheet. Wrapped in Rammen's wolf-skin coat, Ulrika lay beside him. Her suitcase, all packed, was still open. On top was her weaving book, the one she had begun as a girl.

"Ulrika," I whispered and touched her cheek. "I know what happened. He told me."

Her voice was surprisingly steady. "He was a good man. We mustn't hold it against him."

The doctor had warned us. A shock could cause such a moment of clarity, but then it would get even worse. It was not unusual for patients who suffered from neurasthenia.

"Father told me I'd be fortunate to marry such a man," Ulrika said. "He said he was superior to Adolf."

"And your mother?"

"She said I must consider the child. It was the only way I could keep it."

As I sat in the armchair beside the bed, Ulrika talked more than I would ever hear her talk again. She kept assuring me that her life with Rammen had been good. What was at first a violation became a thing that bound her to him. After the first time, when he had been too eager to prove himself, she had come to enjoy their nights as much as he did, touching him in hidden places and making him follow.

"But you never loved him?" I said, unable to hold back my tears.

"I tried but he wouldn't let me. Said he had no right."

Hours later, light began to spill through the windows. "Your child," she murmured. "He told me. Said you made him proud."

A few hours later the doctor arrived in a motorcar, a nurse at his side. When Disa noticed that Ulrika had pinned her ruby brooch to her hair she first made a motion as if to remove it. Then she caught my gaze and refrained.

We all stood around as Ulrika took her seat next to the chauffeur and called him Adolf.

"I thought you'd never come," she said. "Your brother is dead but we don't have to stay for the funeral."

The doctor and the nurse rode in the back.

TEKLA CAME ALONE and brought Erling's regrets. "You carry it well," she said when the two of us prepared for the funeral. "Just stand tall, wear your long shawl, and no one will know."

Wilhelm and Emma arrived from Nybo, Emma more beautiful than ever, her auburn hair loosely pinned up, as it had been the first time I saw her. I noticed Björn was watching her. Wilhelm looked ill, the skin under his eyes dark and thin. He had written to Adolf, telling him that Rammen was dead.

While Björn and Wilhelm talked in Rammen's office, I joined Emma as she unpacked. Wilhelm's room looked much the way it always had. A photograph on the wall showed Democrate de Bogaerden, a famous Ardenner stallion, weighing two thousand pounds and standing seventeen hands high. A stereopticon lay on the desk. Adolf had sent it to Wilhelm for his fifteenth birthday.

Emma placed the clothes in the bureau drawers, folded to conceal the places where they had been mended.

I inserted one of the photographs into the stereopticon. Called "Orange Grove in Florida," it showed a Negro posing next to a tree full of oranges. A second showed the New York City Post Office, a building so large that the people were mere specks. A third, called "Subjugation," showed a woman reading a newspaper while the man wore an apron and minded the children.

"Does he still play the fiddle?" I asked.

"Not any more."

Ever since Wilhelm hit his head against the washtub, his headaches had worsened. When he was no longer able to farm, he and Emma had moved to the second floor of a house near the Nybo railway station. The owner, an elderly widow, lived underneath. To make a living, Wilhelm sold insurance to farmers. Emma would watch him from the window as he returned on his bicycle. He always sat down to rest before he came inside. There were times when he declined supper and went straight to bed.

That evening we all gathered in the parlor.

"The forest is still there," Björn said, pacing as he talked.

Disa spoke first. "Rammen would never approve."

"Rammen is dead," I said, as if she needed reminding.

"What did you have in mind?" Wilhelm asked Björn, who stood before us now, rocking slightly on the balls of his feet.

"Agnes and I have a son. I saw her yesterday and she accepted my proposal. The boy is with foster parents in the north. We'll go fetch him next week."

He looked at everyone but me.

Disa leaned my way and whispered, "Did you know?"

Still staring at Björn, I shook my head.

"I'll keep Elias and Gustafa," he said. "Sara must go. Disa can help Agnes in the kitchen, Gustafa not being much help as it is. And then of course we'll have Nils and Lina. The rest of the work will be done by day laborers, as needed, and as I can afford them."

And so he laid it out, step by step, his plan for saving Ramm. "I knew that Rammen was running the farm into the ground. Told him to start felling the forest. He said it would have to be done over his dead body. Apparently he meant it."

Through the haze of it all, I realized how well he knew the land, not just the forest but every single field, where there was need for more drainage, and where the soil was more suitable for one crop as opposed to another. He said we could expect difficult times after the war was over. Land values would go down and many farmers would be caught with heavy liabilities and not enough assets. He intended to be prepared. On some of the pastureland, once covered by forest, he was going to plant spruce, which would increase the value of the farm. He would also start felling the old forest, replanting as he went along. He had been following Fredrik's progress at Prästgården. "Otter's ideas will also work at Ramm."

He still seemed determined not to look at me. "I won't be able to buy any of you out. Perhaps some time in the future, but not now."

We could all have insisted that Björn pay us for our shares, but this was about Ramm, not about us, and we all knew it.

Later that evening I sat by the upstairs window, waiting for the morning. It was past midnight when Björn joined me. The moonlight slanted through the window and formed squares on the wooden floor.

"Not proud of what I did," Björn said, loosening his collar.

"You should have told me."

"I knew Agnes would be better off with Otter. She knew it too. I had nothing to offer a wife, much less a child. Now all that has changed."

He pulled up a chair next to mine and sat.

"Did Rammen know?" I asked.

"I certainly didn't tell him. And I knew that Otter wouldn't talk."

"So Fredrik knew?" I said.

"Not at first."

"What happened?"

"I missed her."

"Yes?"

"One evening I walked over to Prästgården and knocked on the kitchen window. Agnes met me in the garden. Otter caught us. She insisted on telling him the truth."

"He never said a word to me."

Björn scoffed and lowered his voice. "Not surprised."

I knew in an instant that he was holding something back. Had Rammen been told, he would have insisted that Björn marry Agnes, and he would also have sent him away. No marriage, no land. It would have applied to Björn, just as it had applied to Wilhelm. In the end I might well have been the one to take over Ramm, and yet Fredrik had never breathed a word.

Björn too seemed to ponder this. He was quiet, his arms folded across his chest.

"Have you met the boy?" I asked.

He shook his head. "She gave birth in Gothenburg. The woman running the cooking school knew all along and agreed to put her up."

For all his apologies, he could not conceal the joy he took in finally being able to talk about his son. Bringing the boy to Ramm seemed to have given him a whole new sense of purpose. "Eight years old by now. Agnes says he's got my build."

"I went to see her," I said. "The day she was churched. I could see her disappointment when she opened the door. I thought she hoped it would be Fredrik. I was wrong, wasn't I? She was looking for you."

"She's willing to give me a second chance. Question is, are you?"

He flinched when I said I was not, and yet he sat with me until the morning, although by then he had grown as silent as I. Despite my objections he took the reins away from Elias, who shrugged, muttering into his beard.

"No harm done," Björn said as he carried my luggage on to the train. "Otter will be glad to see you."

AT TROTTA, I paid the coachman his fare. The chestnut trees were already turning, yellow leaves against a bleak autumn sky. A brand new motor plow stood by the barn with mud caked to its wheels. It was an Avance. I had seen it advertised in the newspapers.

I knocked on the kitchen door. Dagmar opened, her eyes widening ever so briefly before she asked me in.

"I'm sorry," I said. "I should have let you know I was coming. There simply was no time."

Dagmar nodded but did not smile. "They're in the barn, but they won't be long."

I sat at the kitchen table as Dagmar put out cups. She did not seem to question my long, bulky cardigan.

"They're checking on a cow," she said and placed the coffee pot on the burner. "She just bore twins. I've offered to foster the smaller one, since she appears to reject it."

A black cat stretched in a corner. It had its own small basket, and it looked at me with a curious gaze. At Ramm we never allowed cats inside the house. Nor did anyone else in Hult, at least not as far as I knew.

"When did he buy the motor plow?" I asked.

"A few months ago. Horses are expensive. A team of twelve-year-olds would have cost at least three thousand crowns. Add the cost of feeding them and wages to the driver, and a motor plow was a better choice."

I nodded. She was a farmer's daughter. She understood the advantages of a purchase like that.

"Spring was hard," she said. "Rain or shine, I saw him out in the fields, hands shoved down his pockets. Kept testing the soil with the heel of his boot."

She spoke with urgency now, as if to bar interruptions.

"Day after day he waited for the mail. He couldn't sleep at night. But he's better now. He really is."

Fredrik's voice came from outside, interspersed with the steward's. The door swung open and the two men entered, the steward first, then Fredrik, wearing his wool jacket and black felt hat.

"Anna!" he said, stopping short.

Dagmar told them to sit down but Fredrik did not move. She put two lumps of sugar in his coffee and stirred.

"Anna," he said again. "You've come."

The steward sat, but Fredrik remained standing. My blood was racing and yet I told myself there was no need for concern. Dagmar would understand, would she not? After all, I was expecting his child.

Fredrik placed his hands on the back of my chair, his voice pressing. "Anna, will you join me in the terrace room?"

While I sat on the sofa, he still preferred to stand, his eyes wary in the pale light coming through the window.

"Why are you here?" he asked.

"Rammen is dead."

"I'm sorry. I hadn't heard."

"We're telling everyone it was his heart."

He raised his eyebrows but said nothing.

I had read that pregnant women had no yearnings, but either that information was wrong or I was some grand exception, for I was ready to lie down with him right there on the polished parquet floor.

"Björn and Agnes are about to marry," I said. "Both Ella and the boy will grow up at Ramm."

He walked over to one of the tall windows and looked out.

"After you left—" I began. "I went to the cabin."

"I lost my mind," he said, his back still turned. "As much as I despised Björn, I had no right to attack him. All through the night I stood in the courtyard, watching your bedroom window, hoping against hope you'd come out."

He came toward me now, those golden flecks in his irises still wanting to dance.

I held up my hands to stop him.

"There's more though, isn't there?" I said.

"It doesn't matter now."

"What happened between you and Björn?"

"It's all in the past."

"I have to know."

"It's better you don't."

When he finally spoke, his words were shards of glass grinding through my skin.

"I told him he must marry Agnes. If not, I said I would do to you what he had done to her. Didn't think he'd be able to hold out. Didn't think I'd fall in love. Thought I had it all in hand."

He must have come with me to the kitchen, for there he was, blocking the door that led outside.

"Anna," he said, showing his palms, as if to convince me I had no cause for fear.

When I tried to get past him, I caught a glimpse of Dagmar's horrified face.

Again and again he spoke my name.

"Please, Anna, it doesn't have to end like this."

I stepped back, shaking my head. "I made it so easy for you, didn't I? The more you held back, the more I pushed. What a time you must have had, laughing behind my back!" The black cat hissed in its basket and I was vaguely aware of Dagmar picking it up.

Despite my entreaties, he kept repeating my name. "I love you, Anna. That's all that matters now."

The walls closed in and I felt my fists on his chest, hitting and hitting, until he finally grabbed my wrists.

"Shush," he murmured as he pulled me close, again that scent of clover and earth, his heart pounding against mine. For a moment I must have held still, but the sense of betrayal was too strong.

"Get out of my way!" I shouted, over and over, until at long last he did.

Chapter Forty-Three

ELLA IS HERE. She telephoned several times to tell me she was coming, her eagerness barely hidden behind her starchy nurse's voice.

As always, when she stays over, we drag the old zinc tub out on the kitchen floor and fill it with cold water. I shed my clothes, step into the tub, twist my long hair and hold it up against my head while Ella scrubs my back. I ask her to scrub harder and she keeps scrubbing, shifting the brush from one hand to the other, until her arms hurt and my skin feels almost raw.

After supper, she gives me a report she has borrowed from a doctor.

"It's about a child on the ward," she says. "You must read it."

As she watches me from the sofa, I sit at the kitchen table, reading words that make no sense.

She tells me to keep going. "You'll be glad you did."

The photographs are the hardest. Not that I cannot see what they are—the child's lids are so dry that they are pulled inside out, the eyes themselves a tortured stare for help. Still, I seem unable to make the connection. I copy passages of text onto my spiral-bound notebook, word by word, but even now the words fail to add up.

Ella rises, sits beside me, and gently takes the pencil from my hand.

"Writing it down won't change it," she says. "But at least you know."

I lean back, remove my glasses, and rub the bridge of my nose. It is only then that I surrender to the tears.

This morning I walk with her to the bus stop and watch the bus pull away. Instead of going back to the cabin, I walk over to the lake. Ripe lingonberries spread carpets of red. A wood grouse hen squats next to the path, all but hidden in her mottled gray and brown, so modest compared to the cock that will seduce her in the spring.

As I stand by the lake, the call of a loon pierces the air. Other loons answer, and soon there is a chorus of birds, eerie falsetto cries that ripple across the lake. Is this what wakes me up in the night?

I hear Björn's voice. We are children again, drifting in the rowboat, one of those long summer afternoons.

"Ramm!" he shouts.

"Hult!" I shout back and the game begins.

Sweden! Scandinavia! Europe!

Björn shouts the names of the stars and the galaxies, so loud that anyone standing on the shore can hear us.

He lies on his back and talks about "the great order of things." He says our lives will be over in a flash and no one will know we had even existed. I tell him there will always be stories, just as Rammen said. That is how people live on.

The water laps against the boat, an osprey circles above, and cattle graze on the island. When he catches a perch, Björn takes it off the hook and throws it back. The perch flips its tail and swims straight down, the water swirling green and brown. He says he does not trust the stories. He would rather be remembered by a fish.

Chapter Forty-Four

THE OBITUARY, COMPOSED by the doctor, lay on the sideboard in the parlor.

> *The village of Hult is in mourning. The widely known Grim Larsson is gone. His many friends will remember evenings spent at Ramm, where Grim held forth with a warmth and an intelligence that never failed to move. His battles were fought for the good of all, and the Provincial Council will miss his voice, as will Hult and the villages around it. Even his horses nickered and turned their heads when they heard his steps. A great man has died. He lived well, and at Valhalla he has surely taken his seat at the table.*

On the morning of the funeral, Björn stood in the courtyard greeting the guests. Elias had spread hacked-up branches of fir on the path to the front door. In the bedroom, where white sheets covered the windows and the walls, Rammen lay on *lit de parade*. The coffin was blackened with carbon and a book of hymns propped up his chin.

Upstairs, in the *sal*, the guests served themselves food, mostly eggs and pickled herring. The scarcity of the offerings was in keeping with the times. Not even at Rammen's funeral should there be signs of abundance.

The family was closing ranks.

"So sudden," a farmer's wife said, as she stood by the table. "No signs that his heart was strained?"

"Death comes when we least expect it," Aunt Hedvig said. "It peers through the windows while we feast and laugh."

No one dared ask about Ulrika.

By the time the procession left Ramm, rain was falling. Rammen's warmbloods pulled the wagon with the coffin, Nils Lind at the reins. Walking behind, we all leaned into the wind. The villagers lined the road, which was strewn with fir all the way to the church. Despite the rain, the men held their hats in their hands. Even Erik was there to honor Rammen. He nodded as I passed.

When the bell ringers saw the procession approach, they pulled the ropes. I was told that the wind carried the sound for miles, first the heavy muted sound of the large bell, then the clear light sound of the small. When the pauses between the chimes grew longer, the procession came to a halt. We stopped, bowed, and remained motionless as the bells continued to toll.

When the bells rang faster, the procession started forward. The black blanket on Rammen's coffin was soaked. Rain trickled under my collar and funneled down between my breasts. I felt the child move, a slight nudge, so slight I was not even sure it was there. When it moved again, it was more like a push.

Ahead, barely visible through the rain, stood the church, its spires and turrets disappearing into the lowering sky, its octagonal shape still causing travelers to point and wonder. "Step inside," Rammen used to say when he showed them around. "The soothing colors and the soaring ceiling will convince you that this too is a house of God, be it ever so uncommon."

That was when I knew I must stay. I was not about to run away, pretending to be what I was not. It was not the kind of story I wanted to tell my child.

BJÖRN NODDED WHEN I told him. "Glad to hear it. I can use your help with the books."

Björn and Agnes were married a week later. The following morning Björn and Elias were in the forest at dawn. We could hear the whack of their axes.

Kristina stopped me outside the bank. "Never thought I'd live to see it. Rammen's trees coming down."

It was the same day Agnes went to fetch Ragnar, a small boy who stared at his father in silence. Disa and Ragnar instantly took to each other. It was as if the two of them knew each other on sight. On those rare occasions when Ragnar still visits Hult, he always brings flowers for her grave.

By October, my clothing could no longer hide the fact that I was pregnant. Talk travels widely, and soon Fredrik heard about it too. This time I opened his letter and read. He wanted to know my plans.

I wrote back. *"At first I meant to move to Stockholm but I've decided to stay in Hult. When the child is old enough to decide for itself, I'll take it to Stockholm, if that's what it wants. Perhaps it can spend summer vacations at Trotta. I never intended to keep it away from you."*

One morning, when I arrived at the bank, Miss Rydelius was waiting.

"I wish it could be otherwise," she said, "but I have to dismiss you. My superior in Varberg says we must ensure that all our employees are of irreprehensible moral fiber. Those are his words, not mine."

I thanked her for all her help, packed up my belongings, and left. The women outside the store stopped talking as I passed.

Through the doctor we heard about Ulrika. We were told to stay away as she needed to be around people with no ties to her past. Treatment, in fact, consisted of isolating her from relatives and friends, whose presence might increase her excitement and worsen her condition. The doctor reassured us that she was in good hands, walking with her nurse through the grounds and enjoying the gardens. She seemed to benefit from the routine, meals brought to her room at exact hours, warm baths, regular sleep. But the delusions were still with her and she must not return home, at least not for a long time. Patients like Ulrika could easily regress. He asked if we could find a way to keep her at the sanitarium, and Erling and Tekla offered to pay.

Once I took eggs to the store. They broke as I struggled to get down from the wagon and dropped the basket. The stares of the villagers stung like nettles in the spring. No one came to my aid. Caesar swished his tail, and as soon as I managed to get the basket and myself back onto the wagon, he bolted for Ramm. By the time I turned the broken eggs over to Agnes, there was still enough for a cake.

"Shameless like the Virgin Mary," Andrasson was heard to say. "And yet she's nothing but a common whore."

On November 8 the Kaiser abdicated. In Stockholm, workers marched through the streets, shouting, "Down with the King." When the armistice was signed on November 11, we all went about our lives as usual. It was as if we had stopped reacting to good news as well as bad, or perhaps we were simply overwhelmed by the momentousness of the occasion. The only exception was Gustafa. All she could talk of was the queen, who was imprisoned in a castle in Germany, guarded by a Workers' and Soldiers' Council.

In early December, a north wind packed drifts of snow against the house, which groaned and sighed under the weight. All the stoves were fired up to fight back the coldness that crept through the walls. Elias had built a cradle and Disa brought down baby clothes from the attic. My skin was stretched so thin I thought I could see the child. While Ella watched, Agnes rubbed my legs and ankles. At night she gave me a few camphor drops to slow my heart.

On December 9, my labor started. Agnes put me to bed in the small upstairs room that Ulrika had used for birthing. The head of the bed faced the wall so the light would not bother my eyes. Gustafa padded across the rag runners, adding more wood to the tile stove and heating up the water bottle.

As the hours passed, Gustafa sat by my bed, always so that I could see her, darning socks or dozing. Disa was weaving in the other room and I could hear the creak of the treadle and the faint clicking of wood. From the shed came the banging of the hammer, the echo frozen in the air. Gustafa said there was frost on Elias' beard.

Now and then Gustafa rose to smooth the sheets or shake out the pillow. When the contractions grew stronger, I kept asking if something was wrong. Gustafa put her ear to my stomach and told me to hush. She could always tell by the strength of the heartbeat if it was a girl or a boy, but this time she could not be sure. Outside the door, Björn turned the pages of his newspaper. Each time he changed position, his chair rasped against the wooden floor.

The child was born at noon. Emilia held my knees apart, while I dug my heels into the mattress, straining and bearing down. The pain clutched me so hard I called for Ulrika. As soon as the child pushed out, Emilia told Björn to telephone the doctor.

The doctor said it was the first case of syphilis in the parish. When I told him I had been tested, he said that no test was conclusive.

"Otter's past is well known," he said. "The disease may lie dormant for years, only to surface in the next generation."

He said he would treat me with Salvarsan although he could not promise that I would ever be cured. For the child, there was nothing he could do.

Throughout the nights I paced with the crying child in my arms, asking God to transfer her suffering to me. Her skin was thick and scaly, like that of a fish. I tried to nurse her, but my breasts ran dry. She took the bottle willingly enough, but she did not gain much weight, even though I added cream. I patted her skin with glycerol to keep it from cracking, and I dusted the raw spots with potato flour to soothe the burn. Even so the wounds kept blistering, the pus turning into a yellow crust. On the morning of the seventh day, her fever climbed and we had to send for Wikander. He christened her Ingrid and called her God's child. An hour later the crying stopped.

I have been told that I sat with the dead child in my arms and refused to let anyone near us. Of this I have no remembrance. They said I made no sense at all, even less than Ulrika. I made as if I stood at the gates to the Garden of Eden, pleading to God to let me back in. Then my frame of mind turned even darker. "Come show yourself!" I shouted, holding the tiny corpse high. "Stop hiding behind the cross!"

This, they said, went on for hours. The doctor finally managed to get close enough to give me an injection. I entered into a deep sleep, empty even of dreams, and when I awoke, they had taken the child.

WIKANDER APPEARED PLEASED that I wanted the child buried in the old graveyard rather than the new. Perhaps he thought I wanted her hidden away, at long last admitting that she was a bastard. Truth was, I wanted her close to her great grandfather Lars.

The small, white coffin stood on the table in the *sal*, while I sat by the window looking out at the snowy forest. Gustafa placed the tin box with my caul at the child's feet. Disa, losing patience with Gustafa's ways, reached to remove it.

"Leave it," I said. "It'll be safe with the child."

I overheard Disa's words to Agnes about me staring out the window, like the mare that covered her dead foal with straw and then wanted out.

"Not normal," Disa said. "Unless she gets some sleep, she'll go the same way as Ulrika."

Björn came to tell me that Fredrik was downstairs. I said I did not want to see him.

"*Anna,*" Björn said, as if pleading for himself as much as for Fredrik. "It's his child too."

I watched as Fredrik walked over to the coffin. By then it had been closed and he ran his hand over the lid. His thick wool jacket pulled tight over his back as he sobbed. I told him I could never forgive him for killing our child. I also said I wanted him gone.

Björn carried the coffin to the old graveyard. It seemed even smaller in his large, awkward hands. I walked between Agnes and Disa, slogging through the snow. Gustafa and Elias followed.

Wikander waited at the arched stone gate. The grave was next to Lars', just as I had asked. Klas had actually begun to dig one in the far corner of the graveyard, next to the large oak, the very tree under which Fredrik used to read. Björn had to pay him twice, before he could convince him that a bastard child could be buried out in the open, just like everyone else.

The ceremony was short. Wikander cleared his throat. "*The Lord giveth, the Lord taketh away.*"

When the earth struck the coffin, I steadied myself against Björn. The jackdaws cawed and the branches of the aspens scratched the pewter-gray sky. Later I heard that Fredrik had been watching from the meadow below, a wreath on his arm. Only after the rest of us left, did he approach.

WHEN TIME CAME for my churching, Wikander offered to make an exception. He said it could be done in private, with Björn as the only witness. I told him I wanted it done the usual way, just like all those women who had knelt at that threshold before me.

Still numb from the loss of the child, I stood outside the church, waiting for the service to be over. I walked up to one of the horses, took off my glove, and held my palm to its muzzle, all softness and warm breath. The horse jerked its head away when Klas approached to tell me it was time.

As I knelt at the threshold, I kept my gaze on the hem of Wikander's robe. There were the usual coughs and stirrings from the congregation. Wikander's voice was distant. "*For marriage is honorable in all, and the bed undefiled, but whoremongers and adulterers God will judge. Walk in peace and sin no more."* As the church bells began to ring, I thought of the woman who died in the lake.

In the bedroom, I looked out the window and saw the women coming up the hill. Snow was falling and at first it was difficult to see who they were. I recognized Emilia and Alfrida, and as they came closer, I recognized the others too, wives and daughters of village farmers, some of them arm-in-arm. Agnes greeted them in the hall. By the time I had put on my black dress again and entered the parlor, Disa was putting out coffee and cake. She made excuses for what the house had to offer, and for once she truly meant it, for not even Disa could have foreseen that we would have guests.

The miller's wife gave a short speech. She said they were sorry about the loss of my child. "We shouldn't have shunned you when you needed us the most." Emilia added that it was time to look forward and not to the past.

Agnes, every bit the mistress of Ramm, asked them all to step up to the table, but no one moved until I went first.

None of the women, not even Disa, seemed real to me then. My only company was the woman who had waded out into the lake. She fixed her gaze on the opposite shore, where banks ran steep and a colony of ground swallows would nest in the spring. When her feet no longer found purchase, she fought her urge to swim, the murky water closing above her, not her enemy but her friend. With the stark practicality of someone determined to die, I reminded myself that the lake was frozen and I would have to find another way.

An hour later, shawl wrapped over my head and shoulders, I took my rifle and left for the forest. The women had delayed me and darkness happened early that time of year.

I did not expect the buck. He stood in the middle of the path, his side exposed, snow blanketing his back. He seemed to know that my life could be saved, as long as he would offer his.

I fired at his heart. He did not fall but turned sharply and disappeared among the trees. Tracking the blood that had splattered on the snow, I remembered Björn's words. "If you wound a deer, give it some time. Most likely it won't go very far but find a spot to lie down in."

Björn was wrong. This buck kept going. He even jumped a stone fence. When I finally found him, he was still standing, blood spreading down his leg and blackening his coat. I brought up my rifle and fired another shot, this time aiming at the base of his brain. His legs gave out and he fell on his side. Ready to shoot again, I watched as he tried to rise, his front hooves pawing. Then, as life drained out of him, he put his head down. His nostrils foamed and his eyes dimmed over, those dark, bottomless pupils dilated and fixed.

I set my rifle against a tree and pulled out my knife.

Björn's voice reached me from behind. "Let me help."

I raised my hand and he stood back.

The blood of the buck was pooling in the snow. It was then that I saw the scar. The claw marks ran clear across his buttock and down his right thigh. I thought I could see the lynx in the night, its lips drawn back, its white fangs glowing. Perhaps there had been the faint snap of a twig, perhaps the wind had just turned, but by the time the buck tried to escape, the lynx would have been in close pursuit, its deadly paw reaching out to trip him. Still, the buck had lived. Perhaps he knew that this was not his time and that he and I would meet.

I slit him open and dropped to my knees. Steam rose from his innards, his heart sliding as I cut it loose. Holding it up to the sky, I could feel its firmness and weight. I sliced off the tip and placed it on my tongue. It tasted of heather and sun-flecked moss, of cobweb glimmering wet at dawn. I had taken a life. I had taken it poorly, and yet it had to be so.

The snow was whirling now, and a wild and raucous laughter seemed to issue from the depths of the earth. This was the hardest part, willing myself to go on, knowing that nothing could be changed. I must abandon everything that had sustained me and learn to laugh in the presence of death. When I prayed, I prayed to the fierceness of the buck and to the great indifference of the forest.

Björn helped me cover the buck with branches. "Let's get you home. I'll haul him out in the morning."

Chapter Forty-Five

SAMUEL SITS IN my garden chair and looks out over Ramm. The low autumn sun strikes the red barn, and the wheat stubble is cast in gold.

"It's getting late," I say.

"Is it?"

"There's a low pressure building. I look forward to the storm."

Johan was here earlier and wanted me to spend the night at Ramm. I thanked him but told him no.

Samuel closes his eyes and turns his furrowed face to the sun.

"It wasn't Fredrik's fault," I say. "No more than it was mine."

He waits.

"Ella brought a report," I say. "I wanted to tell you but I haven't been able to talk about it until now."

He nods.

"There's this child in the ward," I say. "Born with a severe type of a skin disease."

I reach into my dress pocket and pull out my notes. "I-C-H-T-H-Y-O-S-I-S. Caused by a mutation of a gene. A rogue event of nature. In the past they may well have mistaken it for syphilis."

Eyes still closed, Samuel loosens the handkerchief around his neck.

"I looked at the photographs. It could just as well have been my child. Scales and blisters all over, and eyelids so dry that they couldn't close. The infection brought on the fever, and with no access to antibiotics, she couldn't survive."

"Well, then. There you are."

He looks back over Ramm and hums, his voice earthbound and full.

"What are you humming?" I say.

"*Ariadne auf Naxos.* We staged it in Salzburg the year the Germans came."

My mind is a divining rod, bending to the ground. "Ariadne? I've heard that name before."

He sips his coffee, this man who has all the time in the world. "The king's daughter. Abandoned by Theseus. Three strings, seven clarinets, eight horns, and tubas. *Sehr, sehr schön.*"

Perhaps it is true what Gustafa used to say. There are other realities, much more frightening than the ones we think we already know. We remember the future as we also remember the past.

Somewhere a young woman will always walk across a field to tend the graves. "Don't!" I want to say as she climbs the stone fence, that same sharp stone snagging her skirt. "Go marry Rikard Lilja. Do anything, but don't do this." But I cannot stop her, any more than she can stop herself. Fate moves her along, like the huge glacier that ground and shaped this land.

Somewhere two men still talk long into the night. One calls on science, the other on faith. A housekeeper with a hairnet and a spotted apron enters the room, nervously eyeing the bottle in the older man's hand. "Jesus alone can save us," the older man says. "We must believe in nothing else, build our hopes on nothing else, when our eyes are opened and we see our sinful and corrupted selves." The younger man rises and puts on a jacket that smells of earth. He says that we ourselves must take on the task to create and destroy, the task we once assigned to God. Faith alone can take us only so far, and even if we have no free will, we must still live as if we do. They shake hands and bid each other good night, the older man patting the younger on his shoulder.

I want to tell them that they both are wrong. There is no meaning in this world or in the one hereafter. There is no accountability in the end. We are still at the mercy of trolls.

The setting sun tints Samuel's hair cobalt blue. When I stand to go to the kitchen, he rests his large hand on my arm.

"No more coffee," he says. "I want you to stay."

Rising high above the stubble field, a lark fills the air with a song of its own.

"Odd," I say. "They shouldn't be singing this time of year."

Black clouds roll in over the mountains but in my garden the sun still shines. The small bird hovers and soars.

"How do we find our way when the map we follow is flawed?" I ask.

"We blunder on."

Epilogue

IN THE AUTUMN of 1974, Samuel Stern found Anna Larsson dead on the path to the old graveyard. They carried her body back to the cabin, where leaves had blown in through the open window. The unicorn lay in pieces on the floor. The lid of the phonograph was open and the needle had stopped midway through the record. It seemed she had left in the dark of the night and was overcome by the wind and the rain.

A note leaned against a cup on the kitchen table. Although the old graveyard was no longer in use, she still wished to be buried close to Fredrik Otter and their child.

The parish council found a way.

Birgitta Hjalmarson lives north of San Francisco, in a house on a hill, overlooking the ocean. When not writing, she walks along the bluff and up into the forest, alone or with friends. Tutoring a nine-year-old boy keeps her grounded. She studied Swedish, English, and German Literature, earning Master's Degrees from the University of Lund, Sweden, and the University of California at Davis. While covering the San Francisco art beat as a contributing editor for *Art & Auction* in New York, she also wrote *Artful Players*, a book on early California art, published by Balcony Press. Turning to fiction, she drew on memories of her native Sweden, where she spent her childhood summers in a village much like the one we encounter in *Fylgia*. Sarah Orne Jewett's words to Willa Cather still hold true: "Of course, one day you will write about your own country. In the meantime, get all you can. One must know the world so well before one can know the parish."